# NO ESCAPE

Also by James D. Brewer

*No Bottom*
*No Virtue*
*No Justice*
*No Remorse*

# NO ESCAPE

## A MASEY BALDRIDGE / LUKE WILLIAMSON MYSTERY

# James D. Brewer

WALKER AND COMPANY

*New York*

First published in the United States of America in 1998 by
Walker Publishing Company, Inc.

Published simultaneously in Canada by Thomas Allen & Son
Canada, Limited, Markham, Ontario

Library of Congress Cataloging-in-Publication Data
Brewer, James D.
No escape / James D. Brewer.
p. cm.—(A Masey Baldridge/Luke Williamson mystery)
ISBN 0-8027-3318-2 (h)
1. Baldridge, Masey (Fictitious character)—Fiction. I. Title.
II. Series: Brewer, James D. Masey Baldridge/Luke
Williamson mystery.
PS3552.R418N615 1998
813'.54—dc21 98-2826
CIP

Series design by Mauna Eichner

Printed in the United States of America
2 4 6 8 10 9 7 5 3 1

# NO ESCAPE

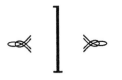

## WEDNESDAY MORNING,
## SEPTEMBER 17, 1873

The smell of death surrounded Masey Baldridge as his horse clopped down the deserted bricks of Market Street. Every fifty to a hundred feet, corpses lay on the edge of the wooden sidewalk, awaiting the steady, plodding approach of the Holst and Brothers undertaker's wagon. An invisible killer moved silently through the streets of Memphis, and though no one knew from where it came, or how to stop it, the stinking human residue on the sidewalks left unmistakable evidence of the predator's power.

"Repent! I say repent ye while ye may," a voice echoed from the alley to Baldridge's right. His horse, Nashville Harry, shied from the sound as Baldridge struggled to make out the speaker through the smoky haze—the residue of last night's tar and sulfur burning. Finally a man emerged from the alley onto Market Street. He was dressed in a long black preacher's frock, his wide-brimmed hat partially obscuring his face as he paged through a worn Bible. With cold, gray eyes he stared at Baldridge as he rode past. "Are you washed, brother?"

Baldridge halted Harry. "Beg your pardon?"

"I said are you washed?" the preached replied, moving up to the horse. He grasped the bridle. "Are you washed in the blood?"

"Preacher, I ain't got time to—"

"You must be washed in the blood of the lamb, brother," the preacher said. He pointed his Bible down Market Street like a pistol, speaking in the resonant voice of a tent revivalist. "God's judgment has descended, brother. Jehovah has judged the city and found it wanting."

A woman emerged from a door half a block east. She approached a body that lay on the wooden sidewalk and covered it with a white sheet. The preacher noticed her, released Baldridge's bridle, and began walking toward her, his declarations still resounding along the nearly empty street.

" 'Lest ye repent and be washed in the blood, ye shall surely be as this one,' " he declared, indicating the body she had covered. "God's judgment has befallen the wicked—"

The woman rose suddenly from the body and spun to face him.

"How dare you!" she shouted. "The fever has taken my husband and you dare to say it was God's judgment?" The preacher began backing up as the woman walked toward him. "My husband was a God-fearin' man, and you . . . you . . ." The woman charged at the preacher and began beating him about the head and shoulders with her fists and cursing him as he attempted to hold her at arm's length.

Baldridge moved Harry forward, calling out as he went, "Move on, Preacher."

The preacher, still holding the woman back, turned and glared at Baldridge.

" 'The righteous shall be known by their words,' " he shouted.

"So shall the fool," Baldridge replied. "Now, I said move along. And leave this woman be."

The preacher forced his way past the woman, who half-heartedly attempted to pursue him, eventually giving up in a flood of tears.

"I'm sorry about your husband, ma'am," Baldridge said. "I lost my wife to sickness back during the war. I know you'll miss him."

The woman lowered her hands from her face and turned slowly toward him. Sunken eyes peered from a thin, hollow face gripped with pain. Her tears stopped suddenly.

"I won't miss him long, mister." Her quivering lip attempted a wry grin. "You see, I got the Bronze John, too." Then she began to laugh, softly at first, then louder as she walked across the sidewalk and entered her door. Even after she'd slammed it behind her, Baldridge could hear her maniacal laughter coming from inside. The preacher had moved on down the street, where the undertakers, wearing full-length aprons, gloves, and scarves tied around mouths and noses, went dutifully about the business of loading the bodies into the hearse.

"Go on and get out of here, Malachi," one of them said. "Go preach someplace else."

The preacher moved on, but Baldridge sat on his horse watching the men from Holst and Brothers.

Tuesday's *Daily Avalanche* listed the death count for Monday at fifty-two, all but three of them dying from the fever, and Baldridge wondered how much longer this horror would last. The dying had begun more than a month earleir—only a few at first, and most of those in Happy Hollow, the shanty section of town. Poor folks mostly, living down by the water. Baldridge recalled how the poor folks dying didn't get too many people excited. But when the fever began to spread from the tin roofs of Happy Hollow to the copper roofs of Madison and Jefferson Streets, people began to worry. Even with the death toll rising daily, the board of health had waited until September 14 to declare a yellow fever epidemic. Baldridge could not help but think that somebody should have done something sooner.

The clock mounted above the door of a nearby jewelry store showed almost nine. The message from the mayor, addressed to the Big River Detective Agency and delivered to the steamboat *Paragon*, had been quite specific: Be at the courthouse at nine o'clock sharp. Tell no one of the meeting. Come prepared to talk business.

Inside the courthouse, Baldridge gave his name to a lady behind a desk and took a seat in a reception room along with eight others—all also waiting to see the mayor. Within a couple of minutes, a rather short, pudgy-faced man emerged from an adjoining office. His full black beard and mustache, peppered with gray, was neatly groomed. Several of those who had been waiting arose and began talking all at once. An older man in the group pushed in front and began complaining.

"Mayor, I've been waiting almost an hour."

"We've all been waiting," another man said.

"Folks, I'll see each of you just as soon as—"

"I must speak with you about the sanitation plan for Happy Hollow," the older man said. "I just don't see how we're going to pay for it all. I insist—"

"Mr. Hensley, please," the man said. "Everyone listen to me. I'll see each of you as quickly as I can. But I must attend to another matter first." He gazed about the room. "Which one of you is Mr. Baldridge?"

Baldridge rose awkwardly to his feet, the stiffness in his left leg obvious to everyone in the room.

"I'm Baldridge."

The man shook Baldridge's hand. "Can I ask you to step inside my office so we may speak in private?"

"Now, see here, Mayor Johnson," Hensley said. "I was here before this man, and I insist that you see me first."

"I was here before him, too," another gentleman said.

"Me, too," a third man added.

Hensley pointed at Baldridge. "This fella just got here."

"I can't see you yet, Mr. Hensley," the mayor said, then turned to the younger man. "Or you either, Mr. Fields." He addressed the entire group. "But I give you my word that I'll be with each of you just as soon as possible."

Several individuals began to protest, but Fields shouted over them, "Don't you realize what we're facing here? The city is at the point of wholesale panic—"

Johnson raised his hands and forced a modest smile. "Now, gentlemen, there's no need to panic."

"Then when is the sanitation going to begin?" Fields demanded.

"I'm more interested in who's going to pay for it," Hensley said. "We've got to talk—"

"We will talk just as soon as—"

"Mayor, we must get this straight now," Hensley said.

"Money or no money, we must begin the sanitation immediately," Fields interrupted. "Don't you realize—"

"Mr. Fields, I assure you I'm aware of the urgency of the situation," the mayor said. "I suspect that I've seen the death toll more recently than you have. I don't need you to tell me what is happening."

"Well, sir, then—"

"But you're still going to have to wait until I've talked with Mr. Baldridge." The mayor eyed the group sternly. "All of you will have to wait."

Hensley stared at Baldridge jealously. "And who, exactly, are you, sir?"

"None of your damn business," Baldridge replied, limping past Hensley and entering the mayor's office.

Johnson whispered something to the woman at the desk, followed Baldridge into the office, and closed the door.

Baldridge surveyed the elegant furnishings, immediately locating the liquor cabinet.

"You've got some mighty upset folks out there," he said, making a quick inventory of the mayor's stock of libations.

"Drink, Mr. Baldridge?"

"Don't mind if I do," Baldridge said, pouring himself a brandy. He offered the bottle to the mayor.

"No, thank you. As much as I'd like to join you, I don't think those good citizens out there would understand liquor on my breath. They're mad enough as it is."

"Sound scared to me," Baldridge said.

"Of course they're scared. Scared of the fever. Isn't everybody?"

"I picked up your message down at Captain Luke Williamson's wharf boat. I understand you wanted to talk with someone from the Big River Detective Agency."

"Yes, that's correct. And I appreciate your respecting the confidence of my message with those people outside." Baldridge sipped his drink and nodded. The mayor offered him a wing-backed chair, then sat behind his desk. "I've followed some of your work over the past year. You seem to know your business, though it's a rather strange setup if you ask me."

"How's that?"

"Well, you being a Southern man—a veteran and all—and teaming up with Captain Luke Williamson. Wasn't he a Federal officer during the war?"

Baldridge nodded. "Gunboat pilot."

"Well, I guess it doesn't matter, as long as the two of you work together."

"We get along," Baldridge said. "Miss Salina Tyner is also with us."

"Tyner. Don't believe I know her."

Baldridge finished his brandy, limped over to the liquor cabinet, and poured another. "What do you want with the Big River Detective Agency, Mayor?"

"Mr. Baldridge, the city of Memphis is facing two problems that I hope you can help us with. You know about our health crisis. . . ."

"A lot of folks are suffering."

"Yes, the mortality figures are rising daily."

"Sounds like you need more doctors, not detectives."

"This meeting is not about the fever," the mayor said. "At least not entirely. As you may know, the board of health declared this past Sunday that yellow fever is in the city."

"I read it in the *Daily Avalanche*," Baldridge said. "Smart boys on that board. It only took a hundred some-odd dead people before they did anything."

"These kinds of things are very delicate, Baldridge. You just can't stop an entire city, ruin the business dealings of thousands of people, and throw a city like Memphis into a panic."

"Still sounds like they should've done something sooner."

"We couldn't be sure it was Yellow Jack. Starting the way it did down in Happy Hollow, it could have been any number of sicknesses. You're from around here. You know as well as I do that the area is not clean, and the people down there . . . well, many of them are transients."

"But—"

"It has never come this early, Baldridge. The outbreak in '55 was much later. And the first cases of fever in '67 didn't appear until about mid-September."

Baldridge placed his empty glass on the edge of the mayor's desk. "The paper claims the first case was spotted early last month."

"I'm familiar with that report. August tenth, to be exact. Some old fellow named Davis got off the tugboat *Bee* up in the Punch area, not far from Wolf River, and died the next day."

"I heard the captain of that boat died within two days somewhere upriver."

"That's not been confirmed, sir."

"You ain't seen him lately, have you?"

"At the time, none of the doctors I talked to thought it was Yellow Jack."

"Well, I guess you know now," Baldridge said. "But what has any of this to do with needing a detective?"

Johnson stood up and walked over to a bookcase. "As I said, we have two matters before us of great importance. The first I shall tell you about here in the office. The other I will discuss with you later at a different location. Are you familiar with the Howard Association?"

"They provide nurses for folks sick with the fever, don't they?"

"Nurses, doctors, money to bury the destitute," the mayor said. "The Howard Association is a wonderful humanitarian organization, Mr. Baldridge. I don't know how the city would survive without it."

"I'm sure they have their hands full right now."

"They do. And that is precisely why I contacted you," the mayor said in a sober tone. "The truth is, Mr. Baldridge, the fever is spreading rapidly through the city. Just this morning, Dr. Nuttall at the board of health confirmed several cases on Third and Fourth Streets, and now even along Exchange Street. The doctors tell me that, historically, Yellow Jack has held on and spread until the first frost, and with that perhaps as much as a month away, I'm afraid the Howard Association may soon be overwhelmed if the disease continues its spread." He paused a moment. "But the city has a serious problem with the Howard Association," he said, adding, "and that, Mr. Baldridge, is where you fit in."

"How's that?"

"The Howard Association exists solely by the good graces of the people, through subscriptions, or contributions, raised in each ward of the city."

"I've seen the gift list in the paper."

"Mr. Baldridge, I'll put it quite simply. I have received an allegation that someone is stealing money from the association, and I want you to find out who it is."

Baldridge was puzzled. "Now, don't get me wrong, because I'm not trying to turn down the business, but ain't this something the police should investigate?"

"I can't involve the police. They are committed down to the last man in just maintaining order in the city. There is no one to spare for such an investigation," Mayor Johnson said, "and even if there were, I couldn't use them."

"Why?"

"Because, quite possibly, the police may be involved in the theft." He explained how subscriptions to the Howard Association were either brought directly to their office at 12 Court Street, or were collected by sanitary patrolmen or elected officials in each of the city wards. Some regular policemen, Johnson explained, had the additional duty of collecting donations for the Howard Association.

"So far, the discrepancies are limited to Ward Two. The chairman is Gerald Roe, a businessman who's had his share of financial troubles over the years. He owns a novelty company that's gone sour. I've got a feeling he may be involved, but I doubt he's the only one."

"We'll look into this Roe fellow," Baldridge assured him.

Johnson expressed his fear that involving the police might tip off the investigation and send the thief into hiding. Then he shared his overriding concern.

"Understand one thing, Mr. Baldridge. The people of the city of Memphis cannot afford to lose faith in the Howard Association. If donations stop, or if well-intentioned people are scared off from contributing because of some scandal, many innocent citizens of Memphis, who might otherwise have received treatment, will suffer and die from yellow fever."

"I see."

"There's more. In just over a week, the city will have liquidated enough bonds to give ten thousand dollars directly to the Howard Association. As mayor, I cannot in good conscience allow that donation if I believe a thief to be at work within the organization."

"Who else knows of this?" Baldridge asked.

"Only the Reverend Dr. Landrum, head of the Howard Association. If your agency agrees to take this investigation, I would suggest you begin by speaking with him. He will be joining me and several members of the board of health tomorrow morning on a tour of the Happy Hollow area. If you take the case, I'll arrange for you to meet him then."

"All right," Baldridge said.

"Again, I can't emphasize enough how important confidentiality is in this investigation. If you agree to take the case, you will report your findings only to me. If we are to have any hope of forestalling a full-scale panic, the people simply must maintain their confidence in the Howard Association. Is that clear, Mr. Baldridge?"

"Crystal clear, Mayor. Now, what about the other problem?"

Johnson checked the clock in the corner of the room. "I want you to meet me at the back door of Holst and Brothers at eleven o'clock."

"The undertakers?"

"That's correct. The coroner and Chief of Police Athy will be joining us."

"This doesn't sound too good. What's the—"

The mayor cut him off. "Mr. Baldridge, I simply will not discuss this situation here. Just bear with me and be at Holst and Brothers at eleven. I'll explain the entire matter then."


HOLST AND BROTHERS was only about five blocks from the mayor's office, so Baldridge took a slight detour down Front Street and into the alley of saloons known as Whiskey Chute, where he stopped off for a drink at Pete Flanagan's. He hated funeral homes, and just being around dead bodies gave him the shakes. The cold, ashen faces of too many young men in the war still haunted him. He wondered what could be so sensitive that the mayor couldn't have just told him right there in the peace and comfort of that elaborate office. So someone was stealing money? It hardly seemed a matter of interest to the coroner. Baldridge had the bartender fill his whiskey flask with Kentucky bourbon, mounted Nashville Harry, and rode to the undertaker's, his mood considerably lightened by the stopover.

After tying Harry to a railing behind Holst and Brothers, Baldridge slipped in the back door, humming an old war tune. He could hear the mayor arguing with someone in an adjacent room.

"I don't give a damn who he is," a deep-voiced man said, "he's got no business in this investigation. My men can—"

"Phillip, you and I both know you're spread too thin," Johnson replied. "We've got to get to the bottom of this, and fast."

"I don't need some half-assed detective—"

"Mr. Baldridge," the mayor said as Masey pushed open the door. "We were just talking about you."

A strong stench struck Baldridge as he stepped into the room. He stopped humming and covered his mouth with his sleeve. "Goddamn!" he said, turning his face away. "Who died in here?" The room fell silent as he grasped the door behind him. "Are you sure you want this closed?"

"Quite sure, Mr. Baldridge," the mayor said.

Baldridge surveyed the room. Beside Mayor Johnson stood a heavyset man with a long mustache that curled at the ends. He wore a badge, and Baldridge noticed a leather strap across his chest that he figured supported a revolver under his coat. Another man stood between two tables, his sleeves rolled up to the elbows, holding some type of medical instrument in his hand. On his left rested a body covered by a bloodstained sheet. On his right a second body clothed in a work shirt and torn trousers occupied a wooden table.

"Gentlemen, this is Mr. Masey Baldridge of the Big River Detective Agency," Johnson said. He introduced the big man beside him as Chief of Police Phillip R. Athy, and the gentleman beside the bodies as J. P. Prescott, Shelby County coroner. "Mr. Baldridge and his agency will be assisting in the investigation."

Athy started to speak, but Johnson cut him off. "Mr. Baldridge, if you'll step over here . . ." Baldridge, having trouble catching his breath, hesitated, the thought of getting closer to those stinking bodies almost making him gag. When he didn't follow Johnson and Athy, the mayor turned back to him.

"Baldridge? Are you coming?"

His first thought was to dash out the door and get some fresh air. Then maybe he would return. And maybe he wouldn't. Maybe he'd just go back to the *Paragon* and tell Luke Williamson the case wasn't worth taking. The whiskey he'd consumed only minutes before churned in his stomach and he felt as if at any moment he would heave its contents onto the floor.

"Baldridge?" Johnson repeated. "If you please?"

He summoned his strength and walked slowly between the bodies, standing just behind the mayor and Athy. He cleared his throat.

"So, uh . . . what's all this about?"

The mayor turned to the clothed body as the coroner stepped around the table and stood behind the head. "Five days ago this man was found dead in an alley on the south end of town," Johnson began. The coroner pointed to some dark, linear markings still visible on the neck as the mayor spoke. "He was strangled." Johnson turned to Athy. "Chief, tell him what you know."

Athy reluctantly produced some paper from his pocket and after giving Baldridge a contemptuous glare, began reviewing his notes. "The man is Deke Stayley. He had been a patient at the yellow fever hospital out near Fort Pickering. One of the sisters who nurse the sick folks out there found him in an alley about two blocks from the hospital. Nobody knows how he got there."

The coroner spoke as he stepped around the table opposite

Baldridge. "Looks like he had the Yellow Jack pretty severe. I noted the tone of his skin the first time we brought him in here."

Baldridge looked at Prescott. "The first time?"

"We had the body exhumed last night," Prescott said.

"You dug the son of a bitch up?" Baldridge said. "No wonder this place stinks."

The mayor spoke up. "The chief here has no clues as to who strangled him. He's got no known address and no family that anyone can find."

"Deke Stayley ain't exactly a stranger, though," Athy said. "My jailer down in Ward Five says he's a drunk. Been in and out of jail down there for years. He says ol' Deke here was a regular repenter down at the Beale Street Baptist Church. He was known to walk the aisle at least one or two Sundays a month and ask the congregation to forgive him his drinkin'," Athy explained. "Then he'd be hard at it again on Monday night. And they'd lock him up for the night to sleep it off."

Baldridge stepped closer to the body for a better look. Maybe he had seen him before. Maybe not. The man was too long dead to be sure, but something about the way Athy was talking angered Baldridge. He looked at him.

"You sayin' you ain't never had a little too much to drink?"

"What I drink isn't the issue here, Baldridge."

"You're talkin' about this man like he was a dog. I just don't think he deserves that."

Athy laughed nervously. "Hell, the man was a drunk. Probably never worked a day in his life."

"You don't know that; you didn't know the man at all. Your jailer told you all this."

"Ain't much to know."

"Listen, Athy. You don't know why that man done what he

done. You never walked in his shoes. I suspect you didn't investigate his death the first time because he was a drunk. Just another dead drunk."

"Now, see here, Baldridge. As far as I'm concerned, you don't have any business in this investigation in the first place."

Mayor Johnson tried to intervene. "Gentlemen, please—"

Baldridge held up his hand. "No, let him talk."

"You don't know what you're doing," Athy continued. "You've got no place involving yourself in police business."

"The mayor thinks different."

Athy looked at Johnson and amended his tone. "I've got no choice in this. If this is what the mayor wants, I'll just have to go along with it." He put his finger in Baldridge's chest. "But I'm telling you right now—"

Both of Baldridge's hands flashed in front of Athy and struck him solidly in the chest, driving him backward and into the table that held the other body. Athy's arm slapped against the sheet covering the rigid corpse as he tumbled to the floor. The coroner watched in horror as Athy, still on the floor, reached for his gun. He stopped abruptly as he stared down the barrel of the .45-long Colt Baldridge drew from the shoulder holster under his coat.

"I don't care if you are the goddamned chief of police, don't you ever put your hands on me again."

"Baldridge! Please!" the mayor shouted. He motioned with his head for the coroner to help Athy to his feet. Athy pushed him away, still glaring at Baldridge as he stood. "You men simply must work together on this," the mayor added. "There's too much at stake." He looked at Athy sternly. "I need to know you're going to give Mr. Baldridge full cooperation on this." Athy picked up his hat and brushed it off. "Chief?"

Athy nodded his head slowly, looking away from the mayor. "He'll have it."

"Good. Why don't you finish telling him what you know about the other victim?"

Athy pulled back the sheet on the other body as the coroner moved to stand beside him at the second table.

"This is Mr. T. R. Lassiter," Athy explained. "He was found by a neighbor who brought soup to his house for his dinner last night. Lassiter's wife died about a week ago from the fever. As far as we know, he was at the house alone. You can see that his throat's been cut. The neighbor told us he was facedown in his living room. From the looks of the place, that's right where he died. Somebody sliced him from ear to ear and he fell right there. Wasn't no sign of a struggle. No weapon. Found his Bible beside him. Prescott here thinks he was praying."

"Praying when he died?" Baldridge asked.

"That would be my guess," Prescott said, leaning over the corpse. "From the shape the body was in, that is, the way the blood had pooled, I'd say the man was kneeling beside his chair. Somebody stepped up behind him and slashed his throat. He dropped to his face. Maybe flailed a bit on the floor from the blood spattering we found, but he expired rather quickly."

"What did you say the neighbor was doing there?" Baldridge asked.

"She'd brought some soup for Lassiter's supper," Athy said. "Seems Lassiter was still grieving over his wife. He had been going next door each evening to pick up a meal the neighbor lady prepared. When he didn't show up last night, she went over to see about him."

"Nobody saw anyone coming or going from the house?" Baldridge asked.

"The neighbor said someone from the Howard Association had stopped by that afternoon. Apparently Lassiter was alive and well when whoever it was left."

"Any idea how long he'd been dead when the neighbor found him?" Baldridge asked Prescott.

"Anywhere from two to four hours, I'd guess."

"Lassiter had no enemies anybody can point to," Athy said. "Doesn't look like he was robbed."

Baldridge walked back over to Stayley's body. "So somebody strangles Stayley in an alley. But why?" He looked at Athy. "Do you think he was robbed?"

"I doubt it. From what I hear, the man was always broke."

"What do you reckon he was doing out of the hospital?"

"Just wandered off, the best we can tell. The nurses say they get delirious sometimes," Athy said.

"That's the damnedest part of it," the coroner said. "From the toll the fever had taken on him, ol' Deke would probably have been dead anyway in a day, maybe two. I can't figure why someone would strangle him."

Baldridge turned to the other body. "And two days later, somebody cuts Lassiter's throat in his own living room. Without his making any effort to fight back."

"Looks that way," Athy said.

Baldridge looked first at the mayor, then at Athy. "What's the connection?"

Johnson nodded toward Prescott, who unbuttoned Stayley's shirt and exposed his pallid chest. Baldridge held his breath and leaned in for a closer look. Just below his heart, perhaps six or eight inches above the navel, was a deep purplish outline. He studied it momentarily. "Looks almost like a cross."

"That's what I figure," Athy said, glancing at Prescott. "Tell him what you think."

Prescott held his finger over the odd marking. "Looks almost like someone imprinted a cross on the man's chest."

"Imprinted? How?" Baldridge asked.

"The best I can tell, they might have placed something like a crucifix on his body, like this," Prescott said, demonstrating, and then lifting his fist, "then pounded it against his flesh. Of course, that would have been after he died from the way the blood pooled around the imprint." Baldridge was puzzled. Prescott stood erect. "Now look over here." He moved to the other table and pulled back the sheet from Lassiter's nude body. Grasping the shoulders while Athy took the feet, the two rolled the corpse onto its side, revealing a similar mark in the center of his back.

"Looks like the same thing," Baldridge said.

"I'd say so," Prescott said.

"So you think the same person killed both these people?" Prescott nodded.

"Looks that way to me, too," Athy said.

"Mr. Baldridge, with all that Chief Athy and his men have to contend with right now, I'm afraid the weight of this investigation must fall on you. I want you to find out who did this before he kills somebody else." Johnson looked down and shook his head. "And I realize what I'm asking . . . but I want you to do it without anyone knowing about it."

When the mayor's eyes met his, Baldridge knew he was talking about more than the murders. From what Johnson had said back in his office, he was being asked to play a dangerous game. He'd have to investigate a murder with the help of a chief of police who didn't want him around, and at the same time look into the role of the police in the theft of the Howard Association funds. If Athy found out about that little matter, Baldridge wasn't likely to get any cooperation.

"I'll talk to my partners."

"Mr.—"

He interrupted the mayor. "I know. I know. Keep quiet about this."

Athy spoke up. "If you think this is a little too much for you to take on, then—"

"Just worry about yourself, Chief," Baldridge said.

Athy and the coroner left through the front door of Holst and Brothers while Baldridge and the mayor went out the back. Johnson stopped beside his carriage.

"I can't risk having you come back to my office," Johnson told him. "Your coming and going might raise more questions than I care to answer right now. And if the newspapers get hold of this . . ."

"How will I contact you again?"

Johnson climbed into his buggy and took hold of the reins.

"Mr. Baldridge, time is of the essence. I need to know as soon as possible if I can realistically expect you and your colleagues to take this case, or if I should contact someone else."

"We'll take the case," Baldridge said quickly.

He knew he shouldn't have said it the minute the words left his mouth, but he kept thinking back to Athy's comment about the case being "too much for him," and before he'd realized it, he had committed the Big River Detective Agency to work for the city.

Johnson looked doubtful. "Are you certain you can speak for Captain Williamson and the rest of your agency?"

"I can speak for the agency. Luke Williamson is my partner, not my boss."

"Very well, Mr. Baldridge. I'll expect you to meet me down at Happy Hollow tomorrow morning. I'll be accompanied by a number of people, so your presence won't arouse suspicion. I'll introduce you to Dr. Landrum then. Tomorrow night I'll be attending the Confederate Relief Association's masked ball. It's being held to raise money for fever victims, and in my capacity as mayor I simply must attend. I want you to come to the ball.

We can find a quiet spot and you can tell me what you find out from talking with Dr. Landrum. The ball will provide the necessary anonymity."

"I hadn't planned on going to any ball. I ain't got a ticket," Baldridge said.

The mayor's horse stirred and Johnson held him in place. "Oh, I'll see to it that you have a ticket."

"You've got to have costumes for those things."

"I understand D'Arcy's on Main Street is supplying costumes. It is rather late, but I'm sure you can procure something."

"Right. But tell me one thing, Mayor. If this is a costume ball tomorrow night, how are you going to recognize me?"

Johnson appeared slightly embarrassed. "You do have a very distinctive gait, Mr. Baldridge."

"I see."

"By the way," the mayor said, glancing down at Baldridge's leg. "If you don't mind me asking, did you get that limp from the war?"

"A Yankee sharpshooter got lucky," Baldridge said.

The mayor leaned out of the buggy, patted him on the shoulder, and in a tone that seemed condescending to Baldridge said, "There's glory in being wounded for your country."

"Glory won't even buy a bottle of good whiskey, Mayor."

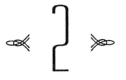

## WEDNESDAY, TWO P.M.

A board his steamboat the *Paragon*, Captain Luke Williamson squeezed through passengers standing shoulder to shoulder on the lower deck as he made his way toward clerk Steven Tibedeau.

"No more," Williamson shouted over the cacophony of voices near the bow. Tibedeau acknowledged him and stepped atop an empty crate on the wharf boat at the end of the landing stage. He raised his hands high in the air.

"Ladies and gentlemen, I'm sorry. But I can take no more passengers. The *Paragon* has reached capacity."

Williamson heard angry protests spread along the line of a hundred or more people that stretched from the wharf boat back to the shore.

"You can't do this!" screamed a woman holding a child in her arms. "You've got to take us on board."

"Ma'am, I can't," Tibedeau said.

"This is outrageous," protested a well-dressed gentleman some ten places back in line. "Surely you can take a dozen more."

"You'll have to try one of the other boats," Tibedeau said.

"We can't possibly get on another boat," an older woman called out. "They're filling up, too."

Williamson glanced up and down the Memphis landing, where the scene in front of the *Paragon* was being repeated at each of the other two boats nosed up to the bank. In a near mob scene, hundreds of citizens attempted to board the *City of Chester* and the *Grand Tower*. Worst of all, Williamson knew the woman was right. If they weren't full already, it would be only a matter of hours, perhaps maybe even minutes, and hundreds would be left on the Memphis landing without passage out of the fever-ridden city.

"Captain Williamson," one of the *Paragon*'s regulars shouted, "it's Harlan Phillips. You know me. You'll take me, won't you? I ride your boats all the time."

The woman with the baby pushed forward. "If he takes you, then he's taking me and my young'un."

Williamson stepped up on the capstan, balanced himself against a cargo pole, and tried to gain their attention.

"Listen to me. Everyone listen." Immediately, the shouting died down to a low buzz. "I know you want to leave. I know you're scared."

"Damn right we're scared," the well-dressed man said. "The fever's killing more every day. Captain, you've just got—"

"I know you're scared," Williamson continued, "and I'd like to take every one of you. But the *Paragon* is already over capacity." He pointed down the deck at the passengers lining all levels, some with hastily packed bags in hand, many of them leaning over the deck rails, watching those onshore. "I've got no place to put anybody else."

"Surely you can take a few more," the well-dressed man said. He waved money over his head. "I'll pay double. Triple, even. Whatever you want."

"Mister, it's not the money," Tibedeau tried to explain.

"You can't just leave us here to die," the older woman said.

Her voice shook with fear, and Williamson wanted desperately to take her and the others across that landing stage and aboard the *Paragon*. "Ma'am, I'm sorry, but I can't safely operate the boat with any more people on board." Voices of angry protest arose again from the crowd. Williamson raised his voice. "The last thing I want to do is get out in that channel and have this boat go down to the bottom of the river. And you don't want that either."

"We don't want to die from Yellow Jack neither," a muscular young man said as he pushed past several others in line, making his way toward Tibedeau and the landing stage.

"Other boats will arrive," Williamson told the crowd, but he doubted his own words, for already the city council was discussing a quarantine of the city. If it passed, no boats would be allowed to stop at the landing, and, perhaps worse for Williamson, none would be permitted to leave.

The young man wrestled past several people, nearly pushing the woman with the baby into the water. "I'm gettin' on this damned boat," he said as he came face-to-face with Tibedeau. "And neither you nor nobody else is stoppin' me."

"You can't come—" Before Tibedeau could finish speaking, the man grabbed his throat and forced him backward along the landing stage. Two deckhands nearby moved to pull the man off Tibedeau, but he struck one of them in the face with his fist, sending him down hard against the planks, and he fought the other off using the strength of one free hand. All the while, the man walked Tibedeau backward toward the deck, the clerk's face turning blue from the grasp on his throat. Emboldened by the man's success, several of the passengers pressed forward in his wake, and Williamson realized that he had to act. Some crewmen began moving toward the landing stage to aid their comrades, but Williamson jumped down from the capstan and cut them off. Drawing a navy Colt from beneath his jacket, Williamson fired a round into the air, then rushed onto the landing stage to meet the man holding Tibedeau. Cocking the weapon a second time, he rushed past the clerk and shoved the barrel squarely into the ear of his assailant. From the dazed expression on the slight-framed Tibedeau's face, Williamson fully expected him to pass out at any moment, and with the smell of gunpowder hovering in the hot September air, he met the man's eyes.

"Let him go," Williamson said. The crowd following the brash young man had halted at the report of the captain's weapon, but the young man held fast his grip on Tibedeau's throat and still attempted to push his way across the landing stage.

"Not until I get on this boat," the man said.

"You're not coming aboard," the captain said, pressing the weapon harder into his ear. "Give it up, mister." Williamson knew that, driven by fear of the fever, he might very well die trying to board, and perhaps kill Tibedeau in the process. Given the general mood and widespread fear along the wharf, a riot would likely ensue.

When Williamson pulled the weapon back from the man's head and pointed it skyward, the man smiled as if he'd won.

"Let go of my clerk."

"Not until I'm on board," the man replied, forcing Tibedeau another step backward. By now, several deckhands, under the leadership of the first mate, Jacob Lusk, had gathered at the edge of the landing stage, ready to wrestle the man to the deck as soon as he boarded. But if he was successful in boarding, even temporarily, it might spur others to try forcing their way aboard.

The man, sensing victory, moved quickly to within two yards of the deck, but Williamson suddenly lowered the revolver and fired a round that passed through the man's right biceps, spattering Tibedeau's face with blood. Releasing his grip, the man grabbed his wounded right arm with his left, and Tibedeau staggered into Lusk's arms. In disbelief, the man stared first at his bloodied arm, then at the captain.

"You . . . you shot me."

The crowd stood in stunned silence as Williamson cocked the weapon again, stepped in front of the man, and with the barrel planted against the man's forehead, began walking him back toward the wharf boat. Williamson released him and jogged back across the landing stage to the *Paragon*, ordering the stage to be raised. As the deckhands cranked the stage up, the man who had attacked Tibedeau called out to Williamson, "I'll see you in hell!"

The landing stage had reached a forty-five-degree angle when a half dozen of the citizens on the landing jumped into the river and attempted to swim the fifty feet out to the *Paragon*. Seeing them approach, Williamson fired two shots into the water in front of them.

"If you try to board, I'll kill you," he called to them. "Don't make me do that." Williamson turned to First Mate Lusk. "Post guards all around. Keep an eye out for Masey Baldridge or Miss Tyner. Anyone else tries to get on this boat, shoot 'em."

"Yes, sir, Cap'n," Lusk replied.

FROM THE WINDOW of the newly built office of the Big River Detective Agency, adjacent to his own quarters, Luke Williamson stood sipping a cup of coffee and watching the sea of desperate, frightened people still swarming about the wharf. He was furious at himself for having shot that man, and even angrier for ever having let the situation develop that far. Jacob Lusk had told him an hour before the incident that the *Paragon* couldn't take many more passengers. But Williamson just kept saying, "We'll take a few more. Just a few more." He should have listened to Lusk. But Williamson was well acquainted with the specter of Bronze John, having watched both of his parents succumb to the horrible fever on one of its earlier calls back in 1853. And seeing them die in the filth and stench of *el vomito negro*, or the black vomit, the captain had determined to help as many Memphis citizens escape as possible.

With New Orleans as its port of entry, the fever had remained anonymous during the first few weeks, much as it had back in '53, masquerading as any number of relatively common swamp fevers. But not more than two weeks earlier New Orleans had announced that the fever was in the city. Then, one by one, the cities north along the Mississippi began to experience cases, the citizens in each believing, hoping, praying it would stop somewhere short of an epidemic. Meanwhile, Williamson and the other riverboat packet owners continued to run their routes, unable and unwilling to paralyze commerce, hoping that sanitary precautions on board would be enough, fearing the advent of the disease on their boats, yet responsible for moving as many people to safety as possible.

The thought of bypassing Memphis entirely had crossed his mind. Three days before, when he'd left Vicksburg on the fourteenth, he'd known from newspaper reports that the board of health in Memphis had officially declared yellow fever to be in the city—as if anyone needed a bunch of doctors to tell them that. If it was like New Orleans, all people had to do was watch the undertakers' wagons, or the flood of refugees packing trains and boats and crowding the roads with their buggies and carts as they attempted to flee the city. Even now, Cairo, Illinois, was considering quarantine, and St. Louis would not wait long. Even if he got to Memphis, there was no certainty he could go farther north or hold to any semblance of a schedule. But still he came. And now he had shot a man whose only crime was being too afraid to stay and face the fever. What kind of man had he become?

Williamson saw Jacob Lusk pass in front of his window, heading toward his cabin. "I'm in here, Jacob."

Lusk entered the office. "Got the guards out like you said, Cap'n."

"Any further trouble?"

"Not so far. I think you made a believer out of the others."

"God, Jacob, I feel bad about that."

"You did what you had to, Cap'n. Them folks is crazy out there."

"Can you blame 'em? Do you have any idea what they're facing?"

"Yes, sir. I know. I lost folks to the fever myself. But you can't worry yourself about what happened out there, Cap'n. You got to control a mob. You always got to control a mob. A mob will kill you in a second."

"How's Steven?"

"Oh, he's all right, I suppose. His neck is all bruised up. Other than being a little peaked, I think he'll be all right. That was one strong fellow you tangled with out there."

"Any sign of Baldridge or Tyner?"

"No, sir. Do you think they'll make it by the time we leave?"

"Masey should. I don't know about Sally. I got a telegram after we arrived yesterday saying she was on her way back from Nashville. She went to see about getting us a state operating license for the detective agency." Williamson walked over to the window again. "With the hysteria out there, frankly, Jacob, I'm worried about her."

"Miss Tyner's a pretty smart woman, Cap'n. She knows how to handle herself."

"I guess you're right."

"And Mr. Baldridge?"

"He should be back any time. He left the boat before lunchtime."

Jacob smiled. "Mr. Baldridge? Leave before lunch?"

"Yeah, that is unusual for Masey to miss a meal. Particularly a meal someone else is paying for. The agency got a message late last night from the mayor."

"The mayor of Memphis?"

"Yeah."

"He lookin' for detectives?"

"Apparently."

"Why would the mayor of Memphis want detectives? Ain't he got his own police?"

"I don't know, Jacob. That's what Masey's gone to find out."

"What if Miss Tyner don't make it back by tomorrow? Are we gonna leave without her?" Lusk asked.

"Damned straight. They both know the rules. The *Paragon* leaves on time."

Or at least they should know the rules, Williamson figured, but you never knew with Baldridge. He had worked with the two of them for almost a year now, becoming a full partner in the Big River Detective Agency only four months back. It had all started when Baldridge had helped find the man responsible for sinking his sister ship, the *Mary Justice*—a wreck that had cost the life of his business partner, Edward Smythe. Several cases had come Baldridge's way since then, and teaming up with Tyner, they had used Williamson's packet line, and the captain himself, to establish a reputation as dependable detectives. So Williamson, in a move he was wont to occasionally second-guess, had offered them room and board on his two boats, the *Paragon* and the newly commissioned *Edward Smythe*, in exchange for a third interest in the Big River Detective Agency.

Williamson finished his coffee and glanced once more out the window. He wished Baldridge and Tyner were back. Even though he had agreed that Baldridge should respond to the message from the mayor, something about the whole matter gave him a bad feeling. But whatever the mayor wanted, Baldridge would return to the *Paragon* and discuss it in detail before committing to anything.

## ≺ 3 ≻

WEDNESDAY EVENING

xcept for an elderly couple, and a sweaty businessman who had subjected her to fifty miles of boring conversation, Salina Tyner was the sole occupant of the passenger car as her train slowed on its approach into the Memphis depot. The last of the travelers who had begun the trip with her in Nashville had disembarked in Jackson, some eighty miles east. She recalled a young mother's concern as she led her child off the train at that previous stop.

"Are you sure you want to go on to Memphis?" the woman had asked. "Folks is dying there every day."

"I won't be staying in Memphis very long. I'm catching a boat for St. Louis."

Tyner remembered how the woman had shaken her head in disbelief. "Well, if it was me, I wouldn't go within ten miles of that town."

Tyner might not have had she not promised to meet Luke and Masey with the business license for the Big River Detective Agency. A week earlier she had left the *Paragon* and headed for Nashville, her sole mission to convince the state to recognize their detective business with a state operating license. They had already been working without one, concentrating on cases in various ports along the river, and she, Williamson, and Baldridge had discussed the possibility of continuing in that way. But Luke, ever the businessman, saw the potential for making money from the state, and with the Reconstruction government in power, he reminded them that they would not stand a chance of getting any work from the state of Tennessee unless they secured a license. Williamson could ill afford to take the time away from the packet line to travel to Nashville, and Baldridge would have no chance in getting the license. Even with a conservative Democrat in the governor's office, Nashville still held enough radical Republicans to guarantee that an ex–Confederate soldier would be denied a license for anything. So Tyner was the logical choice—in fact, the only choice—and even she had met with plenty of resistance.

"Where in the world did you get the idea that a woman can run a detective agency, little lady?" one of the bureaucrats in the capitol had asked her through a patronizing smile. Tyner had gritted her teeth, returned his smile, and assured him that it was a partnership. She made the state's employee feel infinitely better by telling him that a man, Luke Williamson, was the official petitioner for the license.

"Oh, Captain Williamson. Well, he certainly would qualify for consideration," the man admitted.

"Consideration" meant three days of visiting the same office and annoying the clerk until the license for the Big River Detective Agency was signed by the latest carpetbagger to occupy the throne. But now it was done.

"Memphis depot five minutes out, ma'am," a porter said as the locomotive chugged through the outskirts of the city. "Do you need help with your things?"

"Yes, please," Tyner said, pointing at the bag on the seat beside her. As she stood and allowed the porter to secure the bag, he spoke to her as if in confidence, despite the nearly empty car.

"Ma'am, if I was you, I'd be right swift in leavin' the train," the porter said. " 'Cause from what I hear, folks is gettin' down-right rowdy about gettin' on board and gettin' out of Memphis. This here train ain't goin' nowhere until tomorrow morning, but I been hearin' that some of these people are so desperate they're gettin' on the trains and sleepin' there the night before, just so they don't get left."

Tyner smiled. "I appreciate the warning."

"Yes, ma'am."

Having followed events in the Nashville paper, Tyner knew the situation had deteriorated in the last week, but it wasn't until they eased into the depot that she realized just how bad things were. The train jolted to a halt, and the porter barely had the door open to step down to the platform with her luggage when two young men pushed their way past him and nearly knocked Tyner down hustling into the passenger car. She stepped quickly onto the platform just as a half dozen men and women, arms loaded with baggage, dashed for the open door. The porter placed her bag on the siding and futilely demanded tickets as the people rushed past him and crowded up the steps.

A middle-aged woman in a badly wrinkled dress sauntered up to Tyner. "Where's that train headed?"

"I have no idea."

"I reckon it don't matter," the woman said, pushing past her and following the others up the steps. "Long as it's leavin' town."

As Tyner made her way toward the main building she saw

similar scenes played out along two parallel tracks. One locomotive released steam between its wheels that came perilously close to wide-eyed children following their parents in search of an empty seat. With people acting this crazy, getting out of Memphis would suit Tyner just fine, and the sooner she escaped from this bedlam and settled into her quiet room on the *Paragon*, the better.

"Sally," someone called above the fray. "Sally, over here." Standing on her tiptoes, she struggled against the growing darkness to find the source of the sound. "Over here."

Tyner caught sight of Masey Baldridge, riding his horse in her direction and leading a mount behind him.

"Right on time," Baldridge called to her.

"A few minutes early, actually." Before she could reach Baldridge, she noticed a man approaching him.

"How much for the horse, mister?" the man called to Baldridge.

"Not for sale," Baldridge said without looking at him.

"I'll pay all I've got," he said.

"It's not for sale," Baldridge repeated as Tyner reached him.

The man stepped forward and took hold of Baldridge's reins, bringing Nashville Harry to a sudden halt. "I need a horse bad, mister. I got eight dollars. I know that ain't enough, but it's all I've got. Mister, I've got to get my family out of town. I got me a wagon," he said, pointing to an overloaded wagon, the driver's seat occupied by a hollow-faced woman cradling a child in her arms. Tyner saw the fear in the man's eyes as he continued to plead with Baldridge to sell the horse. "But my horse give out. I need to—"

"Let go of the bridle, mister," Baldridge told him firmly. "The horse is for the lady."

"Oh," the man said, appearing suddenly ashamed of himself. "I'm sorry. I thought it was an extra—"

"Don't worry about it," Baldridge said. "Good luck finding something."

As the man turned away, Tyner called to him, "That train just arrived. It'll be leaving in the morning. Maybe you and your family could get a seat."

The man turned and looked at her with a penetrating sadness. "Don't do me no good, ma'am. I got two more young'uns in the back of that wagon. I can't afford no train."

Tyner momentarily entertained the idea of selling him the horse anyway, but it belonged to Luke Williamson, and though she wrestled with the notion of explaining it to him later, by the time she'd made up her mind, the man had disappeared into the crowd.

Baldridge extended his hand. "Let me have your bag." When he had taken it from her, Tyner mounted sidesaddle, folding her dress neatly beneath her and grasping the pommel.

"Let's get out of here," Baldridge said, but Tyner hesitated, her eyes fixed on the woman gently rocking her child atop the horseless wagon that sat like an island amid the flow of people. "Are you coming or not?"

"Follow me," she said, leading her horse through the crowd. "Make way," she shouted when the pedestrians were slow to move. Baldridge trailed along behind her.

"Where in hell are you going? We need to be moving west instead of—"

"Just hush and keep up," Tyner said.

When she neared the wagon, the man who had approached Baldridge about the horse was consoling his wife, her eyes reddened from crying, her arms wrapped tightly about the blanketed child.

"Sir?" she called to him. The man turned and looked up at her.

"Yes, ma'am?"

"I can't give you this horse."

"Yes, ma'am, I understand."

Two dirty-faced children poked their heads through the burlap flap behind the driver's seat, watching in silence.

"I can't give it to you . . . but . . . I can let you borrow it."

"Borrow it?" the man repeated.

"Sally, what are you doing?" Baldridge asked.

"Consider it a loan from Captain Luke Williamson of the steamboat *Paragon*. You can rent the animal."

"Ma'am, are you serious?" the man asked, unable to contain his growing excitement.

Tyner hopped down from the horse, walked around the mount, and passed her bag up to Baldridge.

"What am I supposed to do with this?"

"Hold on to it." She turned to the man and handed him the reins. "I will expect you to return the animal to Captain Williamson's wharf boat at the Memphis riverfront, Mr. . . . ."

"Pegram," he said, taking hold of the bridle. "Will Pegram."

"Sometime within the next month, Mr. Pegram."

"Ma'am, I—I don't know what to say."

"Don't say anything. Just get him hitched up and get your family to wherever you're taking them."

Pegram dug into his pocket. "Here," he said, shoving a handful of dollars toward her. "Take this here as payment toward rent on your horse."

Tyner was in the process of refusing his money when Baldridge leaned down from his saddle and snatched the bills.

"Masey," Tyner said, her eyes flashing at him.

He cut her off. "Luke's gonna expect something in good faith. That's an expensive animal you're handing off there."

"The man's right," Pegram said. "I'd feel better about taking him if you'd accept the money."

"I don't—"

"We accept," Baldridge said, extending his arm to assist Tyner in mounting up behind him. "Now can we get back to the river?"

"Ma'am, I'm in your debt," Pegram said as Baldridge led his horse away.

"No, Mr. Pegram," she called back to him. "Luke Williamson's debt."

"Yes, ma'am. And I'll sure return this here horse. I will for sure," Pegram shouted to her over the bustling crowd. "You be sure to thank the captain for me."

Tyner kept pushing off Baldridge's shoulder, adjusting her skirt in search of some modesty as they worked their way through the crowded landing.

"Would you sit still? I've got enough to handle, what with carrying this bag. You're liable to pull us both off."

"I'm just trying to find some comfortable way to sit," Tyner snapped at him.

"Why, I figured you'd just rest on your laurels," Baldridge said, laughing as one of Nashville Harry's abrupt steps brought forth a moan from Tyner.


AT TEN O'CLOCK that evening, inside the office of the Big River Detective Agency on the *Paragon*, Luke Williamson was livid.

"You gave away one of my horses?" he said, staring at Tyner in disbelief.

"No, Luke, I didn't exactly give it away," she tried to explain. "I rented it out."

"You rented it."

"Yeah. I sort of loaned it."

"Sort of loaned it? To whom?"

Tyner had hoped Baldridge might weigh in on her side, but he could scarcely contain his laughter.

"A man named Pegram," Tyner explained. "Will Pegram."

"Who is this Pegram?" Williamson asked.

"He had a wife and three children, and they had no way of getting out of town."

"Well, that's too bad, Sally, but who is he?"

"I don't really know," she said, averting her eyes.

"You don't know? You handed off one of my best mares and you don't know who you gave it to?"

"He'll return it. I'm sure he will," Tyner said.

Williamson shook his head. "That's one gone horse, that's what we've got here. One gone horse."

Baldridge laughed. "Maybe not, Luke." He handed Pegram's money to him.

"What's this?"

"Advance on the rental."

"Eight dollars?"

"It's better than nothing, ain't it?" Baldridge said. He looked at Tyner, and with a devious smile, added, "She wasn't even gonna—"

"Let him get away without paying," Tyner said quickly. "I was just looking out for your interests, Luke." She tossed Baldridge a menacing stare.

Williamson held the money, eyeing first Tyner, then Baldridge. "You let her do this?"

Baldridge shrugged, a hapless look on his face, but Tyner was growing angry.

"Let me? Let me?" Tyner said. "I'll tell you right now that Masey Baldridge doesn't 'let' me do anything!" She moved closer to Williamson. "And neither do you, Luke. I did what I thought was right. And if you don't like it, I'll pay for the horse myself."

"All right, all right. It's done now," Williamson said. "Masey, tell us about your meeting with the mayor."

Williamson had a steward bring in mint juleps, and over the next half hour, Baldridge described the assignment Mayor Johnson had outlined to him, describing in detail his visit with the coroner and Chief Athy at Holst and Brothers. Williamson, in turn, replied to Baldridge's question about the armed guards he'd encountered on the wharf boat, relating the incident earlier that day.

"So you've taken to shooting the passengers?"

"It's not funny, Masey. There's nothing funny about it," Williamson said. "If I'd had my choice, we would have been under way this afternoon. We've had the ship full since this morning."

"Then why didn't you go?" Baldridge asked.

"I'm not scheduled to depart until tomorrow. I keep my schedule."

"Even if you're fully loaded?"

"Oh, he's just being silly," Tyner said. "He wasn't willing to leave us, were you, Luke?"

"That's part of it."

"Just part of it?" Tyner said.

Baldridge finished his mint julep and leaned forward in his chair. "Ain't much place to go, is there? I heard that Cairo's turning boats away. So is St. Louis."

Williamson appeared disturbed. "Masey's right. All the major ports are locking up tighter than a drum with this fever outbreak. Unless we can land at one of the smaller towns like Chester, Illinois, I'm not sure where we'll stop."

"What about staying right here?" Baldridge asked.

Williamson ran his hand through his hair. "We can't stay here. The passengers will never stand for it, and I'm not even sure it would be the right thing to do. I talked to Augustus Zeigler, master of the *City of Chester*, this afternoon. He figures to put out tomorrow, too. Says he'll take it slow upriver, maybe take an extra day getting to St. Louis, and hope they lift the quarantine in the meantime."

"Is that what you'll do?" Tyner asked.

"Probably. It makes the most sense." He studied both their faces. "If you two don't want to take this case, I'd understand. Nobody could blame you for not wanting to stay here in Memphis. I doubt I'd do it if I were you. Yellow Jack's nothing to mess around with."

As Tyner spoke to Williamson, she noticed Baldridge's growing uneasiness. "Sure, Luke, staying here and working on this case means risking the fever. But it also means making a name and a reputation for the agency."

"You know, Luke, Sally makes a lot of sense. I don't think we should be running from the fever or anything else. Besides, if what I went through back in June didn't kill me, I don't figure ol' Bronze John's got much shot at it."

Baldridge was referring to a fever he had experienced in St. Louis while working on a case a few months earlier. Tyner had helped nurse him through it, and though he had almost died, the nature of the illness remained unknown. Baldridge seemed to have made a full recovery in the intervening weeks. Tyner figured he was gambling that whatever he had contracted would give him some immunity to yellow fever. Maybe it would, but it offered no protection for her.

"I'd like to work the case, Masey, but I just don't—"

Baldridge cut her off. "You'll feel better about it when we meet the mayor tomorrow morning down in Happy Hollow—"

"Meet the mayor?" Williamson said. "You sound like you've already agreed to this."

"I have," Baldridge muttered.

"What?" Tyner said.

"I told him we'd take the case," Baldridge said, glancing away from her.

Tyner came to her feet. "You agreed to take the case without talking to us?"

"Sally, you said yourself how good it could be for business."

Tyner looked at Williamson, who sat shaking his head. "Luke, are you gonna let him get away with this?"

"You had no right to commit us without at least talking it over first," Williamson said.

"The mayor needed a decision, and he needed it right then."

"Politicians always want things immediately."

"I told him I had the authority to speak for the agency."

"But you don't," Williamson said.

"The hell I don't," Baldridge shouted, rising to his feet. "I'm a partner in this every bit as much as you. You're leaving tomorrow, anyway. You just said so."

Tyner stared at Baldridge, still in disbelief at his selfishness. "What about me?"

Baldridge glared at her. "You can leave, too, if you want. I'll work the damn case by myself." He walked toward the door, and stopping just short of it, turned to face his two partners. "This is serious. This city is in trouble. But if you two don't want to do anything about it, that's just fine with me."

"Hold on, Masey," Williamson said, tapping out the tobacco from his pipe into an ashtray. "I'm not saying we shouldn't take the case. All I'm saying," he added, glancing at Tyner, "and I think Sally is, too, is that we wish you would have discussed it with us before committing the agency."

Baldridge held the door open, ready to leave. "I told you. The mayor needed an answer."

Williamson looked at Tyner, and she knew he wanted her opinion. For sure, Baldridge had been impetuous and inconsiderate, but none of that changed the fact that he was right. The situation he had described called for immediate action, and part of Tyner was quite pleased that the mayor of Memphis had thought enough of their reputation to want them. But she'd be damned if she'd let Baldridge off the hook that easily.

"Well," she said, her hand on her hip, addressing only Williamson, "I don't see that we have much choice. Since Mr. Speak-for-the-Agency here has already committed us, I don't hardly see how we can back out now."

"I'm afraid you're right. We'd look bad if we went back and refused the work. But it's the two of you that are going to get stuck with this, so I'd just as soon not make the decision."

"We'll handle it," Baldridge declared.

"Oh, you're real quick to say what *we'll* do, aren't you?" Tyner said.

"Damn it, Sally, are you with me on this or not? 'Cause if you're not, I've got work to do."

She eyed first Williamson, then Baldridge. This was her last chance to say no, and her mind was filled with images of the hundreds of people struggling to leave Memphis, making her wonder if she was mad to agree to stay, and even madder to agree to take work in the fever-stricken city. But there was the quarantine among the ports to the north, and the danger of the fever even greater in the cities to the south. Better to be in Memphis doing something significant than sitting on a boat offshore some disease-infested town, just waiting to get sick and die.

"You're staying. I know you are," Baldridge said with a grin. She should have objected, but it wasn't the first time he had been right. His uncanny ability to identify her thoughts had always intrigued her. She would stay, partly because it was paying work, but mainly because she couldn't bring herself to leave Masey to work the case alone—fever or no fever.

"I suppose I am." She pointed her finger at him. "But I'm telling you right now, don't you *ever* do this to us again. Do you understand? We make the decision together to take cases. Is that clear?"

"Yeah, it's clear," Baldridge said, closing the door and returning to his chair. "Now, we've got some planning to do."

"So, what's next?" Williamson asked.

"Talk to the people running the Howard Association, I suppose. And find out how they receive their subscription money. Then I guess we follow it backward and see who's got their hands in the pot."

"And the two deaths?" Tyner asked.

"I don't know yet."

"Oh, that's a hell of a plan!" Tyner said.

# 4

## THURSDAY, SEPTEMBER 18

The crowd that had lined the Memphis wharf on Wednesday afternoon had thinned by nearly two thirds by morning. With all boats filled and refusing additional passengers, and no others daring to stop, most of those seeking to flee Memphis had disappeared into the night in search of another way out of town. Those who remained along the wharf had spent a hot, humid night sleeping on the cotton bales and stacks of barrels that lined the landing, abandoned by a freight carrier like a bride on her wedding day. When Baldridge and Tyner slipped off the *Paragon* that morning, several of those waiting on the wharf entertained the momentary hope that they might take their places. But yesterday's shooting had been the evening's subject of hasty campfire talk among those who remained; and Luke Williamson's crewmen, armed and standing by the landing stage, soon dashed any hope the stragglers may have held for getting aboard.

Baldridge and Tyner rode to Poplar Street and then toward the river, arriving at the bluff along Front Street. Baldridge leaned over in his saddle and eyed the winding trail that led down the bluff and twisted for some two hundred yards through dozens of shanties and down to the water.

"Do me a favor," he said to Tyner, still gazing over the settlement known as Happy Hollow.

"What's that?"

"When we get to the bottom of this bluff, don't give your horse away today. 'Cause I'm not sure Nashville Harry could get us both back up here, and I sure as hell ain't walkin'."

Tyner followed him as he started down the trail. "Will you just hush about that? What else could I do? The man was—"

"You could've not given Luke's horse away."

"For the last time, Masey Baldridge, I didn't give the horse away. I loaned it."

"Well, I can tell you one thing for sure."

"What, Masey?"

He patted his horse on the neck as he negotiated the turns in the trail. "Don't be askin' to borrow Harry, 'cause I've really grown to like him."

What Tyner's sudden silence suggested was confirmed by a quick glance over his shoulder, as Baldridge saw her tightly set jaw. He'd made her mad. And that brought a smile to his face. She was a hell of a good-looking woman when she got mad.

Baldridge had been to Happy Hollow about four years before, long before so many coloreds and poor white folks began homesteading there.

"Good Lord, Masey," Tyner said, producing a handkerchief to cover her mouth. "This place smells awful!"

"It's a damn trash heap," he replied. "For fifty years, people been hauling every kind of filth you can imagine and dumping it over the bluff. Rain washes it down, spreads it out, and pretty soon you got free land."

"Free? Doesn't somebody own it?"

"The city does."

"And they actually let people live here?"

"They don't stop 'em. The chance of living rent free draws poor folks like horseshit draws flies."

"Just look at these places," Tyner said, surveying the line of shanties that extended along the trail from the bluff. Built on uprights that positioned them above the yearly high-water mark, the collection of squatter dwellings was constructed of every imaginable kind of material. The dwelling nearest them had weatherboarding ripped from some railroad car, siding that still bore a trace of the name "Memphis and Charleston Railroad." Others were little more than abandoned flatboats perched on support poles, few of which had a roof worthy of keeping out a light summer rain. The hot September sun had baked the ground hard, but as they rode toward the river, the earth beneath them softened into a near mush, their horses sinking several inches as they walked.

"I think I see the mayor," Baldridge said, pointing to a dozen or more men gathered near the rickety steps of one of the shanties. Approaching within thirty or so feet, Baldridge and Tyner halted but did not dismount. The mayor was talking to the owner of the shanty.

"Now, I know you don't like it, but I think it's best for everyone," Johnson said to a gaunt-looking man who stood on the steps some four feet above the mayor. A woman stood beside him.

"Ain't best for me," the man said. "I ain't sick." He tugged on one of his suspenders. "Ain't gonna get sick neither."

"You don't know that for sure," Johnson said. "The fever could get any of us."

"Not me."

Johnson turned to the dignified-looking man beside him and with a frustrated sigh said, "Dr. Fledge, explain it to him."

"Mr. Stiles, the board of health has declared that yellow fever is in the city. It was in the newspaper three days ago."

"Don't read no newspapers," Stiles said, folding his arms.

"Sir, this place breeds the disease. It spreads it," Fledge said. "The filth down here—"

"I thought nobody knowed what caused Yellow Jack," Stiles countered.

"Well," the doctor said, glancing at the group standing beside him, "we can't say for sure, but I happen to believe it's the offal. You see, the—"

"The what?" Stiles asked.

"Offal, sir. The rubbish. The trash that's collected here over the years." Stiles's expression was unchanged as the doctor continued, sounding more like a preacher than a doctor, and as Baldridge listened he couldn't help but wonder whether the doctor was talking primarily to Mr. Stiles or to the distinguished-looking gentlemen surrounding him. "The recent rains have soaked all this loose ground quite fully. Then, when the sun comes out and bakes this ground—hot, like it's been these past weeks—it releases miasma. Vapors, sir. Really quite poisonous. Obviously, anyone who breathes these vapors is subject to succumbing to the disease."

"I been livin' down here three years, Doctor," Stiles said. "Ain't had no fever. Neither has my wife or either of my young-'uns. And I been breathin' the whole time," the man added with a chuckle.

"Sir, this is no laughing matter. If you had seen the death I've seen—"

"I have seen it," Stiles said. "Most folks down here has lost somebody to the fever. But I ain't. And I ain't movin' out of the hollow."

Dr. Fledge, clearly losing his patience with the man, placed one hand on his hip and with the other pointed a finger at Stiles. "Sir, you may have no choice. Mayor Johnson here may just force you to move."

"Now, Randolph, I didn't tell this man—"

"Mayor, this entire area should be burned to the ground," Fledge said. "It's breeding a disease that could kill everyone in Memphis."

"Randolph, we don't know that for sure."

"I know it!"

Another gentleman standing nearby interrupted. Baldridge remembered having seen him in Mayor Johnson's office the previous morning. Hensley was his name. "Look around you," the man said, gesturing in the direction of the bluff. "Why, there is not another nest of rookeries to equal this in any other decent city. These squatters should be forcibly moved and this filthy place burned to the ground. Mayor, you owe that much to the citizens."

Johnson pointed at Stiles, who had remained silent throughout the heated debate. "He's a citizen."

"Not for long if he doesn't get out of here," Dr. Fledge added.

Mayor Johnson finally noticed Baldridge, and after acknowledging him with a wave, turned back to the group. "Gentlemen, I've authorized the street cleaning. I've empowered the city to fully fund the yellow fever hospital out at Fort Pickering, and we've established the pest house on President's Island." He looked directly at Dr. Fledge. "Hell, Randolph, I'm even considering the quarantine you're insisting on—even though I don't want to think about what it will do to the business and industry of the city." He eyed the others. "And you all know that I'm doing the best I can to see to it that the city helps the Howard Association. But I'll be damned if I'm going to burn these people out."

"But the city owns the land, Mayor," Hensley said. "You've got the authority. You could—"

"It's not about the authority."

"Mayor, it's what the people of Memphis want," Hensley said.

"Maybe. But the people don't have to do it. I do. And I'm not ready to do it. Not yet, anyway."

"Then when?" Hensley asked, pointing at Fledge. "You've got a medical doctor right here telling you that Happy Hollow breeds Yellow Jack. The board of health has a petition signed by a dozen reputable doctors demanding that we quarantine the city. What more do you want?"

"And I've got other doctors telling me the opposite, along with another petition *not* to quarantine. Those doctors say the fever's *not* contagious. Others say it might be. Gentlemen, I don't know who to believe. But until I do, I'm not going to take such a serious step. Think about this. Shreveport's had an awful time with the fever. So have a half dozen other cities. But they haven't started leveling buildings, have they? For God's sake, man, Happy Hollow here in Memphis didn't cause the Yellow Jack in Shreveport! And until somebody can show me positively that the fever is caused here in Happy Hollow, I'm not running anybody out." He paused for a moment, but neither of the other gentlemen spoke. "Now, if you want to continue along here and try to get these people to move voluntarily, then you go right ahead. I'll support you a hundred percent. But the city is not making anybody move." He motioned for one of the other men to join him and started walking toward Baldridge, his feet sinking in the soft ground. "Now, if you'll excuse me, Reverend Landrum and I need to speak with this gentleman."

Moving out of earshot of the others, the mayor stopped on a slight rise of ground and shook hands with Baldridge.

"I was hoping to hear from you this morning," Johnson said.

Landrum offered his hand to Tyner. "This ground is a bit firmer, if you and the lady would care to dismount."

Once off their mounts, Baldridge introduced Tyner and confirmed again for the mayor that the Big River Detective Agency would take the case.

"That's good, Mr. Baldridge. That's very good. We have no time to waste. People are starting to panic over this Yellow Jack."

"I could tell," Tyner said, glancing at the half dozen men walking in the muck toward the next shanty.

"Oh, they mean well, Miss Tyner. At least I think they do. It's so easy for them. Just move people out. Declare quarantine. Burn down half the city. But they don't have to answer for the actions I take."

"Or the ones you don't take," Baldridge said.

Johnson nodded. "You are a detective, indeed, Mr. Baldridge. You have cut exactly to the heart of my dilemma, sir." Johnson realized that he had not introduced Landrum, and with a self-effacing smile amended the error. "The Reverend Dr. Simon Landrum is head of the Howard Association. It was at his behest that I decided to contact you." He tossed a questioning look at Baldridge, which the latter took to be a check of the confidentiality he had explained to him yesterday morning, then he glanced at Tyner. "Has Mr. Baldridge told you of the serious matters I want him to investigate?"

"Yes, sir. He has."

"Then you realize that we don't need a scandal with the Howard Association on top of everything else."

"I understand. Masey told me that you suspect someone of stealing money," she said.

"That's correct. Reverend Landrum can give you the details. He is the one who approached me with the impropriety. I really should get back to Dr. Fledge and the others before they become suspicious of our conversation."

"Or before they decide to torch half the city," Baldridge said.

"How true, Mr. Baldridge," Johnson replied. "By the way, I have that ticket for you to the ball this evening, and an extra one if the lovely Miss Tyner will be joining you."

"Yes, she will," Baldridge said.

Tyner seemed surprised. "Ball? What—"

"And she's delighted by the invitation," Baldridge added.

"Excellent. We'll talk again tonight," Johnson said, excusing himself and walking through the muck to join the others.

Tyner grasped Baldridge's sleeve. "What ball? What's he talking about?"

"I'll explain later," Baldridge assured her.

Reverend Landrum spoke softly, measuring his words carefully. "I'm very pleased you have decided to help us in this difficult matter. It really is quite awkward, you know. I've been trying my best to manage the benevolent efforts of the Howard Association for almost a month now. And we've done much good work. We've provided nurses for the ill, hired doctors to attend to the suffering, even paid for the interment of many who could not afford it. And, of course, we've raised considerable money in the process. And that, my good people, is where we seem to have a problem."

"The mayor says you suspect someone of stealing money."

"That's correct, Mr. Baldridge. The Howard Association is a charitable organization. It originally existed back in 1867 during the city's last visitation of the pestilence. It was effective in bringing considerable relief. Thus, when the fever again appeared in early August, those of us who had been a part of the Howard Association back in '67 immediately began to put together a skeleton organization."

"But I understand the board of health didn't officially declare that the fever was in the city until last Sunday," Tyner said.

"That's true, Miss Tyner, but those of us who went through Yellow Jack before didn't wait for the board of health. We've seen what the disease can do—how it can devastate the city. When the first cases of fever appeared down here in Happy Hollow, the doctors weren't sure what it was. Many of these malarial fevers have the same appearance initially. It might have been dengue fever, or something else. But as the disease advances, it shows some very specific symptoms."

"Didn't the doctors who treated these early cases recognize the signs?"

"Yes, they did."

"Then why didn't the board of health declare that yellow fever existed a month ago?"

"That is a very good question, Miss Tyner. One that many people are asking." Landrum looked in the direction of the mayor and the others, and as if to ensure he could not be heard, lowered his voice even more. "The truth is, the board of health has failed miserably. It was formed to give early warning to the community in the advent of diseases. It was supposed to keep a close register of mortality, and direct the sanitation efforts in and around Memphis so no epidemic would spread as it did back in '67. The board has done little of this, and what it has done has come much too late."

"But the Howard Association has been active," Baldridge said. "I've seen the news in the paper."

"Yes, I'm proud to say it has. When the disease first appeared, and the first deaths occurred, we got the Howard Association going."

"And the money?" Baldridge asked. "Tell us about the money that you believe to be missing."

"The Howard Association exists only through the charity of the community," Landrum explained. "I am shepherd of a church, and my parishioners have been most generous, but they cannot carry the burden alone."

"How did you discover the money missing?" Tyner asked.

"My treasurer, Mr. Roland, records each donation by the person's name and the amount. A week ago we began publishing contributors' names in the paper each day. It's not just to give credit to the contributor, but to urge others to give money."

"So did this Roland find that money had been stolen from your office?" Baldridge asked.

"No. No money has been taken from our building on Court Street. It seems, Mr. Baldridge, that someone is taking the money before it gets to us."

"How do you know that?"

"One of our benefactors, a Mr. Snowden, contacted me personally about four days ago. He told me he had sent one hundred and fifty dollars to the Howard Association by way of the collection committee. When the first list of contributors appeared in the newspaper, the amount of his contribution was shown as one hundred dollars."

"What happened to the other fifty dollars?" Tyner asked.

"That is precisely what Mr. Snowden wanted to know. Obviously, I was quite shocked by the whole matter, and though I suggested to Mr. Snowden that this might have been a simple misprint in the paper, I assured him I would look into it. I immediately contacted Mr. Roland and had him review his ledger book. The amount of money he received was one hundred dollars. Just as stated in the paper."

"Do you trust this Roland fellow?" Baldridge asked.

"Absolutely, Mr. Baldridge. Thomas Roland is a decent, Christian man. He would never steal money from the Howard Association. He works long hours with no pay to handle the finances of the organization. He was as saddened by this whole matter as I. If this were the only occasion of an impropriety, I might count it an anomaly."

"There have been others?" Baldridge said.

"I'm afraid so. The very next day I had two other contributors contact me indicating a discrepancy between the amount they gave the collection committee and that which appeared in the newspaper. Both of them live in Ward Two."

"And Mr. Roland?" Baldridge asked.

"He confirmed that the published amount was exactly what the Howard Association received."

"Have there been other instances?" Tyner asked.

"No. Not since Monday. But what disturbs me, Miss Tyner, is that we only discovered these discrepancies once we began listing donors in the newspaper. What if this has been happening for two or three weeks? Unless the amount of the gift is published in the paper, the benefactor does not know how much money we actually received."

"Do you think that's true?" Tyner asked. "Do you think money disappeared before last Sunday?"

"I don't know. I suppose I could contact the earlier subscribers and verify the amount they say they gave with our record book, but . . ."

"But what?"

"Miss Tyner, I don't want to lose the good reputation of the Howard Association. Our organization may be the only thing standing between Memphis and a scourge of a disease that is biblical in proportion. The citizens simply cannot lose confidence in our organization. And perhaps just as important, they cannot stop giving money for fear of having some or all of it stolen."

"So you want us to find out what happened to Snowden's money, and the others you mentioned, and make sure it isn't still going on?" Baldridge asked.

"Precisely. That is why Mayor Johnson hired your organization. He informed me that he has been authorized to commit ten thousand dollars of city funds to the Howard Association on September twenty-fifth. But he will only do so providing we have these discrepancies cleared up."

"So if there's a hole in the bucket, he wants to patch it first," Baldridge said.

Landrum nodded.

"We'll need to talk to Roland."

Landrum seemed annoyed. "Mr. Baldridge, I assure you that Thomas Roland—"

"If you don't mind, Reverend," Tyner interrupted, "we'll assure ourselves."

Landrum nodded. "Very well, then."

"And we'll need a list of the people on your collection committee," Baldridge said.

"Mr. Roland can provide that for you. I'm afraid I'm not close enough to that end of our operation to name those people."

"Thank you, Reverend Landrum," Tyner said, offering him her hand. He assisted her in mounting, then turned to Baldridge, who had already mounted Nashville Harry.

"Just one moment, Mr. Baldridge," Landrum said, removing a piece of paper from his pocket. He scribbled something on the page, folded it, and gave it to Baldridge.

"Here is a note by way of introduction when you arrive at our office on Court Street. Father Martin Walsh administers the office in my absence. Present this to him when you arrive and he'll see to it you talk with Roland. Martin is aware of none of this disquieting affair, and I've simply referred to you in my note as 'interested citizens.' "

"Thank you," Baldridge said.

"And, Mr. Baldridge, please let me remind you and Miss Tyner of how sensitive this whole matter is. If word gets out about your investigation, I shudder to think of the consequences for the health of the city."

"We'll keep it quiet, Reverend."

On their ride to the Howard Association, they were joined part of the way by Dr. Randolph Fledge, who had taken leave of the mayor and his party to make rounds at the yellow fever hospital at old Fort Pickering, then gone on to the pest house on President's Island. He would be the rest of the day and well into the night attending to patients, but he seemed tireless and more talkative than Baldridge expected. All the way up the bluff and well into town, Fledge expounded upon his views of the current scourge, describing in more detail than Baldridge desired the most disgusting details of the illness. Baldridge allowed him to believe, as Landrum had suggested, that he and Tyner were exploring the possibility of assisting the Howard Association in caring for the sick, and he wondered if Fledge, at least in his own way, was trying to prepare them for what was to come. Fledge continued south when Baldridge and Tyner turned east, but by that time Fledge's descriptions of black vomit had killed what appetite they had for lunch, so they proceeded directly to the Howard Association, where they found Father Martin Walsh.

Walsh received them in the office, a modestly furnished

room with three wing-backed chairs and a rolltop desk. Walsh nodded slowly as he read the note from Landrum.

"So you folks want to help?"

"That's right," Baldridge said. "Miss Tyner and I want to learn more about what the Howard Association is doing."

"Well, we certainly can use nurses. Yesterday alone we were contacted for twelve," Walsh said, his penetrating eyes locking on Tyner. "It's incumbent upon every citizen to do whatever he or she can at a time like this."

"I agree, Father," Tyner said. "But I'd like to talk to some of the people around here first. I want to know what I'm getting myself into."

Walsh nodded. "That's certainly reasonable. We don't actually treat patients here. This is just our administrative office. I man this office in Reverend Landrum's absence. We receive volunteers, assign nurses and doctors, mainly coordinate activities from here. But you could certainly speak with Sister Naomi. She's our chief of nurses." Walsh leaned out the office door and looked to the right. "I think she's with a young woman right now. Sister Naomi?" he called down the hallway.

"Yes?" a woman replied.

"When you've finished with your guest, could you join me in the office?"

"Certainly, Father," she replied. Walsh turned to Baldridge. "And you, Mr. Baldridge. How do you wish to help?"

Baldridge leaned back and ran his fingers along the lapels of his jacket. "Father, I am a man of no small means," he declared. Tyner looked at him, trying to contain her surprise. "I'm prepared to make a sizable contribution to the Howard Association as soon as I have a better understanding of the organization."

Walsh's eyes brightened. "I see. What kind of understanding

do you seek, sir? We treat victims of yellow fever. There's really not much more—"

"I'm talking finances, sir. As a businessman, I like to be comfortable about where and how my money is being spent. Whether it's real estate, shipping—whatever the investment—I'm accustomed to having a thorough look at the project before I commit funds." He was laying it on thick, and from Tyner's look, he knew he would hear about it later.

"Mr. Baldridge, the Howard Association is not an investment. I don't know what Reverend Landrum told you, but we're a relief organization. There will be no return on your money. Your only return will be the knowledge that you may have helped to save some lives and perhaps ease some suffering."

Baldridge hesitated. "Well, of course. I understand that." He cleared his throat. "But like Miss Tyner here, I still want to know what I'm getting into."

"Very well, then. What do you want to do?"

"I'd like to talk to your Mr. Roland," Baldridge said, noting Walsh's surprise.

"You know Thomas Roland?"

"I understand he handles your finances."

"That's true, but—"

"Then he's the man I want to see."

"All right."

Walsh was interrupted by a knock outside his door. A short, middle-aged woman stood in the doorway, her hands folded in front of her, her eyes gazing down at the floor.

"Oh, good. You're free," Walsh said, rising from his chair to meet her.

"Mr. Baldridge, Miss Tyner, this is Sister Naomi, our chief of nurses here at the Howard Association. She works directly for Reverend Landrum."

"Sister," Tyner said. Baldridge nodded.

"Sister, Miss Tyner is considering assisting us as a nurse. If you have time, she would like to speak with you about what the duties would involve."

Sister Naomi smiled and spoke softly to Tyner. "I always have time for someone who strives to help the suffering."

The front door of the building slammed hard, and the wooden floors rumbled with the heavy tread of a man Baldridge could hear grumbling as he approached.

"Reverend Landrum, Reverend Landrum, we've got to talk!"

Sister Naomi stepped out of the doorway and into the room, narrowly avoiding a collision with a broad-shouldered, burly man Baldridge estimated to be at least six feet four.

"Oh, Sister! I'm sorry," the man said, grasping her arm to steady her. "I didn't see you standing there." He glanced at Baldridge and Tyner, and without addressing them, gazed directly at Walsh.

"Where's Reverend Landrum, Father?"

"He's on a tour of Happy Hollow with the mayor and some others."

"I bet I know who, too—that goddamned idiot Randolph Fledge!" The man's face reddened with embarrassment. "I'm sorry, Father. But it's true." He walked over to a cabinet. "You got any wine in here?"

"I think Simon keeps some communion wine," Walsh said.

"That'll do. I pronounced three dead already this morning." He located the wine bottle. "I don't suppose the good Lord will miss this, do you?"

Walsh didn't answer, but though unsettled by the man's intrusion, soon introduced him to Baldridge and Tyner as Dr. Frank Rice. Once Rice discovered the communion wine,

Baldridge moved over beside him and recovered a second glass from the cabinet. "Mind if I join you?"

Dr. Rice looked him over from head to toe without offering the bottle.

"Uh, Dr. Rice, Mr. Baldridge is a businessman who's interested in making a considerable contribution to our relief effort."

Rice still hesitated momentarily, then poured about two fingers of wine into Baldridge's glass.

"Baldridge, huh? I know a lot of people here in Memphis, but I never heard of you. What business are you in?"

"Horses," Baldridge said.

"Shipping," Tyner said.

"Shipping horses," Baldridge added. "Among other things."

Rice turned immediately to Walsh. "Fledge is out of control. I ran into him on his way to Pickering. He's practically convinced the mayor to quarantine the whole city. And God only knows what ridiculous treatment plan he'll subject the patients to today. Every day it's different. And not a goddamned one of them works." He waved his glass at Walsh, then glanced at Sister Naomi. "Sorry, Sister."

In a soft voice, barely audible across the room, Sister Naomi addressed Rice. "Begging the doctor's pardon, but Dr. Fledge told me he's had some success with his ice treatment—"

"Ice treatment?" Rice shouted. "Do you have any idea how absurd that is? These patients should never be packed in ice! If anything, they should be given a bath in hot mustard to sweat out the fever. But why should anybody be surprised? Fledge's whole approach to medicine is absurd."

"So you disagree with Dr. Fledge about the treatment of yellow fever?" Tyner asked him.

"Treatment. Cause. Prevention. Quarantine. I think Randolph Fledge is full of . . ." Rice caught himself. "The man's wrong. He's just plain wrong. And worst of all, he's got half the city listening to him."

"I've met Dr. Fledge," Tyner said, "and he seems like he knows what he's talking about."

"Oh, Randolph knows all the right words. He talks a good treatment. Only problem is, none of the old bastard's patients survive. He starts talking about effluvia and—"

"Offal," Tyner said. "He told Masey and me that yellow fever is caused by animal offal."

"See what I mean? That's what I'm talking about," Rice said, nearly shouting. "Ma'am, do you know what 'animal offal' is?" He paused for Tyner to answer. When she offered no reply, he continued. "It's shit! Randolph Fledge actually believes ol' Bronze John is caused by animal shit." Rice stood there with his now empty wineglass in his hand, staring out the window and shaking his head incredulously. "Oh, he's got all the Eastern educated words. He talks about effluvia and poisonous vapors—"

"So if Fledge is wrong, where does the disease come from?" Tyner asked, her voice shrill. Baldridge lifted his hand and motioned for her to calm down.

"Ma'am, I don't know," Rice said, his voice revealing a terrible sadness. "I honestly don't know." He placed his glass on the cabinet and picked up his hat. "But I'm damned sure it ain't cow shit." On the way across the room, he paused in front of Walsh. "If you see Fledge again before I do, please tell him to keep his mouth shut. And ask Reverend Landrum to talk to him. The people are beginning to panic. I'm going to a house over on Jefferson Street where it sounds like we've got two new cases." Rice looked back at Baldridge. "We can use your financial support." He glanced at Tyner. "And we can definitely use another nurse. Sister Naomi here will show you what you need to know."

An awkward silence descended when Rice left the room, broken only by the quiet voice of Sister Naomi.

"God has truly blessed us with physicians who care. Miss Tyner, if you'll come with me, I'll tell you more about our relief effort."

"I'll ask you to pardon Dr. Rice's gruff nature," Walsh said after the women had left. "He's just seen so much suffering in the past two weeks. I think he's angry because they wouldn't listen to him on the board."

"The board of health?"

"Yes."

"Rice is on the board?"

Walsh nodded. "He tried to get them to declare the fever present in the city a week ago, but the others wouldn't hear of it. I think he blames them for a number of needless deaths. He speaks his mind, as you can tell, and that does not make him a popular man with the board."

"I've always figured that any man who says what he really thinks had better keep a horse saddled," Baldridge said, returning his wineglass to the cabinet.

"Do you think the truth is that dangerous, Mr. Baldridge?"

"Dangerous as hell, Father."

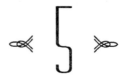

FUN, HUMOR, AND CHARITY

GRAND FANCY DRESS
AND
MASKED BALL
OF THE
CONFEDERATE RELIEF ASSOCIATION
AT THE
EXPOSITION CENTER
ON
THURSDAY EVENING
SEPTEMBER 18, 1873

he had seen the advertisement in the *Memphis Appeal* the day before she left for Nashville, but with the fever running rampant in the city, Salina Tyner figured the ball would be canceled. It wasn't that she was afraid to go, she just wished Masey had given more notice. Of course, he had a ready excuse—the mayor not coming up with a second ticket until Thursday morning—but then, he always had an excuse for his inconsiderate actions. Baldridge and her attending the ball was the mayor's idea. Naturally. Masey wouldn't have thought of anything so elegant. His idea of an evening out would have been a poker game in one of the saloons along Whiskey Chute.

For the past hour she had been at D'Arcy's Store on Main Street while their seamstress adjusted the hemline and took in the waist on the last costume in the building. The last costume. Now she was Marie Antoinette whether she liked it or not, her pink, ruffled dress cut low in the front, her chest underneath covered with a not so narrow weave of lace that reached to the neck. She could feel her head already sweating beneath the cascading curls of her platinum wig. Masey had probably been dressed for an hour and had found some place to have a drink while he waited. She heard a knock on the fitting-room door.

"You decent in there?" Baldridge called.

"Sir, the lady is—"

The seamstress was cut off in mid-utterance as the door swung open to reveal Baldridge wearing a green archer's hat, a black mask covering his eyes and nose, a forest green jacket whose top two buttons struggled to remain fastened, and holding a bow and arrow in his hand. He wore the same pants he'd had on that morning.

Tyner stifled a laugh. "What if I hadn't been dressed?"

Baldridge's eyebrows danced. "Then I'd probably be smiling right now." He glanced at the seamstress, down on her hands and knees, making the last correction, then looked up at Tyner. "Who are you supposed to be?"

"Can't you tell?"

"Nope."

"I'm Marie Antoinette."

"Oh."

"And you?" Tyner tilted her head to the right, lifted her mask to her face, and peered through it. "Let's see . . . how about Little John in Robin's shirt and Masey's pants?"

"Robin Hood," Baldridge said. He lifted the mask and rested it on his forehead. "And I ain't about to wear them sissy pants."

"I don't know, Masey, they might look rather attractive on you."

"Are you ready yet?"

The seamstress got to her feet, and standing on the far side of the fitting room, began to nod slowly.

"Miss Tyner, I believe that's about got it."

"Thank you so much for doing this," she said, giving Baldridge a withering look, "on such *short* notice."

"I hope you and the gentleman have a delightful evening," the woman said as Tyner walked over to take Baldridge's arm. But Baldridge had already started across the main floor of D'Arcy's, babbling about having to pay the carriage driver to wait for her. Tyner looked over at the seamstress, who just shrugged and offered a sympathetic smile.

"I liked to have never found a carriage in this city," Baldridge said as they clip-clopped toward the Exposition Center. "When I got dressed, I went on over to the ball and found one of the drivers who'd already put off his passengers."

"We're using someone else's carriage?"

"Got him for half price."

He seemed quite pleased with himself, and Tyner was frankly surprised he'd gone to the trouble of getting a carriage at all.

"I suppose we could have walked," she said.

"Too hot. Besides," he added, looking her over, "Marie Antoinette never walked anywhere in her life." Sometimes, though rarely, Tyner thought she sensed a tiny trickle of consideration amid the dry, barren wasteland that was Baldridge's manners.

"Tell me again why we're going to this ball?"

"The mayor wants us there. He wants to talk."

"Then why not talk in his office?"

"He says it's too risky. He says people watch his office. He wants this investigation kept quiet, and I guess he's willing to go to any extent to keep it that way."

"I think it's silly," Tyner said. "Don't get me wrong. I like a good party—at least when I have some notice that I'm going."

"Sally, you were there when the mayor—"

"What if people are afraid to come? Afraid of catching the fever?"

"A lot of the money from this ball will go to people suffering from the fever. It'll pay nurses, buy medicine. People will come." He looked at her again. "Are you afraid?"

Tyner stared out the window. She wasn't sure whom to believe. That Dr. Fledge had sounded so convincing, and yet Dr. Rice seemed so sure that the fever wasn't contagious. Would the board of health let a ball take place if they really thought you could catch Yellow Jack from other people? And yet the mayor was considering a quarantine. Either way, Tyner figured she had placed her bet on not catching the fever when she'd agreed to stay in Memphis and work the case. Traveling around the city all day and wandering around in Happy Hollow wasn't the behavior of a woman afraid of catching the fever.

"No," she said in a near whisper. "I'm not afraid."

Baldridge and Tyner made their way up the steps of the Exposition Center and through the receiving line where they shook hands with several former Confederate generals, city officials, and, eventually, Mayor Johnson. She overheard him lean in close to Baldridge and indicate that they would talk after he had some refreshments.

Strains of "The Bonnie Blue Flag" emanated from a stringed quartet at the far end of the room, mingling with the conversation and laughter of the growing crowd. Baldridge disappeared momentarily and returned with punch for the two of them—one taste of which brought tears to her eyes. She held the cup at arm's length, clearing her throat.

"I can't believe they serve this stuff so strong."

"They don't," Baldridge said, smiling and patting his pants pocket, which bore the rough outline of his whiskey flask. She should have known. They stood and watched the crowd for several moments, neither saying a word. Tyner was tapping her foot to the music of a fiddler and wishing for the opportunity to dance —an opportunity that, she assumed, would not come from Masey Baldridge. A minié ball from a Federal sharpshooter had shattered Masey's knee three days before the war ended, leaving him with an awkward limp and nearly constant pain. Some days it was better than others, but there were times—like the night she saw him squeeze the deck railing aboard the *Paragon* until his knuckles turned white—when the pain was almost unbearable. During those times, Masey drank to dull the ache. But in the year she had known him, it seemed to take more and more whiskey to tame the torment.

"Little crowded out there, don't you think?" Baldridge said, finishing off his punch.

"A little," she replied.

"Here, let me get you some more," he said, taking her cup.

"Without the flavoring this time," she called to him. Baldridge offered an abbreviated bow and moved off to the refreshment area.

"Let them eat cake!" a man said, stepping up behind Tyner.

Holding her mask to her face, as was the custom, she turned to face him. "A lady like you would never say such a thing to the people of France, would you?"

Tyner recognized the voice from that morning at the Howard Association.

"Dr. Rice?" She examined his costume. "Or do you go by Christopher Columbus?"

"Frank will be fine."

"Good evening, Frank."

"Miss Tyner."

"Was I so easily recognized?" she said.

"No. But the gentleman with you—"

"You mean Masey."

"Nasty limp he's got there." Rice glanced off toward the refreshment table. "I must admit to a certain professional curiosity. Some kind of accident?"

"Wounded in the war."

"I see. I assume he's had someone examine him. To see what they can do . . ."

"Several. I must confess to being surprised to see you here. With so many cases of the fever—"

"Life must be more than pain and death, Miss Tyner. Besides, it's important that people see me here." He smiled. "Even if it is in this gaudy costume. We've got to get people past the fear that Yellow Jack is contagious from person to person. Otherwise, people will hole up in their homes breathing stale, possibly diseased air, and they might very likely come down with the disease."

"So the fever is carried in the air?" Tyner said.

Rice shook his finger at her. "You're trying to trap me. That's not what I said."

"But people believe it can be carried on a ship—"

"Miss Tyner, yellow fever is not contagious from person to person. You must believe that yourself or you wouldn't be here tonight. I admit it can be carried aboard a ship because a ship may carry a section of atmosphere. But then, the port to which the ship goes must be rife with the conditions for the propagation of the disease. Otherwise, its germs will not be strong enough to cause an epidemic."

"I'm not following you."

"Until we know more about the disease, fear is our greatest enemy. Dr. Rush of Philadelphia said almost a century ago that a panic-stricken people are more susceptible to an epidemic." Rice stopped abruptly. "Let me apologize for going on about this matter at a social function. This is the second time I've seen you today, and both times I have been inconsiderate."

"That's quite all right, Dr. Rice."

"Please call me Frank." This tall man had a disarming smile that a woman could appreciate at her bedside. "You didn't care much for me when you met me today, did you?"

"I wouldn't say that," Tyner replied.

"I must apologize for my language. But I've been under a great deal of strain the past two weeks. On the one hand, I feel so helpless that I can't identify the cause of Yellow Jack—though I have some ideas. But I also get angry—as you saw this morning—when people like Randolph Fledge frighten the community."

Tyner looked about the crowded room. "Well, they don't look too frightened."

"As they shouldn't be. Of course, we'd have much better attendance if half the city wasn't trying to flee."

"Are we fiddling while Rome burns, Doctor?"

"No, Miss Tyner. We're just getting on with life." He offered his hand as the band struck up a waltz. "Would you honor me with a dance?"

She took his hand. "I'd be delighted."

Rice turned out to be an excellent dancer, though he spent the entire waltz complaining about Dr. Fledge and a host of others on the board of health who disagreed with his views. As much as she welcomed the dance, Tyner was glad when the song ended. Rice rattled on about his theory on treating the fever, and with that discussion came more gory details than a woman ought to have to listen to on an evening out on the town. Baldridge walked up to them holding two drinks.

"Good evening, Mr. Baldridge," Rice said.

Baldridge studied him momentarily. "You're the doctor," he said, handing a drink to Tyner. "From this morning."

"Frank Rice," he said, shaking Baldridge's hand and eyeing his drink. "My good man, could you by any chance tell me where you found that punch?"

"Other side of the room, over near that far entrance," Baldridge said.

"Thank you." Rice turned to Tyner. "Miss Tyner, I appreciated the dance."

"My pleasure, Doctor."

"Good to see you again, Baldridge," Rice said, eyeing Baldridge's bad leg before moving off into the crowd. Baldridge took a sip of his punch and grinned at Tyner. "Was it?"

"What?"

"Your pleasure?" Baldridge said.

"Actually, it was. At least until he started talking about vomit. Though I must admit," she added with a smile, "he is a very good dancer."

"Don't hardly see how he's got time to be dancin' with all these sick folks around," Baldridge grumbled. Tyner wasn't sure his concern was for the suffering or something else. There were times, albeit infrequently, when she almost believed Masey

Baldridge was jealous. Then he would do something incredibly inconsiderate, and any notion she had that he might appreciate her beyond her contribution to the Big River Detective Agency would quickly melt away.

A gentleman, in a loud carnival voice, announced the Confederate hat dance. Baldridge suggested they participate. More of a game than a dance, Tyner sensed it was probably the only one Baldridge felt comfortable enough to try, so she agreed and took her place in a line of ladies across the floor.

A row of three chairs occupied one end of the ballroom, with a line of ladies extending down one side and a line of gentlemen down the opposite side facing the ladies. Someone donated a gentleman's hat and the music began, with the first lady in line taking the middle seat. Instantly, the first two gentlemen from their line dashed over to the chairs and occupied one on each side of the lady. With the hat in her hand, she studied the two gentlemen briefly, then placed the hat in the lap of the gentleman to her left. Grasping the hand of the gentleman to her right, she sashayed with him between the two lines, each of them returning to their respective lines. The gentleman who was left holding the hat slid to the middle seat, as the next two ladies in line each occupied the seats on either side of him. He surveyed first the lady on his right and then the lady on his left, then placed the hat in the lap of the one on his right, took the other lady's hand, and sashayed up the line. The crowd would chuckle when the younger ladies would dash away with one of the older Confederate veterans, leaving some young man holding the hat.

It was a silly game, Tyner thought, but one she had seen light the spark of romance or fan the flame of anger, depending on who ended up with the hat.

The dance progressed through two circuits of the line, and both times Tyner had been taken by the hand and danced to the end of the line by an admiring gentleman, an outcome never in doubt for Tyner. But as the third time around came, she noticed Baldridge almost directly across from her in the gentlemen's line. She saw him looking at her as their turn at the chairs approached, and she figured it would be just her luck to end up beside him. A rather hefty woman dressed as a Pilgrim had been abandoned with the hat in her lap as a couple went dashing down the line. As the disappointed woman slid over to the middle chair, Tyner watched Baldridge take a seat beside her while another gentleman occupied the opposite side. Tyner tried to keep from laughing when, as the woman eyed Baldridge carefully, his face poorly disguised his concern for the impending consequence. The large woman examined the gentleman to her left, taking longer than usual, before quickly tossing the hat in Baldridge's lap and skipping away with the other gentleman. Tyner was sure she saw relief on his face as he plopped into the middle chair, his left leg extended rather awkwardly. The woman in front of her took the seat beyond Baldridge, and Tyner, still a bit surprised it had worked out this way, slipped into the chair next to him. Tyner turned and offered her most alluring smile, certain that he would toss the hat in the other direction and take her by the hand. But something in his eyes startled her. Maybe it was the emerging grin, maybe that devious sparkle she had seen before—something gave her the terrible feeling that he might not choose her. That was ridiculous. She was always chosen. She couldn't remember the last time she'd been left holding the hat. The seconds it took Baldridge to decide seeming like minutes, Tyner caught herself stealing a glimpse at the woman on the opposite side to size up the competition.

*He wouldn't dare. He has to choose me. He would never choose that woman. She's as plain as a biscuit.*

Suddenly Baldridge lifted the hat up level with his face, and in dramatic fashion started toward the other woman with it.

*Finally.*

She reached to receive his hand, but he stopped suddenly and tossed the hat into Tyner's lap, and with the best skip-step his bad leg would allow, sashayed down the line with the other woman.

*That bastard!* She realized she had been staring at Baldridge the entire length of the floor when one of the two gentlemen waiting to take her seat spoke.

"Ma'am?"

"What? Oh, yes," she said, offering an abrupt smile. She slid to the middle seat, and without even bothering to look at either of the gentlemen, tossed the hat into the lap of the one who had spoken and danced away with the other. All the way down the line she kept watching over the man's shoulder to see Baldridge take his place at the end of the line. She scowled at him as they passed, but when she peeled off to join the ladies' line, she saw him laughing.

*How dare he laugh at me?*

She could not believe she had been left behind. She was never left behind. Who did he think he was? It shouldn't matter, she told herself. It was a stupid child's game. Just a silly game. Nobody cared who ended up with the hat. Why should they? There was absolutely no reason she should care either way. What difference did it make who Masey Baldridge went limping away with? It was a wonder he didn't trip and send the both of them tumbling across the floor. She would probably have been embarrassed to go with him, anyway.

*Look at him. Having a good laugh. I hope he enjoys himself. He'll be sorry he did that to me.*

Tyner began counting the number of women between her and the chairs, then the number of men. She tried to estimate when he would reach the chair. She tapped a lady on the shoulder two places ahead in line.

"Pardon me, but would you mind terribly if we switched places?"

"Well, I don't—"

"Thank you ever so much," Tyner said without waiting for an answer. She virtually pushed the surprised woman out of the line and took her spot. If she had figured correctly, she'd end up in the middle chair with Masey Baldridge on one side. Then they would see how funny it was. But her plans were dashed as the music came to an end when she was within four people of the chairs. The dancers applauded the band and the lines broke up. She turned and hurried over to the refreshment table and was pouring a glass of punch when Baldridge caught up with her. He was still chuckling as he slapped her on the back.

"You should've seen the look on your face," he said.

Tyner wheeled about to face him, determined to give him a piece of her mind, but she caught herself. Why should she care? He would think her childish or, worse, upset. But her face must have given her disappointment away, for Baldridge's smile began to fade.

"Hey, you're not mad, are you?"

"Mad? Me? Whatever for? I could not possibly care less who you chose in that silly game."

"You didn't?" Baldridge asked.

Tyner's fake laugh bothered even her. "Ha! It doesn't matter to me." She lifted her cup in a mock toast.

"You're mad."

"I'm *not* mad."

"Yes, you are."

"Don't be silly. Why would I want to dance with you? I see you all the time as it is. Now, if Dr. Rice had been dancing . . ."

"Oh, yes." Baldridge's smile returned. "Maybe you could have learned how to lance a boil."

Tyner clenched her jaw and took a deep breath. "So are we going to talk to the mayor tonight or not?"

"Yes. I saw him a moment ago. We're to meet him out on the balcony in five minutes."

"Then let's go. It's getting stuffy in here."

"We could sashay out if it would make you feel better," Baldridge said.

"You're just so funny, Masey. So incredibly funny," she said, heading for the balcony.

A refreshing breeze swept the balcony with the aromas of early autumn. Immediately, Johnson began asking them what they had discovered at the Howard Association and seemed disappointed by the results of their discussion with Father Walsh.

"That's *all* you found out?"

"We only spent about an hour there," Baldridge told him. "Anyway, between you and Landrum wanting to keep a lid on this thing, I can't really come out and ask the kinds of questions I want to ask."

"Of course. I understand," Johnson said.

But Tyner wasn't sure he did.

"I'm going to join the Howard Association," she explained. "I'm hoping that if I offer my services as a nurse, I can find out more about Mr. Stayley's death. Sister Naomi—she's the head of the nurses—keeps a pretty sharp eye on what's happening around there. I'm hoping I can use her to find out what we want."

"All right. That sounds like a reasonable approach," Johnson said. The mayor then came up with the name Gerald Roe, chairman of the city's Second Ward Relief Committee. Johnson had learned that Roe was in financial trouble over what he claimed were some bad business decisions made in the past year. While he admitted to having no direct evidence, the fact that it was

Ward Two money that had disappeared made Johnson believe they should at least talk to Roe.

"I can't tell you two how important it is for us to get to the bottom of this quickly. There have been some developments today that—"

"What kind of developments?" Tyner asked.

"Three new cases of the fever. I'm having to take steps that . . . well, the situation with the fever is growing more difficult every day."

"What kind of steps?"

"I'm not at liberty to say right now, Mr. Baldridge," Johnson replied.

"Look, Mayor, if you expect us to help you, you've got to tell us what's going on."

"Mr. Baldridge, I'll tell you whatever is pertinent to your investigation. Just continue with your work and keep me informed."

"But—" Masey tried to challenge him, but the mayor continued.

"I hired your detective agency to investigate these crimes, not run the city. I'll do my job and you do yours. And that reminds me, it's better that we not meet in public anymore. There's a newspaperman who's been hanging around my office looking for a story. In the future, I want you to send a courier with any information you uncover, and if you need to talk with me in person, let me know and I'll arrange a suitable place."

"What are you afraid of, Mayor?" Tyner asked.

Johnson gazed out into the darkness. "I'm afraid of what could happen to Memphis if this fever isn't stopped, Miss Tyner. That's what I'm afraid of. And I'm afraid of losing support for the Howard Association." He turned back to Tyner. "I'm afraid of what panic can do to people. I'm afraid of a lot of things, Miss Tyner."

Panic. Dr. Rice had used that word, and as much as she

shared Baldridge's concern that the mayor wasn't telling them everything, Tyner remembered all too vividly what she'd seen on her arrival back in Memphis. If panic didn't describe the behavior of those people at the depot, it surely took a close second. Maybe Johnson was right.

Baldridge, on the other hand, was less sympathetic.

"I don't like being kept in the dark. You hired us to—"

"Masey," Tyner said, touching his sleeve. "Let's work with what we've got. We've more than enough to do just following up on what the mayor's told us. I'm sure he's telling us everything he can."

"I don't think he is."

"Please, Mr. Baldridge," Johnson said, a look of desperation in his eyes. "Just accept the information I've offered you and continue your investigation. And keep me informed."

Tyner was certain Baldridge would have pressed the mayor had they not been interrupted by a short, nervous-looking man approaching from the tall double doors leading into the ballroom. He wore no costume.

"Mayor?"

Johnson turned and acknowledged the man. As he approached, Johnson looked back at Tyner and Baldridge and, cupping his hand over his mouth, whispered, "Let me do the talking."

Johnson introduced the man as Miles Washburn, a reporter for the *Daily Avalanche*, who wasted no time in getting to the point.

"Mayor, do you have a statement about how the street cleaning went today?" Washburn asked, producing a notepad from his pocket.

"Miles," Johnson said impatiently, "we're at a social gathering here."

"True, Mayor, but the readers will want to know how it went." Washburn seemed unfazed by the mayor's hesitation. "Everything go as planned?"

"Yes. It went just fine. Now, if—"

"Do you think we'll see a drop in the number of cases?"

"The board of health believes so. Miles, we really—"

"But what do you say, Mayor?" an expectant Washburn asked.

"I'd say I really don't want to talk about this right now."

"And the quarantine? Have you made a decision about the quarantine as yet?"

"Miles, I'm not going to answer that right now."

"But you have made a decision?"

Johnson tugged at the collar of his costume, smiled awkwardly at Tyner and Baldridge, and said, "We're considering all our options." He took Washburn by the shoulder and attempted to lead him away. "Miles, if you'll excuse me, I'm having a conversation with some friends—"

Washburn held his ground. "Miles Washburn," the little man said, interrupting. *"Daily Avalanche."* He tipped his hat to Tyner and shook Baldridge's hand, clearly expecting an introduction.

"This is Mr. Baldridge and Miss Tyner," Johnson said. "They're, uh . . . friends of mine."

Washburn gave them the practiced eye of a newsman, holding his gaze on Baldridge momentarily. "Baldridge. Seems like I should know that name."

"Don't believe we've ever met," Baldridge said.

"You live in Memphis?"

"I'm just here for a few days."

"Listen, Miles," Johnson said, ushering him away, "why don't you come by my office about nine tomorrow morning? I'll give you a full story then." After a few words of reassurance, Washburn went back inside the building and Johnson returned to the balcony, where he pounded the railing with his fist. "Miles Washburn is the last thing we need right now," he said. "He's the most persistent, obnoxious little worm I've ever dealt with."

"You're going to quarantine the city, aren't you?"

Johnson did not answer. He pointed his finger at Baldridge, then realized the impropriety and lowered his hand to his side. "Keep your distance from Washburn. If he gets wind of what you're investigating, it'll be all over the front page. Then we may never catch our thief."

"We'll keep our eyes open for him," Baldridge said, returning to his question. "So are you going to quarantine?"

Johnson offered no reply, but excused himself and returned to the ballroom, leaving Tyner and Baldridge alone in the night air, with more questions than answers.

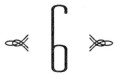

## THURSDAY EVENING

I don't see that we've got much choice, Luke," declared Augustus Zeigler, master of the steamer *City of Chester*. In his navy blue jacket he stood in front of the window of his wharf boat, on the Memphis landing, his foot propped up against the window seat, the smoke from a pipe swirling about his head. "I figure—"

"Oh, I've got a choice, all right," Luke Williamson replied from a table across the narrow room. "I can secure my lines and be making steam north within an hour."

"To where?" Zeigler said. "You can't land at Cairo. St. Louis is under quarantine."

"Hell, I'll go all the way to Minneapolis if I have to."

Zeigler peered back at him. "Will you? And then what? Do

you really think any city along the Mississippi is going to let a boat land that's been in port in Memphis?"

"Zeig is right," offered Captain R. C. Lennox of the *Grand Tower*. His voice had always grated on Williamson's nerves, but tonight the words bothered him even more than the sound. "Nobody's going to let us land. They'll figure we're carrying the fever for sure. And frankly, Luke, we don't know that we're not."

"I haven't had one case of Yellow Jack among any of my passengers or crew," Williamson argued.

"I'm glad for you," Lennox said. "But that's not to say you won't."

"It doesn't mean I will, either."

Zeigler took a puff on his pipe. "They carried three people off the *City of Chester* this afternoon, Luke. R.C. has two cases on the *Grand Tower*. The doctors are pretty sure it's the fever."

"Then *you two* go into goddamned quarantine," Williamson said, rising to his feet. "The *Paragon* is leaving tonight."

"Going where?" Zeigler asked.

"I don't know."

"You can't just sail up and down the river for the next week. Hell, it could be a month before this clears up," Lennox said.

Williamson walked over to a washbowl and poured some water into it from a ceramic pitcher. He'd never expected this when Steven Tibedeau had come to his cabin an hour earlier with a note to meet Zeigler and Lennox. He had just gone over final instructions with Jacob Lusk to make ready for departure at nine o'clock. He was fully prepared to steam for St. Louis in the hope that in two days, by the time he arrived, the quarantine on boats docking in the city might be lifted. It wasn't as if he hadn't thought about what they were saying. He might be turned away from Cairo and St. Louis. Maybe even Keokuk if he went that far north. But he had to do something. Sitting at the Memphis wharf watching the city come apart at the seams was driving him and his passengers crazy. A boat full of people demanding to travel somewhere, anywhere, out of the reach of Yellow Jack, made every hour he stayed in port more difficult than the one before. He had already delayed his departure in the hope that some port would open up, but if anything, cities along the river were closing to any ships from Memphis, Shreveport, and any of a half dozen cities with serious yellow fever outbreaks. That the *Paragon* had revealed no cases of the fever was a miracle, but even Williamson knew it wouldn't be enough to provide him with access to the wharf of the cities along his route. He splashed some water on his face and felt for the towel hanging on a bar at the end of the washstand as he addressed Lennox.

"Tell me again what they want."

Lennox produced a note from his jacket pocket, unfolded it, and pressed it flat against the table. From another pocket he removed his reading glasses, and with them resting on the end of his nose, read aloud the note.

> The board of health, acting in concert with the mayor of Memphis, hereby declares the city of Memphis in quarantine against yellow fever effective nine P.M, September 18, 1873. The quarantine shall pertain to the arrival and departure of all modes of public transportation to include, but not be limited to, riverboats, trains, and stagecoaches. Companies operating commercial passenger steamboat vessels, passenger trains, or carriages will be denied docking or depot rights until further notice by the board of health. Said modes of public transport will be halted before entering the city and, if necessary, forcibly detained. Private citizens will not be prohibited from leaving the city on

an individual basis, but, in an effort to limit the spread of the yellow fever, modes of public transport now in the city will be detained in the city until further notice.

"So let me see if I've got this straight," Williamson said, drying his face with the towel. "People can leave Memphis as long as they do it in twos or threes on their own horses and carriages. But if they try to do it on a steamboat, they'll be stopped. What kind of sense does that make?"

Lennox replied in his raspy voice. "It's just the way things are, Luke. The city ain't worried about stopping folks from coming to Memphis. Nobody in their right mind's gonna stop here during a fever epidemic anyway."

"We're here," Williamson said.

His comment brought a chuckle from Zeigler. "Don't that say something about us?"

Williamson didn't think it was funny. "The city wasn't under quarantine when we stopped. Hell, the board of health only recognized this as an epidemic a few days ago."

"Things like this move fast," Lennox said. "The board of health knows damn well they can't stop people from leaving if they're determined to." Lennox motioned with his head toward the shore. "And from the way folks have been behaving the last two days, there's no doubt they figure to leave. The only thing the board of health and the mayor can control is our boats and the damn railroad. What they're doing may or may not stop the fever from spreading, but in the eyes of the folks in Cairo and St. Louis, it sure as hell makes it look like they're doing *something*."

"R.C., read him the rest of the message," Zeigler said.

Lennox read on. "All boats now docked at the Memphis wharf must move with their passengers to a temporary mooring at Forrest Landing on President's Island until cleared to proceed by the board of health."

Williamson stood silent for several moments until Zeigler addressed him.

"What are you gonna do, Luke? R.C. and I have talked it over, and we've got our own idea of what ought to happen, but we wanted to talk with you first."

"They can't stop us from leaving," Williamson said. "I mean, if we want to head north, they can't physically stop us."

"You mean board us?" Lennox said.

"They wouldn't dare," Williamson said. "Anyway, they don't have the manpower. It's taking all the law they've got just to keep the city from turning into a stampede."

"So are you saying you're leaving?" Zeigler asked.

"I didn't say that. I mean . . . hell, Zeig, I don't know. I swear, I don't know what to do."

"Luke, Zeig and I figure that since the three of us have the only boats docked here right now, whatever we do, we ought to do together. Now, we're competitors, that's for sure. But Zeig and I figure all us rivermen ought to stand together on something like this."

Williamson pondered his dilemma. His instinct was to secure his lines, bring up the steam, and go find someplace that would allow him to dock. But would he really be any better off? What if he couldn't land? What if no one would take his passengers ashore? How would he feed them for a week, maybe two? And what if someone then got sick on board? How would he treat them? He could lose his ship and everyone on it. What if he already had Yellow Jack on board the *Paragon* and it just hadn't shown up yet? Wouldn't it make more sense to remain here, even at President's Island, where people at least had some experience in treating the fever? Williamson walked over to the window where Zeigler stood and stared outside. Intermittent campfires still burned along the landing, and though the crowds had dwindled, he could see a hundred, perhaps a hundred and fifty, people huddled around the cooking fires in groups of five, six, perhaps ten. By now word of the quarantine must have surely reached them. Bad news travels like wildfire along a river landing. Yet still they waited and watched the black ribbon of water that stretched before them on this moonless night, hoping against hope to see the distant glow of a new boat as it steamed toward the port.

"Gentlemen, Forrest Landing is two miles south. If it wasn't pitch black out there, I'd race the both of you." He slapped Zeigler on the back. "And you know I'd beat you. I'd beat you bad."

Zeigler grinned broadly. "That's what me and R.C. figured to do. We hoped you'd see it our way."

Williamson shook first Zeigler's hand, then Lennox's. "I just hope we're doing the right thing."

"Me, I'm hoping for an early frost," Lennox said. "That's about the only thing that seems to send ol' Bronze John a-runnin'."

BACK ABOARD THE *Paragon*, Williamson briefed his officers on his decision to respect the quarantine, and by ten o'clock they, in turn, had spread the word among the passengers. Almost fifty people—all of whom had boarded at Memphis—refused to go to President's Island and demanded to be put back ashore. Since the request in no way violated the order from the board of health, Williamson complied with their wishes. But with the removal of the fifty, the mad rush to find a spot on the *Paragon* that had so plagued him the previous day did not materialize. Once the squatters along the wharf found out the boats were going to President's Island only for quarantine, Williamson figured they thought it best to take their chances where they were. And even though none of the passengers who had boarded in New Orleans or Vicksburg or other ports dared to go ashore in Memphis, they did not all accept the quarantine quietly.

When a commotion broke out in the dining room, one of the stewards sought out Williamson and brought him to the scene.

Three men were angrily abusing one of his officers about the change in itinerary when Williamson arrived.

"What's the problem here?"

"I'll tell you what the problem is," a tall, bearded man replied. "I came aboard this ship in Natchez and bought a ticket to St. Louis. Now I hear we're not going to St. Louis. We're going to some island to sit like a toad on the water. I'm not going to stand for it."

"Mister, I'm sorry you don't like the quarantine, but none of us like it either. I, perhaps more than anybody on this ship, would like to be steaming for St. Louis right now."

"Then by all means, Captain, get us under way," the man said.

"Yeah. Let's get moving," a second man said.

"They can't force you to stay here," a third man added, tapping a bulge in his vest pocket. "I'd like to see 'em try."

"Gentlemen, I can't do that," Williamson said.

"Sure, you can," the bearded man said. "You're the captain. You can do anything you want."

"Well, let me say it differently. I won't do that. It is my intent to comply with the quarantine."

"Then, sir, I demand you allow us to secure passage aboard one of the other ships docked here."

"Both the *City of Chester* and the *Grand Tower* are observing the quarantine, too," Williamson explained. "They'll be going to President's Island with us."

"This is preposterous!" the bearded man said. "I demand that you immediately—"

Williamson moved to within inches of the man. "Mister, you're not in a position to demand anything. I'm the captain of this ship and you, sir, are a passenger on it." He noticed the two men with him approach as if to back him.

"I tell you I'll not be stuffed away on some island with a bunch of sick and dying people—"

"You needn't go ashore unless you want to, sir. We're simply mooring until we are cleared to leave by the board of health. You and your friends can remain on the ship."

"This is just unacceptable." The man poked his finger into Williamson's chest. "We paid to be taken to St. Louis, and I demand—"

Williamson grabbed his finger and twisted it backward until the man groaned.

"Goddamnit, I just told you that you don't demand anything from me!"

The man in the vest moved beside his friend. "Be careful. The crazy son of a bitch shoots his passengers."

Williamson released the man's finger and stared the second man down. "Not unless I have to," he said, "but I tell you what I will do." He turned to the officer the bearded man had been chastising. "Mr. LaFollette, please secure this gentleman's baggage and see to it he's put ashore immediately."

"Put ashore?" The bearded man took a step back, almost falling over his friend. "Now—now, see here. I don't want to go ashore in Memphis. I told you, I don't want to be around the fever. I don't—"

Williamson closed the distance again, almost touching the man. "Then you shut your goddamned mouth, and you do exactly what I tell you to do. Otherwise, I'll personally throw your ass off this boat." He turned to the other man. "That goes for you, too." He held out his hand. "And I'll have that derringer from your vest pocket."

"Sir, you have no right—"

"Give me the gun."

For several seconds, Williamson wasn't sure the man wouldn't try to pull the weapon on him, but he figured that even if he did, he could grab his hand before it cleared his vest. Two other crew members gathered on each side as the man reached slowly for his pocket.

"Butt first, if you don't mind," Williamson said, his eyes still locked on him. And though the man surrendered a two-barreled derringer, Williamson saw something in his eyes that told him that unless the quarantine ended soon, he had not heard the last of this.

## 7

FRIDAY, SEPTEMBER 19

In her room at the Overton Hotel on the northwest corner of Main and Poplar, Salina Tyner ran a brush through her dark hair once more and, holding a hairpin between her teeth, began working the hair into a tight bun. Though she had bathed with a washcloth about an hour earlier, having to put on the costume she had worn the night before made her feel still dirty. It was bad enough that she would have to wear the same clothes, but having to go out in public in broad daylight dressed as Marie Antoinette made her feel ridiculous.

"I'm buying a dress first thing," she muttered under her breath, the hairpin clenched between her teeth. Her clothes and personal items, along with everything belonging to Baldridge, were still aboard the *Paragon*—where they would likely remain, given the events of the evening before. She recalled how she and Baldridge had left the masked ball about ten last night and had ridden to the landing to spend the night in their rooms aboard the *Paragon*. She'd known something was wrong as soon as they encountered a column of more than a dozen Memphis policemen galloping down Front Street. Baldridge had urged Nashville Harry along to catch them, and Tyner, not wanting to be left out, followed behind. She'd heard Baldridge shout an inquiry to one of the policemen at the tail of the column.

"Quarantine," he'd called out over the clopping hoofs of the column. "The city's closed." The officer had continued as Baldridge slowed down and reined up near a gas streetlight in front of a mercantile store. Tyner had moved her mount to join him.

"Did he say what I think he said?" she'd asked.

Baldridge had nodded.

"Then why didn't the mayor tell us?"

"I don't know, Sally, unless he was afraid word would get out. Maybe he was afraid of a stampede out of town."

"Or maybe he just doesn't trust us."

"Could be," Baldridge had said, leading his horse back into the street. "Come on," he'd called to her, snapping the reins against the animal's shoulder. "Let's cut through some back streets and see if we can get to the *Paragon* before the law does."

They had ridden hard the several blocks to the landing, but two mounted policemen some five hundred feet from the *Paragon*'s wharf boat had confronted them.

"The landing is closed," the officer had told Baldridge, whose horse stirred nervously from the sudden halt. "You and the lady will have to leave the area."

"But our things are on that boat," Baldridge had said, pointing to the *Paragon*.

"I'm sorry about that. No one can enter any of the steamers still moored at the landing."

"But what will we do?" Tyner had asked. "We must have our clothes and personal items."

"You'll just have to stay somewhere else."

"For how long?" Tyner had asked.

"Can't say, ma'am. Could be a few days, could be weeks."

"Weeks?" Tyner had echoed.

"I'm afraid so."

"What happens to the *Paragon*?" she'd asked.

"She'll go down to President's Island, along with the other two," the officer had said. "They'll remain there until the quarantine is lifted."

She'd turned to Baldridge. "I'm surprised Luke Williamson would stand for this."

"I doubt he had much choice," Baldridge had said, slipping his whiskey flask from his jacket pocket. In the darkness he'd carefully unscrewed the top and taken a swig, offering the container to Tyner.

"Yeah," she'd said, "I believe I will."


THE WHISKEY BALDRIDGE had offered her from his flask last night had been rough and bitter, and as she completed the final touches on her hair, she could swear the taste was still in her mouth. Tyner heard a knock on the door.

"Come in," she said. "It's unlocked."

"You ought to keep your door locked. I could have been anyone out there. What if—"

"But you weren't just anyone. I knew it was you."

"How? How did you know it was me?"

"I heard you walking down the hall."

"Oh." Baldridge looked down at the floor self-consciously. "By the way, French royalty never looked better," he said.

"I've simply got to get out of these clothes."

"I'd be glad to help."

She winked at him. "I'll keep your offer in mind, but right now I think we've got work to do."

Their plan for now was simple: Tyner would attempt to track the money that had disappeared from the Howard Association while Baldridge developed more information on the two bodies he had seen at Holst and Brothers. But first they searched for an open clothing store, where they used some of the mayor's advance money for Tyner to purchase a modest dress and Baldridge a new pair of trousers and a shirt.

Baldridge rode off to talk to the neighbors of the late T. R. Lassiter and Tyner went in search of Snowden, the Howard Association contributor who Reverend Landrum said had first raised an allegation of missing money. Depending upon what he said, she figured the next stop would be Landrum's accountant, Roland. Maybe he was a good Christian man as Landrum had indicated, but with all that money coming in to support the Howard Association, Tyner suspected he might well have succumbed to temptation.

She finally located Snowden at a dry-goods store on Jefferson Street. Only one other customer was present, an older woman who was busily giving instructions as to exactly how she wanted a piece of cloth cut from a bolt of material.

"Are you Mr. Snowden?" Tyner called across the room.

"Yes, ma'am. I'll be right with you," the gentleman at the cutting table replied. The older woman tossed Tyner an annoyed glance, as if her question had interrupted her concentration. Tyner watched Snowden, a short, balding man with a pencil poised behind his ear, as he patiently followed the woman's instructions. The fact that they were the only two customers in the store was spooky, and given the general fear in the city, she wondered how a businessman like Snowden would survive. The exception had been the ball the night before. She was surprised by how well attended the event had been. Maybe people just wanted to contribute to the relief association. Maybe they were just tired of holing up in their homes and waiting for the fever to find them. Or maybe they just didn't care anymore. Either way, last night had provided the largest gathering she had seen that didn't amount to a mob trying to get out of town.

Snowden eventually satisfied the woman and walked across the floor of the store.

"I'm Carl Snowden," he said cheerfully. "Would the lady be interested in some material today? I have some broadcloth on sale."

Tyner introduced herself and told him she was looking into fund-raising by the Howard Association. Snowden's smile quickly disappeared.

"Why did you come to see me?"

"Because of the charges you raised with Dr. Landrum."

"Charges? What charges?" Snowden said, busying himself by straightening a bolt of cloth on the table beside them.

"Your contribution to the Howard Association," Tyner said. "Reverend Landrum said you approached him about a difference between what you gave to the Howard Association and the amount that appeared in the newspaper listing."

"Oh, that," Snowden said, smoothing the cloth with his hand. "I'm so sorry about all that." He shook his head. "There's no discrepancy. It was a mistake."

"A mistake?"

"Yes, Miss Tyner. I must have looked at my books incorrectly. I fear I was hasty in my judgment."

"But Reverend Landrum said you came to him quite upset. He said your one-hundred-and-fifty-dollar contribution only showed up in the listing as one hundred. He said you suspected that someone had stolen the money."

Snowden looked away from her, his nervous laugh leaving her in doubt of his sincerity. "It was all an error on my part, Miss Tyner. I take full blame for the misunderstanding. I will contact Dr. Landrum and straighten this out."

"So no money is missing?"

"No. Absolutely not. My donation was for only one hundred dollars. I mistakenly thought I had given one hundred and fifty. But I hadn't. The newspaper account was correct. I owe Reverend Landrum an apology for my hasty words."

"Tell me, Mr. Snowden, exactly how was your money collected on behalf of the Howard Association?"

"How is it that you work for the Howard Association?"

"I've been asked to look into the collection of contributions," she said matter-of-factly. "The collection, Mr. Snowden. How was it done?"

"Miss Tyner, I've already told you that this was all a mistake." He removed the pencil from behind his ear and scribbled some numbers on a piece of paper near one of the cloth displays. "I fail to see how—"

Tyner smiled. "If you don't mind, I'd like to know anyway. Just because you caught your mistake doesn't mean it couldn't happen to others."

Snowden's head jerked up from the paper. "There are others?"

"Possibly. Perhaps if you tell me how your contribution was handled I could find out."

"It's general knowledge, Miss Tyner. A person can give to the Howard Association either directly or through the local ward representative."

"What did you do?"

"I gave through Mr. Roe, chairman of the Ward Two Relief

Committee. But I assure you there was no impropriety. It was all a—"

"Mistake. Yes, I know. So did Mr. Roe receive the money directly?"

"Uh, yes. Yes, I gave it to him. *One hundred* dollars," he said firmly. "Not one hundred and fifty."

"I understand." Tyner offered her hand. "I appreciate your taking the time to talk with me, Mr. Snowden."

Snowden shook her hand. "No problem, Miss Tyner. Please come again . . . when you're in the market for some broadcloth."

"I will, thank you," Tyner said, leaving. Once outside on the street, she moved to her horse and untied him from a hitching rail.

"Nice animal." She turned to see a Memphis police officer standing on the porch in front of Snowden's store.

"Thank you," she said, grasping the mane with her left hand and the saddle horn with her right.

"Allow me," the officer said, stepping forward to steady the horse as Tyner pulled herself up and twisted to her left so as to land sidesaddle.

"Thank you again." She gathered the reins and backed the animal away from the hitching post.

"Don't see many ladies like yourself in this part of town, what with the fever broke out like it is."

"Fever or no fever, life goes on."

"Yes, I suppose it does. At least for some. But you might not want to tarry too long in this section of town." He tipped his hat. "You have a nice afternoon. And please be careful out here alone. With the streets so deserted, there's no telling what you might run into."

She thought it an odd comment, but took it at face value and rode for Court Street. Once at the Howard Association, she spoke with a clerk in the front office and got the address of Gerald W. Roe, chairman of Ward Two Relief Committee. About an hour later, Tyner rode up to an elegant house on Gayoso Street. In front, she saw a man adjusting the harness on a buggy and eased her mount up to him. She answered his greeting with a nod of her head.

"I'm looking for Gerald Roe."

"That would be me. How may I help you?"

Tyner leaped to the ground and adjusted her hat, which had canted awkwardly upon impact.

"Mr. Roe, I'm here on behalf of the Howard Association."

"If you're here about the subscriptions, the money's right here in my valise." He touched the brown leather pouch. "I just haven't had a chance to come by there today," Roe said defensively. "That's why I was rigging this buggy. I'll need to make a few stops first; otherwise, I would give you the pouch right now. You're one of the nurses, right?"

"Yes, sir. You have the contributions?"

"Well," he replied, still working on the harness, "such as they are today. Folks haven't been particularly forthcoming." He made a last adjustment to the harness. "You know how Ward Two is."

"Good ol' Ward Two."

Roe looked over at her. "It's gonna pick up, though. I'm sure of it." He extended his hand. "I don't think we've met."

"Salina Tyner's my name." They shook hands.

"I'm . . . well, you already know who I am." He climbed into the seat of his buggy. "Tell Reverend Landrum I'll be along later this afternoon. I do appreciate your coming by," he said, placing his hand firmly over the valise, "but I prefer to deliver it in person."

"I see." She brought her hand up to her nose and pretended

to sniffle, her eyes averting his, issuing forth what sounded like a mild sob.

"Ma'am, you all right?"

"Oh, it'll be all right. I suppose." She looked up at him as she pretended to wipe away tears. "You don't think the reverend will be angry with me, do you?"

"Reverend Landrum? For what?"

"Well, Mr. Roe, I'm supposed to go on duty this evening," she said, making it up as she went along, "but he asked me to find out how the money raising was going first. I'm afraid he'll be disappointed in me if I don't go back with the information."

Roe lowered the reins. "Ma'am, I've never known Reverend Landrum to send someone out here like this. Oh, I've been a little late getting the contributions in before, but I always get them there. Surely, he won't be angry with you."

"I certainly hope not," she said, her face the picture of despair as she turned to grasp her reins.

"Reverend Landrum has to realize that these things take time. I have to wait until the money is brought to me. It's not as if I collect it myself."

Tyner turned to him. "You don't collect the money? But you're chairman of the relief committee for this ward, aren't you?"

"That's right. The chairman. Surely, you don't think I go door-to-door soliciting money, do you?"

He seemed indignant at her suggestion, but his answer only confused the matter.

"If you don't collect the money, who does?"

"For being with the Howard Association, you sure don't know much about how things work."

"They don't tell us nurses very much."

"Well, sometimes it's brought directly to me by the donor,

and the rest of it comes by way of the sanitary patrolman."

"Sanitary patrolman?"

"A police officer designated to patrol the areas of town where the fever is rampant. If you're nursing people with the fever, you must have seen them."

"Yes, yes, of course."

Roe eyed her suspiciously. "I would have thought Reverend Landrum or one of the others at the Howard Association would have explained all this to you. Particularly if he sent you out here to see after the donations."

Tyner feared her guise was wearing thin, but she pressed him with one more question.

"Who's the sanitary patrolman in your ward?"

Roe was growing more impatient.

"Officer Deaves. Now, young lady, I really must be going. I have a very important appointment." He kept staring at her curiously. "I want you to know I intend to speak to Reverend Landrum about this. Your coming here is irregular. Now, if you'll excuse me . . ." He paused for a moment to allow her to lead her horse out of his path, then, snapping his reins, drove off in the buggy.

Tyner wondered what business Roe could possibly have that was more important than getting the money as quickly as possible to the Howard Association. Maybe he was out to find more. Maybe he wasn't. At any rate, if the mayor was suspicious of him, as Baldridge had told her, she felt fully justified in following Roe for a spell. Tyner hadn't believed Snowden. Something was happening to the Howard Association's money between the time it was donated and the time it got to the association. Roe and Deaves were part of that process, and it was as important to Tyner to rule them out as suspects as it was to catch them in a crime. But even as she followed Roe, she was steaming. If there was anything Tyner hated, it was being lied to. Snowden, for whatever reason, had done precisely that, and she wasn't about to let him get away with it. As soon as she found out what Roe was up to, she was determined to pay another visit to Snowden.

WITH SO LITTLE traffic on the streets, Tyner had no difficulty following Roe's buggy at a distance until he eventually turned into an alley off Jefferson Street. Pausing a moment to see if the buggy would return, she eventually eased her horse slowly foward and peered around a corner, where she saw Roe's buggy abandoned near a mimosa tree that grew close beside the back door of a brick building. Tyner scanned the vacant lot immediately behind the building, and finding no sign of Roe, she reasoned that he must have entered the solitary back door. Leading her horse back around to the front of the building on Jefferson, she secured the animal, noting a sign that read "Roe Novelties." Only one or two people moved about on the street as Tyner stepped up on the wooden sidewalk and tried the front door. It was locked. She cupped her hands around her face and tried to see through the glare of the storefront windows. A large room, it was silent and vacant except for a half dozen figurines and children's toys on a rack of shelves on the far side of the room.

Tyner next moved around the side of the building, into the alley, and to the back door, Roe's buggy horse nickering at her approach. The first-floor windows were boarded shut on the back side of the building; trying the back door, she found it locked also. She heard someone coming down the alley, so she hurried away from the door and squatted behind the mimosa tree, barely reaching the hiding place before a disheveled-looking man in a dusty hat and worn boots stepped up to the back door of the building. He glanced back toward the alley, then in Tyner's direction. Tyner ducked lower, and peered around the base of the tree to see the man retrieve something from underneath a crate beside the door. He unlocked the door, then replaced the object beneath the crate and went inside.

Waiting a few moments to see if others might come, Tyner crept toward the door. From beneath the crate she removed a door key, cleared the lock, and slowly opened the door. The room was dark, the boarded windows blocking most of the light except for what came through the open door and an occasional ray that pierced a gap in the boarding. Tyner closed the door behind her, securing it. Immediately, she heard voices coming from the floor above; feeling about in the near darkness, she found her way to a staircase along the outside wall. She could identify at least four, perhaps five, different men talking. Sometimes they shouted, occasionally they stomped, and then there came a strange rattling sound, as if someone were tossing something on the floor. Tyner eased up the stairs, pausing when one of the steps creaked loudly under her weight. But the noise of the men on the floor above had drowned out the sound, so she continued until she reached the landing. The voices were clearer now, and she could tell from the conversation that the men were playing a game, a game Tyner did not recognize until she heard something strike the floor and rattle up against the wall not ten feet from the door. Dice. They were playing dice. She dared not open the door, attempting to see through the keyhole instead. But from the angle where the men stood, she could make out only two in the room, and neither was Roe. Moving three steps down the staircase, Tyner lowered herself to the floor, where a gap almost an inch wide offered a view of the room that captured each of the men, at least from the waist down.

"Eight," someone said. "Fifty dollars on the eight."

Tyner watched as greenbacks fell on the floor in piles. Someone scooped up a pair of dice and she heard them clicking together. Then came Roe's voice.

"Come on, six! Come on, six!"

The dice danced across the floor, ricocheted off the wall, and came to rest.

"Seven!" someone shouted.

Roe cursed his luck. Hoping to actually see him, Tyner drew her face as close as possible to the crack beneath the door. When a pounding sound behind her startled her, she jerked her head back and scratched her nose on the door. The noise in the room ceased suddenly, followed by someone again pounding on the back door below.

"Pick up the money," she heard Roe shout. "See who it is."

Tyner heard footsteps move across the room and figured someone was looking out the upstairs window.

"It's Martin," a man said.

"Well, why in hell doesn't he come on up? Did you put the key back?" Roe asked.

"Hell, yes."

Instantly Tyner looked at her left hand, where she still tightly grasped the key to the back door. The rumble of footsteps moving toward the stairwell door prompted her hasty retreat down the stairs and into the darkness of the first floor. She ducked under the stairwell just before someone came jogging down the steps. His boots echoed loudly as he walked across the vacant room, unlocked the back door, and opened it.

Tyner drew in tightly against the wall as the light from the open door illuminated the room. A tall, slender man stepped inside. "Where's the damn key?"

"Fremont said he put it back."

"Well, it ain't there."

The man who had come downstairs stepped outside. "Are you sure?"

"Damnit, I ain't blind."

The man moved the crate, searched around in the dirt momentarily, then stood up sharply. "We better tell Roe."

When the two of them rushed up the steps, Tyner dashed out the back door; she had made several steps toward the alley when she halted abruptly. Rushing back to the door, she bent down and slipped the key under the edge of the crate, then, grasping the hoops of her skirt, she ran for the corner of the building. Once around the corner, her back pressed against the wall and out of sight, she listened as several men came out the back door. They argued momentarily, then upon discovering the key beneath the crate, one of them laughed at the others, and they reentered the building. Tyner moved quickly to her horse and mounted.

SNOWDEN WAS SURPRISED to see her back so soon.

"Miss Tyner!" he said, peering from a kneeling position behind a counter. "Twice in one day. Did you change your mind about the broadcloth?"

"No, Mr. Snowden," she said, moving to the end of the counter. "I changed my mind about you."

"About me?"

"Yes. You see, when I left here earlier, I just *thought* you were a liar. Now I know you're one."

Snowden rose up sharply, bumping his head on a shelf. "I beg your pardon!"

"You should. You should always beg a lady's pardon after you lie to her."

"Now, see here, young woman—"

"Why did you tell me Gerald Roe picked up your Howard Association donation?"

Snowden rubbed his head. "I—I don't understand."

"You told me Roe picked up your donation. You also told me there had been no mistake. There was no shortage of funds."

"Yes, that's correct."

"Well, you and I both know that Roe didn't pick up your money. So does that mean you also lied about the shortage?"

Snowden removed a handkerchief from his pocket and pressed it against his scalp, checking it for blood, then returning it to his head.

"Miss Tyner, you don't understand. I really can't talk to you anymore about this matter. It's difficult, you see, and—"

"Who picked up your donation?"

Several moments of awkward silence passed, and she sensed that Snowden had something to say, indeed, that he was on the verge of saying it, when the bell over the front door revealed the Memphis police officer she had seen earlier.

"Officer Deaves!" Snowden called, scurrying from behind the counter. "Pardon this handkerchief," he said. "Seems I had an encounter with a shelf a moment ago."

Tyner noticed that Deaves looked at Snowden rather coolly before his gaze came to rest on her.

"I guess you didn't feel the need to follow my advice."

"I tend to come and go as I please," she replied, moving to within a few feet of him. "Aren't you what they call a sanitary patrolman?"

"That's right. I work this ward. Do my best to make sure folks are keeping clean, burning sulfur like the board of health says."

"Must be very difficult work," she said.

"I do my best."

"Does that apply to collecting donations for the Howard Association, too?"

"Yes, ma'am. I do that too."

Snowden tried to speak. "Deaves, I don't—"

Tyner cut him off. "So you collect for Ward Two?"

"I do."

"Did you collect from Mr. Snowden here?"

"I'm afraid I fail to see how any of this is your concern."

"I work for the Howard Association," Tyner said. "I'm always concerned when money that's supposed to go to fever sufferers comes up missing."

"Are you suggesting that such a thing has happened?" Deaves asked.

"I was just talking to Mr. Snowden here about his Howard Association donation." She looked at him. "Seems he changed his mind rather suddenly about a discrepancy he reported."

"Discrepancy?" He looked at Snowden. "Is that right?"

"Deaves, I explained to the lady that I was mistaken. I only thought I'd contributed—"

"Seems Snowden here thought he gave you a hundred and fifty dollars," Tyner said. "Turns out he was wrong. He only gave a hundred—at least that's all that got to the Association."

"Ma'am, I don't think I like what you're saying," Deaves said.

"I'm sure you don't."

Deaves took a small notepad from his pocket and, after flipping over a few pages, held it up for Tyner to see. "This would be Mr. Snowden's gift. See? It says right here: 'one hundred dollars.' "

When she turned to him, Snowden would not look her in the eye. "Do you still say you made a mistake?" she asked him. He shook his head.

"Now, ma'am, if you're here to shop in Mr. Snowden's store, then I think you should do so. And if you're not, then you don't need to be here in my ward harassing honest businessmen."

With no admission from Snowden, and Deaves's producing his handy little record book, the matter was stalled . . . at least for now. She pushed past Deaves and out the door, leaving Snowden still blotting his scalp and watching her as she mounted and rode away.

s he rode Nashville Harry across town to the house of the late T. R. Lassiter, Masey Baldridge caught himself staring down at the Nicholson pavement, consisting of wooden blocks covered with creosote. Two years after the war ended, Baldridge had actually worked on the street crew that laid much of this poor man's substitute for cobblestone. He remembered it as though it had been yesterday—the smell of the creosote as he stirred the boiling mixture and swathed it on the rows of wooden blocks his coworkers placed in the roadway. But that was just one more job he'd had to quit because of his knee. The minié ball that remained in his leg would occasionally press against the nerves and, without warning, render his entire lower leg numb. He had collapsed into the sticky creosote one too many times to suit the foreman of the road crew, and that, like a half dozen other jobs, had disappeared as quickly as it had come. A farrier before the war, he'd given up his business within six months of the surrender, when he could no longer stand for long periods without pain. Some days were better than others, and the warm weather seemed to give him greater mobility, but the late fall and the winter would bring on the inevitable stiffness, and the ever-present pain. Just the recollection of those days on the street crew sent him feeling for the silver flask in his pocket. He lifted it high and took the last swig, shaking it for the few drops that lingered inside before returning it to his pocket.

He recalled reading in one of the newspapers a day or two earlier about some doctors on the board of health actually blaming the streets for the fever, that the Nicholson pavement was decaying and "sending forth a poison that none in the city could avoid." Were they all crazy? He'd spent weeks laying that pavement and had suffered no ill effects, if you didn't count smelling that damn creosote every day. When he read medical opinions like that, it wasn't hard to figure out why the city was in quarantine.

Dismounting at Lassiter's home, Baldridge knocked on the door hoping someone might answer. Perhaps a relative, or someone who might show him where Lassiter died. When no one responded, he went immediately to the house next door, where a young, pregnant woman was attending to a bed of chrysanthemums.

"Pardon me, ma'am," he said, removing his hat. "I was wondering if I might talk with you about your neighbor, Mr. Lassiter."

The woman, rather advanced in her term, turned awkwardly to face him, adjusting a straw garden hat to shield her eyes from the sun.

"Terrible thing about T.R. Simply terrible," she said, sizing him up as she spoke. "Are you with the police?"

"Well, yes, I am. Somewhat." Baldridge wanted to be direct, yet he remembered Mayor Johnson's warning. "I've been asked to assist the police in looking into Mr. Lassiter's death."

"You some kind of detective?"

"Some kind."

She more waddled than walked a few steps from her garden, eyeing the Lassiter home. Baldridge noted her extended abdomen.

"When's the baby due?"

"Probably not more than a month," she offered, "if the moon's right. Of course, it's not the best time in the world to be having a baby, what with the fever and all." She offered a brave smile. "But the good Lord doesn't give you much say in that, now does he?"

"I suppose not," Baldridge said. "Frankly, I'm a little surprised to see you outside. Most folks seem to be staying in with ol' Yellow Jack on the prowl."

"Not me. I believe in fresh air. That's the key to staying well," the woman declared. "If you stay in the house all the time and breathe that old, stale air, you'll get Yellow Jack for sure." She pointed next door. "That's what Mr. and Mrs. Lassiter did. It didn't help them. Mrs. Lassiter come down with the fever as sure as the world. I would've nursed her, you know, if I hadn't been pregnant. But she wouldn't hear of it. Insisted I stay out of the house. Didn't want me and the baby anywhere around her." The woman shook her head. "No, sir, staying inside didn't help them a bit."

"But Mr. Lassiter didn't die from the fever," Baldridge said.

"Yes, I know. I'm the one who found him, poor soul. Somebody split him open like an October hog."

"Were you the one who sent for the police?"

"Yes."

"Would you tell me what happened?"

"Well, it was this past Tuesday. I hadn't heard anything from Mr. Lassiter all day, and that surprised me. His wife died a little more than a week ago, and he was taking it real hard. So I'd been making him supper every evening. For the past several nights, he'd walk over to the house about six o'clock and pick up a plate I fixed him. He was awful sad, bless his heart. When he hadn't shown up by six-thirty, I figured something might be wrong. I was afraid he might have come down with the fever himself. Now that I think about it, that might have been more merciful."

"So you went next door and found the body?"

"Yes. I knocked on the door, which was standing partway open, and when he didn't answer, I just stepped inside. I called his name, but he still didn't answer, so I walked farther in. That's when I saw him."

"Where, exactly, did you find him?"

The woman looked up at Baldridge. "Would you like to see?"

"You can get inside?"

"Oh, yes. After they took Mr. Lassiter away, the police left the key to the house with me. I guess they figured his family would come here to see after the place. Nobody's shown up yet. He has a grown son who lives down in Hernando, Mississippi. I met him once. Now, with this quarantine, there's no telling when he'll show up."

Upon Baldridge's request, the woman struggled up the three steps onto her porch and disappeared inside her house, emerging momentarily with the key to Lassiter's home.

When the woman propped the front door open, the house emitted a strong odor of stale vomit and blood. "If I wasn't so far along, I'd have come over here and cleaned up some," she said. "My husband wouldn't hear of it. He'd probably be upset if he knew I was over here right now. But he's at work down at the mill." She winked at Baldridge. "I won't tell him if you don't."

"We won't stay long," Baldridge said.

"Oh, don't worry about it. I needed a break from stooping over those flowers anyway. And I ain't scared of the fever. Being pregnant increases a woman's resistance to disease," she said confidently.

Baldridge wasn't about to tell her how many pregnant women Yellow Jack had claimed. "That's good. Real good. Can you show me where you found him?"

She led him into a room just off the tiny entrance hall of the modest home and pointed to a bloodstained spot in the hardwood floor. "Right there. He was lying facedown right there." Baldridge moved closer and squatted, his bad left knee—as uncooperative as ever—extended awkwardly out to the side.

"I understand from the police that his throat was cut."

"Slit wide open." She pointed at the floor. "He was facedown, probably drowned in his own blood. You can see for yourself how it's all stained there."

The floor was marred with dried blood in a rough circle some four feet in diameter. Baldridge recalled Athy theorizing that someone had stepped up behind Lassiter and caught him by surprise. He remembered also that the coroner had suggested that perhaps the man had been kneeling. The only reason Baldridge could figure that a man would be kneeling in his living room would be either to pick up something he had spilled, or, perhaps, to pray.

"Did you notice anything being spilled on the floor when you found Mr. Lassiter?" Baldridge asked.

"Other than half the blood in his body, no."

"No, I'm talking about food or drink, or something he might have stooped or kneeled to clean up."

"I told you, he hadn't picked up his supper yet. Besides, there wasn't anything spilled on the floor that I remember."

Baldridge rose to his feet and walked once about the room,

noting an inexpensive painting that hung behind a worn sofa, a well-used rocking chair, the stump of three candles on top of a sewing case. He picked up one of the candles.

"Did you notice if these were burning when you arrived that day?" Baldridge asked.

The woman thought for a moment. "Yes. Yes, they were. I remember one of the policemen blowing them out after he arrived."

"What else can you recall? What else do you remember seeing in or around Mr. Lassiter's body that day?"

"His Bible. It was on that short table there by the sofa. I told the police about it."

"Mr. Lassiter was a religious man?"

"Catholic. Pretty regular about it, too."

Baldridge moved back across the room and stood beside the woman, taking in the entire room in a long, slow examination. Candles burning, Lassiter perhaps kneeling on the floor, the Bible open on the table—Baldridge reasoned that he might well have been praying when his killer approached him. He glanced back at the open front door.

"Did Lassiter lock his front door?"

"Never," the woman said.

The killer could have crept inside, grabbed Lassiter by the head, and slit his throat from behind. That would have caused him to fall forward, where the woman had found him. Baldridge caught himself acting out the motions he was contemplating, with his female companion eyeing him curiously.

"Sorry, ma'am," he said. "I was just trying to figure out what happened."

"Well, good luck. The police sure don't seem to know. They asked a lot of questions, too. But not the same ones you asked—more about who I saw coming and going around here that day."

"Who *did* you see that day?"

"Well, like I told the police, I don't exactly sit around all day and watch the Lassiter house to see who they have for company."

"I understand. But anything you might have seen could help."

"I told the police that the only people I saw over here that day were a couple of nurses from the Howard Association. I didn't actually see them come, but I saw them leaving about four o'clock."

"Did you see Lassiter?"

"Yes. He stood on his porch and waved good-bye to them, then went back inside. That's the last time I saw him alive."

"Why would the nurses from the Howard Association be here if Lassiter's wife had already died? You said he wasn't suffering from the fever."

"Well, not that I knew about. But I hear those nurses are real good about seeing after families even after a loved one has died."

"How many nurses did you see?"

"Two of them. I'd seen them here before—back when Mrs. Lassiter was sick. T.R. thought they were practically saints, the way they helped him care for his wife. I guess in a way they were. At least much more so than me. I didn't even enter the house while the woman was sick."

"You were pregnant. You said Mrs. Lassiter forbade it."

"I could have come over. I could have helped," she added, her face displaying a growing sadness.

"So, to the best of your knowledge, the nurses from the Howard Association were the last people to see Lassiter alive."

"As far as I know. I mean, somebody else could have come inside, I suppose, but I didn't see whoever it was. I told the police the same thing."

"Do you think the police talked to the nurses?"

"I'm afraid I wouldn't know. But they sure talked to that street preacher who's by here all the time."

"Street preacher?"

"Yes. You must have seen him around, always shouting about the judgment of God coming down on people because of the fever and all."

"Are you talking about old Malachi?"

"Yes, Malachi Baine, that's the one. I don't pay him no mind, but T.R. didn't care for him one bit."

"Did they ever argue?"

"Oh, yes, several times," she said. "I told the police about it. The preacher would come down the street shouting all this hell-fire and brimstone, and quoting the Bible, and T.R. would shout at him and quote it right back. He knew his Bible, Mr. Lassiter did. And he could hold his own with the preacher."

"Did you hear them argue recently?"

"I'm afraid so. This Baine came by two days after Mrs. Lassiter died, spewing out all this judgment talk, and it must've been more than Mr. Lassiter could stand. I was working in my garden, trying not to pay any attention to Baine, when I heard the door over here slam and I saw Mr. Lassiter storm out on the porch. Him and Baine exchanged some words—no, more scriptures than words—and Mr. Lassiter called him the child of the devil."

"What did Baine do?"

"Nothing, really. The two of them just kept a-judgin' each other until Baine moved on down the street to find another sinner. I could tell T.R. was upset. I swear, you could feel the steam coming off him from all the way over at our place. He eventually went back in the house."

"When was that?"

"About four days ago."

"The day before the murder."

"That's right."

"Do you think Malachi Baine killed your neighbor?"

The woman shook her head. "I can't see it. Men like Baine are bigmouthed, finger-pointing troublemakers. But I don't think he'd have it in him to kill somebody."

"Even if he got mad enough?"

"Baine never really got mad that day. It was T.R. who was mad. Baine just got that holier-than-thou look on his face and kept walking." The woman grabbed her stomach and grimaced.

"What's wrong?" Baldridge asked.

"Oh, this young'un just let me have a good, strong kick. Guess it's his way of saying I need to get off my feet."

"We can leave now if you'd like," Baldridge said, starting out the door. "How do you know it's a boy?"

"Look where I'm carrying him. Way too low to be a girl. At least that's what everyone tells me."

"I appreciate your talking to me and showing me the house," Baldridge said as the woman locked the door.

"Oh, I didn't mind. Sometimes it helps to talk about things."

"Is there anything else you can think of that you saw or heard that day? Anything you might have picked up or failed to show to the police?"

"Not that I can think of. There is the Bible—the one that was on the table—but I showed it to the police. They gave it to me and told me to keep it in case somebody in the family wanted it. I can't see why they would. There's blood all over the pages."

"You've got the Bible that Lassiter was using that day?"

"Yes. Would you like to see it? I've got no use for it. And nobody's showed up yet to even go through the Lassiters' things. Even if they do, I can't imagine them wanting it with it being so messed up and all."

Baldridge wasn't sure why, but something told him to at least have a look at it. Maybe it was that cross-shaped mark on Lassiter's and Stayley's bodies, or maybe it was just morbid curiosity, but he stood fast outside the house as the woman went inside and brought him the black leather Bible. Dried blood had warped the pages and caked along the edges. Baldridge opened the book to a blood-spattered passage in the fifth chapter of Matthew and asked the woman if she recalled whether or not the Bible had been opened to that page the day she found it.

"Sure looks like it—given the way the blood is all over the pages," she determined.

He scanned down the page, struggling to read the text through the dark, crimson-stained page.

> And seeing the multitudes, he went up into a mountain:
>      and when he was set, his disciples came unto him:
> And he opened his mouth, and taught them, saying,
> Blessed are the poor in spirit: for theirs is the kingdom
>      of heaven.
> Blessed are they that mourn: for they shall be comforted.
> Blessed are the meek: for they shall inherit the earth.
> Blessed are they which do hunger and

Lassiter's blood obscured the remainder of the text on that page, so Baldridge reverently closed the Bible.

" 'Thirst after righteousness,' " he said in a near whisper.

"Beg your pardon?"

"The beatitudes," Baldridge said, handing the Bible back to the woman. "This is probably what Lassiter was reading when he died."

A horse came thundering down the street behind them, the rider reining up beside Nashville Harry. A young man not more than twenty, dressed in a dark business suit, rose up in the stirrups.

"Are you Mr. Baldridge?"

"Yes, I am."

"I'm an assistant to Chief Athy," the man said, leaning over in the saddle and whispering to Baldridge. "There's been another killing. You should come with me right away."

Baldridge thanked the woman for her assistance, mounted, and rode off with the young man. But he was ill prepared for what he would find some eight blocks across town.

"I might have known I'd see you here," Chief Athy said to Baldridge as he dismounted. Athy stood in the open doorway of a two-story boardinghouse, cigar in his mouth, hand on his hip.

"I understand there's been another killing," Baldridge said as he limped up the eight steps to the porch of the boardinghouse.

"You sure you want to see this?" Athy asked.

"I'm here, ain't I?"

Athy shook his head and led Baldridge inside and up the stairs to a room on the second floor. A uniformed policeman stood beside the door, and just inside two women comforted a third who was grieving loudly. Athy began trying to speak to one of the women as Baldridge recognized Coroner Prescott kneeling beside a bed near the window, examining the body of a young girl. As Baldridge moved closer, Prescott glanced up at him but said nothing, returning his attention to the corpse. The child's long blond hair lay tangled about her head and her face was ashen, with a glassy stare into nothingness from blue eyes that once had danced with the joy of youth. Baldridge stood beside Prescott, then leaned over and touched her hair. It felt soft and silky.

"What happened?" he whispered.

"She had the fever," Prescott said, keeping his voice low. He paused momentarily, then added, "But that's not what killed her."

Baldridge leaned over closer. "What do you mean?"

"She was smothered." Prescott pointed across the bed. "Probably with that pillow right over there."

Baldridge was stunned. He'd seen his share of death during the war, cradling the head of more than one young soldier felled by a Yankee bullet. But the sight of this little girl—not more than twelve—turned his stomach.

"Why on earth would someone smother a child?" Baldridge asked.

"Maybe to keep her from suffering," Prescott replied. "I watched the fever kill a sweet little thing like this, and I can tell you it's horrible."

"Do you think the mother did it?"

"I think the chief does," Prescott said, "but I'd bet against her."

"Why?"

"Because of this," Prescott said, gently lifting her rumpled bangs off her forehead.

The outline was only partial, revealing perhaps just the top and the crosspiece, but it bore an unmistakable resemblance to something Baldridge had seen earlier."

"Is that a cross?" he asked.

"Sure looks like it was going to be one."

"Do you think that's the same mark you found on Stayley and Lassiter?"

"Not exactly," Prescott said. "I don't think the killer had enough time to create the entire impression." He pointed to the slight indentation in the child's skin. "Athy can give you the details when he finishes with the mother, but it looks to me like someone came in here and held that pillow over this little girl's face. Weak from the fever, she probably couldn't fight off whoever it was. Looks like the same person who killed the other two."

"No wonder he sent for me."

"Athy didn't send for you," Prescott said, rising to his feet and returning a small probe to his medical bag. "I did." Baldridge seemed puzzled.

"The young man said he was with Athy."

"Yeah, yeah, I know. I told him to say that. Listen, Baldridge, I've known Athy for almost ten years. He's a good policeman. But he's proud—too proud sometimes. He and his department are completely overwhelmed right now, but he doesn't want to admit it—any more than he wants to admit he's got somebody running around Memphis murdering people. But the mayor's right. Athy and his department need all the help they can get." Prescott closed his bag. "Now, I don't know you, but I trust Mayor Johnson. And if he hired you, then you must be pretty good at your business." He picked up the bag. "Just do one thing for me."

"What's that?"

"Find the son of a bitch who's doing this before I have to look into another dead child's face. I'll be downstairs for a few minutes if you need me, then I'm leaving out the back door. No telling who's watching out front."

Following close behind Prescott, the uniformed policeman led the mother, accompanied by the other two women, out the door and down to the first floor.

Athy moved over beside the body. "That's a damn shame, right there."

"Prescott believes it's the work of the same person who killed Stayley and Lassiter," Baldridge said.

"We don't know that for sure," Athy said, tapping a pencil on the paper in his hand.

"The hell we don't! Look at this mark," Baldridge said, pointing to the child.

Athy stood silent for a moment. "I've got to rule out the mother," he said.

"What does she say?"

"The woman and the child were traveling back from Jonesboro, Arkansas, to their farm in Huntsville, Alabama," Athy explained. "The little girl came down with the fever three days ago, after staying in this boardinghouse for one night. They were supposed to catch the train the next evening for Alabama."

"Where's the father?" Baldridge asked.

"In Alabama. Bringing in crops, I figure."

"Who found the girl?"

"The mother and the nurse. In fact, she says they surprised the killer."

"What did he look like?"

"It was too dark," Athy said. "The mother is too torn up to tell me much, but I talked to the nurse, who says they came in here just before daylight to check on the girl and that's when she saw a shadow—the outline of somebody next to the bed—leaning over the child."

"I'd like to talk to the nurse," Baldridge said.

"I've already interviewed her. She says—"

"I want to talk to her myself."

"Baldridge, listen to me. You don't—"

"Either you get her in here or I will," Baldridge demanded.

Athy motioned for one of the uniformed officers, and momentarily a short, rather chubby woman in her mid-thirties cautiously entered the room. Athy waved for her to join them and the woman approached slowly, her eyes locking on the body of the young girl behind them.

"This is Miss Chriswell," Athy said. "Ma'am, this is Mr. Baldridge. He's assisting me in investigating this child's death."

Baldridge noticed the redness in the woman's eyes. Her hands shook and her lips trembled as she spoke.

"I—I just don't know how this could have happened," she said, still staring at the body. "I was gone only a few minutes. I went to wake up her mother. She told me to wake her by daylight." The woman looked at Baldridge, her eyes a picture of pain and disbelief. "Nothing like this has ever happened to me."

"If you don't mind, Miss Chriswell, would you please tell again what you saw this morning?"

"Whoever was in here must have been right in the middle of killing that child," Chriswell said. "I had left the lamp burning when I went downstairs to get her mother. I noticed that the light was out when we got to the top of the stairs a few minutes later. I thought maybe the wind had blown it out, or maybe the oil ran out."

"How long were you out of the room?" Baldridge asked.

Athy interrupted. "Not more than five minutes." Baldridge glared at him and motioned for the nurse to continue.

"That's right," Chriswell said. "About five minutes. Just long enough for her mother to get dressed and for me to tell her how the night had gone."

"How did it go?" Baldridge asked.

"What difference does that make?" Athy blurted out.

Baldridge leaned close to Athy's face. "Shut the hell up and let me talk to this woman." He turned back to the nurse. "How did the night go?"

"The child slept some, but she was restless for the most part. And she was awful weak. I've been nursing for the Howard Association almost a week now, and I've seen several cases of Yellow Jack. I didn't think she was going to make it."

"So you and the mother came upstairs and found somebody in the room," Baldridge said.

"I was walking over to light the lamp when someone stood up sharply from beside the bed, pushed her mother down to the floor, and ran out of the room. I hurried to get the lamp lit and that's when we found the child dead, that pillow still halfway over her face."

"What became of the person who ran out of the room?"

"Disappeared out the back of the boardinghouse, the best I can tell," Athy offered. "The mother started screaming, and Miss Chriswell here was trying to revive the child, so I don't think we know for sure how the attacker got away. But pretty soon a half dozen people were up and came down here to see what had happened. Most of them wouldn't come in, though, given the child had Yellow Jack."

"I don't understand why she wasn't at the hospital," Baldridge said.

"The hospital's full," Miss Chriswell replied. "When there are enough of us available, the Howard Association sends us out to people's homes, or wherever they're staying. Often we stay during the night to help the mother get some rest. I was here the night before, too."

"Are you sure you don't remember anything about the person you saw in the room?" Baldridge asked.

"I'm so sorry. I wish I could," Miss Chriswell said. "But it was dark in here. I only saw the shadow next to the bed. It all happened so fast. Maybe the mother could—"

"I don't think she's up to saying much of anything," Athy said. "She's torn all to pieces."

"I'm sure she is. She had a beautiful little girl," Miss Chriswell said, still staring at the body. "I don't have children myself. I've yet to be married. But I can imagine what it must be like to lose something so special." She began to cry. "What must she think of me?" She looked up at Baldridge. "She must hate me for letting this happen."

"Miss Chriswell, I wouldn't say this was your fault."

"I should never have left the room."

"You were just doing what she asked of you."

Baldridge noted the terrible sadness in Miss Chriswell's eyes as she spoke. "What will Sister Naomi and the people at the Howard Association think of me? I told her just yesterday what a beautiful child this was and how I so hoped she'd recover. They may never let me nurse again."

Athy took the nurse's address, indicating that he might want to speak with her again later, then thanked her for her help. She turned to leave, but paused momentarily, looking back at Baldridge.

"I can't help feeling responsible. The child was under my care."

"We'll talk to Dr. Landrum. We'll explain what happened," Baldridge said.

Athy seemed annoyed. "Baldridge, I haven't got time to—"

"*I'll* talk to the folks at the Howard Association myself," Baldridge said. "I want to ask them some questions anyway."

Baldridge spoke briefly with Athy, but he quickly had all he could stand of the horror in that tiny boardinghouse room. He went downstairs, and as he stepped out onto the porch, he saw a crowd of perhaps twenty to thirty people gathered on the lawn.

"What's going on in there?" one man shouted.

"I heard somebody's dead in there," another man yelled.

Baldridge offered no answer, and had begun limping down the steps when Athy emerged onto the porch, behind him.

"The fever," he said, addressing the crowd. "A young girl has unfortunately died of the fever."

"Ain't what I heard," the first man said.

"Well, you heard wrong."

The man persisted, and as he passed him, Baldridge recognized him as Miles Washburn, the reporter the mayor had introduced him to at the ball.

"Then why are the police here?" Washburn asked.

"I want this crowd to disperse right now," Athy ordered, and though the people began to move away, Baldridge sensed from the rumblings among them that they weren't inclined to believe the chief. He thought he had slipped past Washburn when he felt a gentle tap on his shoulder.

"Sir? Sir? Aren't you Mr. Baldridge?" Baldridge glanced back at him but kept up his irregular stride toward the tree where he had tied Nashville Harry. "From the ball the other night? The mayor introduced us. I'm Miles Washburn with the *Daily Avalanche.*"

"I remember you," Baldridge said as nonchalantly as possible. He untied his horse, and moving around to the right side, as was characteristic of him, he placed his good right leg in the stirrup, pulling himself up by the saddle horn, then swinging his stiff left leg over and plopping into place.

"You were in the house, weren't you, Mr. Baldridge?"

"Yeah." He tipped his hat to Washburn. "You have a pleasant day, sir."

Washburn called to him as he led Harry away. "What happened in there?" Baldridge offered no answer, but waved his hand without looking back. "What were *you* doing in there, Mr. Baldridge?"

Amid Washburn shouting questions, Baldridge heard a booming voice coming from an alley.

"For the hurt of the daughter of my people am I hurt; I am black; astonishment hath taken hold on me."

Baldridge reined up. *What's he doing here? Why is he always around when people are killed?*

"Is there no balm in Gilead?" Baine shouted. "Is there no

physician there? Why then is not the health of the daughter of my people recovered?"

He knew he should talk to Baine, but not with Washburn around. He wasn't sure how much longer Athy and the mayor would be able to keep Washburn from finding out what was happening, and he wasn't about to question Baine anywhere near such a determined reporter. He would pick his time and place. But as he rode away, he saw Chief Athy move through the crowd and initiate a conversation with Baine. Washburn was standing nearby. Surely Athy would choose his words carefully.

# 9

An egg-shaped mass of delta soil, sand, scrub oak, and cotton-woods, some four miles across, President's Island had for centuries sat defiantly in mid-river, splitting the Mississippi into two separate channels. With the sun well up in the eastern sky behind him, Williamson could see several hundred yards across the westernmost channel from the landing where the *Paragon* and the other two ships were docked. He noted the spot where the rebel gunboat *Jeff Thompson* had gone down back in 1862. He had watched her sink—a victim of artillery fire from a Union gunboat. But she had taken her vengeance; for by 1867 her wreckage had become such a challenge to navigation that the steamer *Platte Valley* had ripped her underbelly on the remains and had sunk nearby. That wreckage later claimed the steamer *Molly Boyd* in 1870, and on more than one occasion the current and the shifting channel had carried

Williamson's own *Paragon* perilously close to these underwater skeletons.

President's Island had few visitors, for the Freedmen's Bureau had tried to colonize the island with some 1,500 emancipated Negroes in the two years following the conflict. But with the demise of the bureau, so went the colony, leaving the Negroes to fend for themselves. Many took jobs working the expansive cotton fields owned by former Confederate general Nathan Bedford Forrest—the only planter who felt the rich yet shifting delta soil to be worth the effort to farm it. But as Williamson passed the island during the years following the war, he noted that most of the Negroes had migrated elsewhere, leaving only a handful of residents in shacks near the Memphis side. Now perhaps only a fourth of the island remained planted in crops.

The captain did not recall exactly when President's Island was selected as the location of the pest house, but it was a choice that clearly satisfied the citizens of Memphis. Created to treat people, in isolation, with highly contagious diseases, the pest house consisted of a half dozen whitewashed buildings abandoned by the Freedman's Bureau and renovated by the city of Memphis, connected with a series of elevated wooden walkways designed to survive limited flooding. And the three steamers that presently nosed up to the shore about a half mile away represented the most traffic the island had hosted for years.

As he peered over the flat terrain toward the white clapboard buildings, Williamson pondered how long this quarantine might last. The *Paragon* had been first to arrive yesterday, followed shortly by the *Grand Tower* and the *City of Chester*. After only one night in quarantine, the passengers were already growing restless. Williamson had attempted to shave some of the edge off the situation by offering a special midnight meal after arrival the night before. As expected, almost everyone stayed up until early in the morning, the main dining area having been converted to a ballroom, and danced until Williamson was certain the fiddle player's fingers were nubs. But instead of sleeping late and recuperating today, many of the passengers had been up since daylight, moving on and off the boat in a steady stream, curious about their new surroundings. Some wandered the narrow streets that had once passed for a village, but all kept a safe distance from the pest house. It had made no sense to restrict the passengers to the boats; indeed, Williamson was certain such an effort would have caused a mutiny. No sane person could expect people to remain for an undetermined amount of time cooped up in staterooms.

Both Captains Zeigler and Lennox agreed; thus the passengers from the three boats had spread out along the shore to create their own temporary city, returning to the boat to eat, sleep, and perhaps play a round of cards. Some of the more enterprising travelers had even set up lamps in a couple of the abandoned cabins and, with Williamson's approval for his band to participate, determined to have a follies that Saturday night. The only thing missing were the printed pamphlets, but among such a small settlement, word of mouth proved sufficient. Williamson never ceased to be amazed by how some people could find something positive in the most difficult of situations. He wished he felt so jovial, but he just kept thinking about what that midnight dinner had cost him, along with all the subsequent meals he would have to furnish—if he was able to keep enough food on hand. Unless supplemented from shore, he figured his supplies would last three, maybe four, days at the most. And when he saw his chief clerk, Steven Tibedeau, returning from the *Grand Tower*, he hoped to get some answers to how they might handle the situation.

Tibedeau had met with the clerks from the other ships to coordinate a plan for resupply and communication with the shore. The characteristic jauntiness in Tibedeau's step was missing as he walked across the planks of the landing stage.

"Steven!"

"I'll be right up, Captain."

Tibedeau, somewhat out of breath, made his way up the steps and leaned over the rail next to Williamson.

"Did you run back from the *Grand Tower*?"

Tibedeau shook his head, still trying to catch his breath. "No, sir. I guess I was just up a little too late last night—and way too early this morning."

"I know what you mean. I didn't get more than a couple of hours myself. So, what's the plan?" Williamson asked. Tibedeau took a deep breath and steadied himself against the rail. "Are you all right?" Williamson asked.

"I'm fine, Captain," Tibedeau assured him. "I'm just worn out. Anyway, here's what we agreed on. The three ships will combine to make one supply run every morning and another at night."

"Do you figure the Memphis authorities will give us any trouble about that?"

"Not as long as none of our people go ashore—at least that's what a representative of the Howard Association said."

"Somebody from the Howard Association was there?"

Tibedeau nodded. "They're pretty much calling the shots out here. They're already making two trips out to the island every day, bringing medical supplies, food, relief nurses, whatever they can."

"Then it's not a real quarantine," Williamson said.

"As far as folks coming and going from here to the shore, it is," Tibedeau said. "Only nurses and doctors can move freely. They'll be allowed to come and go as needed."

"Then how do we get supplies?"

Tibedeau removed a handkerchief from his pants pocket, lifted his blue officer's hat, and daubed sweat from his forehead. "It seems they leave the supplies on a dock below the bluff out at old Fort Pickering. The people from the Howard Association pick up the supplies in their boat and row back across with them. Usually takes two or three trips."

"The Howard Association can't possibly bring enough supplies for these three boats."

"That's what we talked about. We agreed that each ship will furnish four deckhands—all in good health, the Howard Association mentioned that twice—to man a skiff that the *Grand Tower* will provide. They'll pick up the supplies for all three boats, and for the Howard Association, plus the doctors and nurses to relieve the shift on duty at the pest house."

"This sure seems like a lot of trouble to isolate people when half the doctors in Memphis don't even believe you can catch yellow fever from another person."

"It's more than I understand, Captain. But then, I'm not a doctor."

Williamson sensed that Tibedeau was discreetly suggesting that the good captain didn't know what he was talking about, and perhaps ought to keep his mouth shut—an approach uncharacteristic of his clerk. "Speaking of doctors, don't we have one on board?"

"Yes, sir." Tibedeau allowed himself a weak smile. "The one who treated the fellow you shot."

"I still feel bad about that."

"You shouldn't, Captain. That fellow would've strangled me for sure," Tibedeau said. "You saved my life."

"I wouldn't go that far."

"Made a believer out of the others, too," Tibedeau added.

Williamson changed the subject. "I want to know what cabin that doctor's in, and I want him available just in case."

"I thought you didn't believe folks could catch Bronze John," Tibedeau said.

"No, I didn't say people can't catch the fever. I'm just not sure you can catch it from another person, Steven. At any rate, I want to be ready in the event any of our passengers come down with something."

"Understood, Captain." Tibedeau put his handkerchief, now fully soaked, away in his pocket. "I've got to find Jacob and set up that supply crew. Will there be anything else, Captain?"

"Yes," Williamson said, patting his clerk on the shoulder. "Slow down. Take it easy."

"I will, Captain. Just as soon as—"

"We're likely to be here for a while."

"I understand, Captain."

"And see to it you get some sleep tonight. Let me know if I need to assign you some help."

"No help necessary, Captain." Tibedeau started to leave and halted. He reached in the pocket of his uniform jacket and took out a sealed envelope. "I almost forgot. The man from the Howard Association gave this to me. It's addressed to you. He said it came over with this morning's supply run."

Williamson thanked him and Tibedeau moved off, leaving the captain opening the envelope. Inside he found a note from Baldridge and Tyner, the handwriting, as it was readable, clearly belonging to the latter. It was dated Friday night, and Williamson read it slowly, hoping to glean from its contents the status of the investigation. He learned of Baldridge's visit to the home of the late Mr. Lassiter, and of the unfortunate death of the young girl at the boardinghouse.

*Three bodies. This is quickly going to get too complicated for Baldridge.*

He skipped down the page to where Tyner described her

encounter with the store owner and detailed her suspicion about Roe and Deaves.

> Maybe these two are working together and maybe they aren't. But Snowden is afraid of Deaves, and I'm sure that if we look under that rock, we'll find a bug. The only question is whether or not someone in the Howard Association is involved.

Tyner went on to explain that she had arranged to start working for the Howard Association as a nurse on Saturday. It was the only way she could think of to get inside the organization for a close enough look. According to Tyner's note, Baldridge, too, had some questions for the Howard Association—specifically, he wanted to know more about the two nurses who were supposedly at the Lassiter home the afternoon he died. She indicated in the message that they would keep him posted by messenger on developments over the next couple of days and wished him good luck in putting up with the quarantine.

Williamson folded the letter and slipped it inside his uniform pocket. Leaning over the rail and looking ashore, he noticed eight or ten young boys running around amid the stubble of an abandoned cotton field. One was swinging a stick at a makeshift baseball. Several adults had gathered to watch the action, and Williamson wished that he were down there, too. He'd been able to hit a ball a reasonable distance back during the war, and he wondered aloud to himself if he could still do it.

*Maybe later.* There were rounds to attend to.

# ❖ 10 ❖

unday morning broke clear and fair and slightly cooler than usual, and Tyner got that first hint of fall that permeates the morning air. The summer had been hot and rather dry—a stark contrast to the rainy spring before it—with no distinct Indian summer. The entire Mississippi Valley had seen a steady parade of hot days and stuffy, humid nights, with air so moist you could almost wring it, all amid the constant hum of the relentless mosquitoes. But today seemed different, and Tyner wondered as she left the hotel whether or not her mood had come about because of what she was to do that day. It would be her first day nursing fever patients for the Howard Association, and while she had attended to her share of sick people in her life, working with Yellow Jack patients would be new—new and frightening. Baldridge had been his usual nonchalant self about the whole matter. The man actually believed he couldn't catch the disease. She only wished she were that confident. As she rode toward the office of the Howard Association on Court Street, she wondered what she could have been thinking when she agreed to help Baldridge work on this case. It was one thing to chase down the missing money—and after conferring last night both she and Baldridge had felt they had a good idea of what was happening—but getting in the face and the breath and the excrement of people dying with the fever was a different matter. Even if she wanted to back out now—and at moments she did—her mind kept returning to the man she had loaned Luke Williamson's horse to at the train depot. His face, his eyes, his irrepressible fear were burned into her memory. So many people like him were suffering and dying and watching loved ones perish in front of them that someone had to help. And investigation or no investigation, Tyner figured that that someone might as well be she. Her past as an entertainer of gentlemen, even if it were known, wouldn't matter to these people. They just needed someone to care about them and be there for them, either in recovery or in their last moments. And though her fear was real, her pride at doing something that mattered was greater.

In the hallway of the Howard Association, Tyner saw Sister Naomi giving directions to two women dressed in the blue and white apron that signified the benevolent assistance of the Howard Association nurses. Sister Naomi smiled when she saw her.

"Good morning, Miss Tyner," Sister Naomi said. "I received word yesterday afternoon that you would be joining our nurses this morning. God bless you."

"We'll see how it goes, Sister."

"I'm sure it will go just fine." Sister Naomi opened a closet door and removed two neatly folded blue and white aprons. "You'll need these today."

"Two of them?"

Sister Naomi smiled and nodded. "The fever is a nasty illness, Miss Tyner. Black vomit, you know." Tyner took the aprons. "Your first name is what, my dear?"

"Salina. But people call me Sally."

"Very well, then, Sally. You'll probably get to see firsthand today why I gave you two aprons. I only hope that's enough. Our supply of freshly laundered aprons is running a bit low. We depend on people donating their time to wash the garments."

*Wash the garments. Maybe that's what I should be doing.* Tyner figured she could stake out a spot by a washboard. Some lye soap would be a little rough on the hands, but she'd get used to it.

"You *are* a nun, aren't you?" Tyner asked.

"Yes, my dear," Sister Naomi replied.

"Then why don't you wear a nun's habit?"

"I do in normal times," Sister Naomi replied. "But I wear the Howard Association apron because of my work. People see this blue apron and they know someone is there to ease their suffering. It's important that I give them a sense of peace."

Tyner tied the apron behind her.

"Where will I be working today?"

"At the yellow fever hospital out by Fort Pickering. I find it's best that new nurses get used to dealing with the disease there before they do any visits in the home, or before they work at the pest house on President's Island. There will be other nurses around to help you."

"I see."

"Have you ever been a nurse?"

"Sure. I mean, not a school-taught nurse or anything, but I've tended to sick folks."

The two nurses Tyner had seen earlier entered the hallway.

"We're ready, Sister Naomi."

"Excellent." She introduced Tyner to the other two ladies, who she said had been nursing about four days, then addressed Tyner again. "During our buggy ride out to the hospital I'll go over the treatment procedures for the disease and try to answer any questions you may have." Tyner started walking toward the door and realized that no one was following her. When she turned around, Sister Naomi and the other nurses were standing, hands clasped together, looking at her.

"Aren't we leaving?" Tyner said.

"Sally, we always begin our day with a brief prayer," Sister Naomi explained.

"Oh." Tyner released the doorknob and joined the circle of hands.

"Gracious Lord and Heavenly Father, we commit this day our efforts to Thy glory," Sister Naomi began, "and we ask that Thou extend through us, Thy servants, Thy healing hand to those we touch. And for those who suffer, we ask that Thou bless them with the peace only Thou can provide—the peace that passeth all understanding—even as they walk in the valley of the shadow of death. We ask this in the name of Thy blessed Son, who for our sins was crucified, on the cross. Amen."

"Amen," echoed the two nurses.

"Amen," Tyner added.

In the carriage ride to the yellow fever hospital, Sister Naomi spared no detail in trying to prepare Tyner for what she would see; and yet, in spite of her thoroughness, Tyner spent the first hour at the hospital trying to recover from the shock. As soon as she entered the two-story wooden building, almost a city block long, the smell of bile and stale urine made her gag. A row of beds scarcely more than a yard apart lined both walls as no more than a half dozen blue-aproned nurses attempted to care for what seemed to be at least a hundred patients on the first floor alone.

The sound of muffled conversation mixed with moans, groans, and the sound of vomiting was a cacophony of horror for which Tyner was ill prepared.

"Quick," one of the nurses yelled to Tyner, "we need you

over here." She froze momentarily, the nurse calling again to her. "Are you coming? I need you to support this patient." Tyner left Sister Naomi and the others and rushed to place her hands against the back of a patient who was leaning over the side of the bed. The nurse who had called her braced her hands against the forehead of a young man not more than twenty. His hands against his abdomen, his guttural groan shaking his entire body, he heaved and lurched forward, spewing vomit that splashed into a pan on the floor beside the bed. Tyner gagged again, mustering all her willpower to not herself add to the mess. The black fluid that slapped against the basin emitted an odor like nothing she had ever smelled, and it almost overpowered her and left her dizzy.

"Careful," the nurse said. "Don't let him fall." Tyner adjusted her grip on his sweat-soaked bedclothes just as the man heaved another spray of black vomit into the bowl.

*El vomito negro.* That's what Sister Naomi had described on the way to the hospital. It was the telltale sign of Yellow Jack, indicating, along with the sweating, that the liver was fully consumed by the disease. "When you see that, they're often near the end," Sister Naomi had told her.

The young man's strength gave out and she eased him back against the pillow, his pale blue eyes—floating almost like pools against his gaunt, yellow skin—seeming to beg her for help. And in that moment she forgot about her fear, and the investigation, and how many aprons she brought, and over the next four hours worked to ease the fear and suffering of that young man, and more than twenty other patients.

Outside the building at a wash point, at about one o'clock that afternoon, Tyner busily cleaned vomit off her hands as Sister Naomi approached.

"You certainly received an abrupt baptism this morning,"

Sister Naomi offered, rolling up the sleeves of her dress and taking a bar of lye soap from a wooden shelf.

Tyner was staring down at her fingers as she scrubbed each of them carefully, and she did not look up as she spoke.

"I wasn't ready for that. That was just too much."

"You did very well," Sister Naomi said. "The other nurses—some of whom have been here for days—said you pitched right in and did good work."

"It didn't seem like it. I mean, I did everything I could, and I did what the other nurses told me, and what the doctors who came in this morning told me to do . . ." Tyner glanced over at Sister Naomi. "But I don't think I helped any of them. I mean, I'm afraid they're still going to die and there's nothing I can do about it."

"All of them won't die, my dear," she said. "But it's true that most of them will." Sister Naomi's eyes met Tyner's. "About all you can do, Sally, is relieve their suffering. The rest is in God's hands. He and He alone will decide who among those people will leave this hospital alive."

"But I want so badly to help them," Tyner said.

"So do the doctors," Sister Naomi said. "How do you think they feel? They've got medical training and even they are powerless against yellow fever."

"Then what the hell are we doing here?" Tyner snapped, the pressure of the morning telling in her angry tone. She felt terrible as soon as the words left her mouth, but Sister Naomi seemed to take no offense.

"The best we can," Sister Naomi said. "The best we can to minimize suffering and work in God's will."

"God's will?" Tyner said, holding her hands in the air, dripping with water and soap. "Now, I know you're a nun and everything, but surely you don't believe all this is God's will."

"Suffering happens for a reason, Sally. I can't say what that reason is, but I trust God to work His plan."

"I'm sorry, but I don't think a twenty-year-old boy puking his very innards out falls neatly into God's plan."

"I understand how you feel," Sister Naomi said, "but we of the faith must attribute to God that which is His domain."

Tyner dried off her hands. "If you ask me," she said, pointing at the hospital, "that place in there is the devil's domain."

"It may well be, but we serve a merciful, yet vengeful God who will separate the sinner from the blessed. It is not our place to say who should live and who should die."

Tyner looked at Sister Naomi for a moment and wondered how she could have this overwhelming look of peace on her face. Tyner had been in there only four hours and she was shaken to the core, but for the sister to have endured what she must have endured in nursing these patients for so long, and still possess such a sense of peace, baffled Tyner. Maybe it was faith. Whatever it was, she would have given anything to have some of it as she walked back into that hospital.

For the remainder of the afternoon and into the evening, Tyner attended to patients. Sister Naomi left by midafternoon to secure a relief shift for that evening, and though the other nurses were helpful, she felt rather alone and unprepared without Sister Naomi. Perhaps her view of God's will was a bit hard to accept, but her skills as a nurse were without peer, and Tyner stood in awe of her ability to handle patients and get results that few could match. It was well past seven that evening before Sister Naomi returned with a relief shift of nurses, and Tyner, exhausted from the day, climbed into the carriage along with the other nurses on her shift and prepared to return to the Overton Hotel. During the ride back, she learned that Sister Naomi had trained as a nurse at a hospital in Philadelphia. Her religious order demanded a vow of service, she explained, and she had selected the ministry of nursing to fulfill that vow. Tyner listened intently as she spoke of her experience and training, as the sister's confident, knowledgeable manner impressed her. *What a strong woman*, Tyner thought, particularly liking the respect Sister Naomi commanded even among the doctors. So taken was she by the sister's words that Tyner scarcely even noticed when the other nurses were dropped off. As the carriage pulled up in front of the Overton, only she and Sister Naomi remained inside.

"I want to thank you for teaching me so much today. I don't know how I would have made it without you. When you left this afternoon, I got a little worried. But I just remembered what you'd told me this morning and I guess I made it fine."

"You made it more than fine, my dear," Sister Naomi said. "In fact, you've done better than most on the first day." Sister Naomi laughed. "Some never come back for the second."

The carriage driver unfolded the step and Tyner climbed outside. "I'll be ready in the morning," Tyner told her.

Sister Naomi smiled and nodded approvingly. "I know. I can see it in your eyes."

"See what?" Tyner said, closing the carriage door and peering in through the window.

"The gift," Sister Naomi said. "The gift of mercy."

The driver bid Tyner good night, climbed back in the driver's seat, and with a snap of his whip drove away.

Tyner stood under the gas streetlight for a moment, watching the carriage disappear down the street.

"The gift of mercy," she muttered. Nobody had ever accused her of that before.

asey Baldridge wasn't convinced that Malachi Baine had killed anyone, but he certainly seemed to be in the right place at the right time, at least for two of the killings. But Baldridge figured that even if he didn't do it, he might have seen something. So for three hours Sunday morning he rode the streets of Memphis, concentrating his search on Ward Two, and with the streets deserted, he expected no difficulty in finding the wandering prophet of the people. But the man who had been everywhere pronouncing judgment was now nowhere to be found, and by lunchtime Baldridge was so frustrated he ducked into Pete Flanagan's for some liquid encouragement.

Flanagan's was nearly deserted, with only a couple of men standing at the bar. The owner, Pete, walked over to Baldridge's table.

"How you doin', Masey?"

"Fair to middlin'," he replied, pouring himself a second glass of whiskey.

Flanagan looked forlornly around the room and let out a long sigh. "You were lucky to find a table with this crowd."

Baldridge laughed. "Yeah. Some crowd."

"We don't usually have many folks around here in the middle of the day. The problem is that nowadays we've got about the same bunch at night, too."

"Business fallen that much?"

"It's the fever." Flanagan shook his head. "The only way I'll get customers back is if the fever lifts, or if it gets a whole lot worse."

"Worse?"

"Yeah. Seems there are two times folks frequent a saloon—very good times and very bad times."

"Kind of like a church," Baldridge muttered.

"You know, that's right, Masey." He glanced around the room. "This place is like a church. I've sure got plenty of people coming in here confessing their sins."

"I suppose."

"Except for you," Flanagan said. "I ain't seen you around much this last week."

"I'm working."

"You still with that detective business?"

"Yes."

"You and that Captain Williamson, right?"

"Yeah. And Sally Tyner."

"What could you possibly be working on in the middle of a fever epidemic?" Flanagan grinned. "You investigating a cure for Bronze John?"

"There is a cure," Baldridge said.

"Yeah? What's that?"

"Dyin'."

"Hell of a cure, ain't it?" Flanagan said. "So, what are you investigating?"

"Well, Pete, I'm working on . . ." Baldridge hesitated, sensing that the whiskey was loosening his tongue. "I'm working on some missing money."

"Somebody stealing from folks in the midst of all this suffering?"

"Yeah, and from people who need it the most."

"Damn shame."

"Sure is."

"Are you gonna be wanting another bottle?" Flanagan asked.

"I don't think so."

Flanagan's tone grew formal. "I'll need you to be payin' cash money today, Masey."

Baldridge glared at him. "I can't run a bill around here no more?"

"Well, things are kind of tight right now."

"Yeah, yeah," Baldridge said, tossing a coin on the table.

Flanagan retrieved it. "I'm sorry to have to ask you for cash, Masey, but, frankly, I can use the money during these lean times."

The growing ache in Baldridge's leg had scarcely lessened since he'd started drinking. He held the whiskey glass up to the daylight that poured through the open door. "You ain't took to waterin' this stuff down, have you, Pete?"

"Hell, no, Masey. You know me better than that."

A few moments of silence passed between them before Baldridge asked Flanagan if he knew anything about Malachi Baine.

"Oh, yeah. The self-appointed prophet of God. He used to come around here about once a week preaching that hellfire and brimstone. Made the customers uneasy. I had to run him off."

"Seen him lately?"

"No. Not for several weeks. I hear he's got his hands full right now."

"How's that?"

"Well, with all this disease to judge folks over, it hardly leaves any time to point your finger at a man for drinking him a little whiskey."

"You've seen him around town?"

"Hell, Masey, everybody's seen Baine."

"Got any idea where I can find him?"

Flanagan pointed out the door. "Out on the streets, I reckon."

"He ain't there."

"Of course he's there. He's always there."

"Not today. I've about wore ol' Nashville Harry out looking for him this morning."

"Then maybe he's in church. It *is* Sunday, you know."

"From what I've seen, Baine is his own church."

Flanagan scratched his head. "Well, maybe the Lord's done struck him down with the fever."

"Could be," Baldridge said, filling his silver whiskey flask with the remaining contents of the bottle.

"Wouldn't that be a hoot?"

Baldridge shook his head. "I don't think the fever is—"

"I'm just saying, wouldn't it be ironic if that old fool caught what he said was a judgment of God for sin?"

Baldridge let the comment pass. "Do you have any idea where he lives?"

Flanagan picked up the empty bottle. "I believe that somebody once told me he kept a shanty over around the three hundred block of Front Street, behind Fontaine's Cotton Factory and Grocery. I believe Fontaine lets him stay back there with the understanding that he don't do no preaching around his store."

"Maybe you should have offered him that deal," Baldridge said.

"No thanks, Masey. I've got enough characters showing up around here—at least in normal times."

"Well," Baldridge said, "I've got to go. Thanks for the whiskey and the information."

"Take care of yourself, Masey," Flanagan said. "And stay away from Bronze John. I can't afford to lose another customer."

Baldridge checked the shanty behind Fontaine's store and found no sign of Baine. He stood on the street in front of the store for several minutes, trying to figure out where to look next. The only way a street preacher like Baine would not be harping at the top of his lungs on a Sunday would be if he was sick or dead, Baldridge figured. Nothing else could keep him off the street.

Baldridge snapped his fingers.

"Except jail," Baldridge mumbled as he adjusted Harry's stirrup. He mounted. "I'll bet Athy's got him locked up."


"CHIEF ATHY'S NOT here," the officer at the desk said, looking at Baldridge contemptuously. "He said you might come by. I'm supposed to let you talk to Blaine if you want to." Baldridge could hear Malachi Baine's earsplitting, rhythmic rhetoric through the closed door to the cell block.

"I want to."

"All right," the officer said, taking keys from a drawer and unlocking the cell door. "But you'll have to talk to him through the bars. You can't go in the cell with him." Baine's voice echoed from the hallway as the officer opened the heavy cedar door. "He's been carrying on that way since daylight."

"When did they bring him in?" Baldridge asked.

"Late last night, I think. I wasn't on duty. I didn't get here until five this morning."

"What was he arrested for?"

"They said it was for being a public nuisance."

"All of a sudden he's a nuisance?"

The jailer shrugged. "To tell the truth, I think the chief just wanted to question him."

Baine's voice grew louder as he saw Baldridge and the officer.

" 'Draw nigh unto my soul and redeem it. Deliver me because of mine enemies. Thou hast known my reproach, and my shame, and my dishonor. Mine adversaries are all before Thee.' "

"Here," Baldridge said, opening his coat and handing the jailer his .45-long Colt revolver.

Baine reached through the bars and pointed his finger at the jailer.

" 'Reproach hath broken my heart, and I am full of heaviness.' "

"You're full of shit," the officer said, shaking his head and turning away.

" 'And I looked for someone to take pity,' " Baine continued, growing ever louder, " 'but there was none; and for comforters, but I found none.' "

Baldridge wasn't sure if the officer left because he was satisfied that Baldridge was no threat, or because he couldn't stand any more of Baine, but he walked back down the corridor and slammed the thick door shut. Baldridge noted only one other prisoner—a drunk still sleeping off the previous evening's libation. Baine's harangue had not broken his steady snoring in the cell opposite.

Baine was still shaking his finger at the now departed officer. " 'Pour out Thine indignation upon them, and let Thy wrathful anger take hold of them. And render Thy—' "

"Hold on there, Malachi," Baldridge said, shouting to be heard over the sermon. "Hold on a minute." Baine grew silent, and leaning his head back, he folded his arms, his Bible in his left hand, thumb inserted to mark his place, his piercing gaze locked on Baldridge. His lips were pursed, as if dangling from the very precipice of speech, his broad-brimmed black hat framing his face like a dark halo. "Before you get to preaching again, I want to ask you some questions."

"My captors have already done that. They do not believe the Lord thy God shall solely judge a man."

"You know, you're right, Malachi. You're absolutely right. The Lord's gonna judge, all right."

"Amen, my brother."

"How will he judge *you*, Malachi?"

"I shall not be found wanting."

"That's good. Because if you killed someone, the Lord would not spare His wrath, now would He?"

"Why do you ask me this? Why do the police ask me this? What demons rack your soul to ask such a thing of a man of God?"

Baldridge spent several minutes explaining to Baine why he thought the police suspected he might be involved in killing Lassiter and Stayley and the young girl.

"I heard you quoting scripture about a young girl that day. How did you know a young girl had been killed?"

"The Lord spoke to me."

"Or maybe you heard people talking in the crowd?"

"Would that be any less the word of the Lord?" Baine denied having anything to do with the deaths, and launched into yet another homily. " 'My tongue also shall talk of Thy righteousness all the day long. For they are confounded, for they are brought unto shame, that seek my hurt.' "

"You're right, Malachi. I'm confounded, all right. I just can't seem to understand why you're around the neighborhood every time people get knifed and smothered."

"I'm simply out doing the Lord's work. Someone has to preach the truth to the people of Memphis."

"Did you argue with a man named T. R. Lassiter last Tuesday?"

"I shared a word from the Lord with him."

"The neighbor said you were shouting at him and he was shouting back. She said you told Lassiter his wife died because of her sin."

"He simply didn't accept the pronouncements of scripture. Neither did the nation of Israel. The wages of sin is death," Baine offered coldly.

"And maybe you've been handling the payroll for the Lord?"

Baine hesitated, appearing momentarily as if he might spew forth some of that hellfire on Baldridge. "I've killed no one," he said in a surprisingly soft voice. "I told the police that. I told them that I'm simply a prophet."

Baldridge peered into Baine's eyes, as wild-looking as they were, and though he might be a person with so little tact as to tell a grieving man that his wife's death from the fever was God's judgment, Baldridge did not figure him for a killer. So he concentrated on determining what Baine had seen in and around the time of the killings. Baine didn't deny the encounter that Lassiter's neighbor had overheard, and though he constantly tended to drift into a sermon about the fever and God's judgment, Baldridge was able to keep him relatively close to the facts. He claimed he had continued on down the street after the exchange with Lassiter, preached to some people loading a wagon on their way out of town, rested for about an hour in front of a stable, and returned to his shanty behind Fontaine's. He said that before the police had brought him to jail the night before and questioned him, he wasn't even aware that anything had happened to Lassiter.

"How did you go home the day Lassiter was killed?"

"I walked."

"No, I mean, what route did you take?"

"I went along Union to Market and then crossed over to Adams."

"So you passed back by Lassiter's home."

"Yes, I did. I already told the police that."

"What time would that have been?"

"Oh, I suppose about six o'clock."

"Did you see anybody or anything unusual when you went past?"

"I didn't see this Lassiter, if that's what you're asking me."

"What about someone else? Did you see anyone else at the house?" Baine shook his head. "What about *around* the house? The neighbor said two nurses visited Lassiter that afternoon. Did you see them?"

"Not at the house."

"But you did see them?"

"No."

"You walked up and down that deserted street and never saw the nurses?"

"I didn't say that."

"Well, did you or didn't you?"

Baine grew anxious as Baldridge's voice became more demanding, and Baldridge sensed that Baine was a man used to doing the accusing rather than being the one accused.

"I've seen the nurses around town. Sometimes I share a word from the Lord with them. They do visit and treat those that the Lord has stricken with His judgment. I believe Jehovah smiles upon them." Baine's eyes brightened. "I've spoken with that sister who sends them out. She is a true woman of God."

"Did you see any of the nurses on your way back home that day?"

"There was one. I saw one nurse that afternoon."

"Where?"

"Just up the street from that house."

"On your way back home?" Baldridge asked.

"Yes."

"Which way was she going?"

"Same way I was going, only on the other side of the street. I called to her. I said, 'Bless you, Sister, for ministering to the least of them.' "

"Did she reply?"

"No. She didn't even look back. She just kept walking. I wanted to share a word from the Lord with her, but I couldn't keep up with her."

"She was in a hurry?"

"Oh, yes. I assume she had some other poor soul to visit."

"Can you describe her?"

"I never saw her face."

"Her clothes?"

"She wore one of those blue aprons the Howard Association nurses wear."

"You're sure she was a Howard Association nurse?"

"I'm sure. That's about all you see moving around on the streets these days. It's like Sodom and Gomorrah. 'Then the Lord rained upon Sodom and Gomorrah brimstone and fire.' "

"But you never saw the nurse actually at Lassiter's house?"

" 'And he overthrew those cities and all the plain, and all the inhabitants of the cities and that which grew upon the ground.' "

Baldridge stared at Baine in disbelief. The man seemed to enter a near trance when he began reciting scripture, and though he was looking directly at Baldridge, his mind was miles away.

"Baine, Baine, listen to me," Baldridge said, grasping his

arms. "On Friday that young girl at the boardinghouse was murdered. You were in the alley when I left the building. I saw you watching the house."

"There were people gathered there," Baine said, his gaze still far away. "They needed to hear a word from the Lord."

"I'm glad you had a congregation, but I'm more interested in what you saw."

Baine smiled strangely. "I see much, brother. More than people want me to see. Jehovah gives me eyes to see the wickedness that men do, so that I may—"

"How long had you been there that day?"

"A half hour, perhaps a full hour," Baine said. "I left after the body of the young woman was removed, and after a policeman had spoken to me."

"There was a nurse from the Howard Association who left the building shortly before I came out. Do you remember seeing her?" Baine nodded. "Did you see her face?"

"Yes."

"Could she have been the same nurse you saw near Lassiter's house?"

"The Lord knows."

"Well, that's just great, Malachi. I'm sure the Lord does know."

"You should ask him, brother."

"We're not on real good speaking terms," Baldridge said, "so I'm asking you. You're the Lord's man. You say you do his work. So start talking for him. Could that have been the same woman?"

"It could have been. I told you. I did not see the face of the nurse near Mr. Lassiter's house. Both of them wore the blue of the Howard Association." Baine's eyes began to glaze again. "'Are not two sparrows sold for a farthing? And one of them shall not fall to the ground without your Father? But the very hairs of your head are numbered.' "

Baine tore off into another sermon and Baldridge figured that little more would come from continuing to talk to him, so he walked down the hall and knocked on the heavy wooden door. He hoped Athy and his men had gotten something more useful out of Baine than he had, but he doubted it. As the officer rattled the keys in the lock from the opposite side of the door, Baldridge heard Baine call out to him.

"Be not afraid, brother. 'For the eyes of the wicked shall fail, and they shall have no escape, and their hope shall be as the giving up of the ghost.' "

Baldridge stepped through the door and the officer closed it behind him.

"Still preachin', huh?" the officer asked.

"At the top of his lungs."

"Well, won't have to put up with that too much longer."

"Why is that?"

"Chief told me this morning that we'd probably release him tonight."

"Release him?"

"That's what Chief Athy said. I don't think they can prove whatever they think he's done. Chief didn't give me any details. Just said we'd probably release him."

Baldridge stared at the closed door. Baine's voice was muffled but still audible from the other side. "Want me to tell the chief you came by?"

"Yeah. You do that. And tell him I want to talk to him tomorrow, at the latest."

"I'll tell him."

Baldridge walked outside and untied Nashville Harry, but before he mounted he heard footsteps on the planks behind him.

"Good afternoon, Mr. Baldridge. I've been looking all over for you." Turning around, Baldridge saw the well-dressed Miles Washburn hurrying toward him. Nothing about seeing this man could be good. Washburn shook Baldridge's hand, nodding slowly and sporting a satisfied grin. "It took some doing. I admit that," Washburn said, "but I finally figured out who you are."

"Is that right," Baldridge said, turning away from him and pretending to adjust the cinch on his saddle.

"Yes, sir. What's it been? Almost a year now?"

"A year for what?"

"Since you linked up with Captain Luke Williamson," Washburn said. Baldridge offered no answer. "You pretty well saved that boat of his—the *Paragon*—according to the account in the paper. That was down around Natchez, wasn't it?"

"May have been," Baldridge said, lowering the saddlebags back over the strap.

"I'm afraid you're a little too modest," Washburn contended. "You and Captain Williamson and that woman—what's her name again?" He thumbed through a notepad. "Oh, yes. Salina Tyner. You all formed this Big River Detective Agency, I understand. What's it like working with those two?"

Baldridge wheeled to face him. "What do you want, Washburn? You didn't find me to talk about my work habits."

"Actually, Mr. Baldridge, that's exactly why I found you. You see, I thought it rather odd seeing the two of you in such serious conversation with Mayor Johnson last Thursday evening at the ball. After all, it was supposed to be a social event and here's the mayor out on the portico carrying on an intense—"

"What do you want to know?" Baldridge said. "I'm in a hurry."

"Well, how about why you're in such a hurry, for starters," Washburn said. "And why the mayor of Memphis is meeting with private detectives, or why these detectives are so interested in the arrest of a street preacher."

Baldridge offered a smile. "Look, Washburn, we're working on a case. It's a private matter and I'd like to keep it that way."

"I'm sure you would, Mr. Baldridge, but where the public's right to know is involved, and city officials are hiring detectives, there's no such thing as a private matter."

Baldridge turned, grasped his saddle horn, and mounted. "I've got work to do."

"What kind of work? And why is your colleague, Miss Tyner, working for the Howard Association if the two of you are on a case?"

"I didn't say that Sally was—"

"Is she investigating the Howard Association? Because if she is, and there's something going on, the public has a right to know." Baldridge began backing Nashville Harry away from the hitching post. "Will you tell me what you were talking to Malachi Baine about?"

"Let this go, Washburn," Baldridge said. "You ain't gonna find a story here."

Washburn seemed unfazed by Baldridge's comment. "Why did the police arrest him? Will you tell me what he's charged with? It has something to do with that child who died in that boardinghouse, doesn't it?"

Baldridge looked down at him. "No."

"I'll just go and talk to Baine myself," Washburn countered.

"Go ahead. May be good for your soul."

"Something's going on here, Mr. Baldridge," Washburn concluded, "and I'm going to find out what it is."

Baldridge tipped his hat. "When you do, fill me in," he said, and rode away.

# 12

MONDAY MORNING, SEPTEMBER 22

"Cap'n, Cap'n, come quick," First Mate Jacob Lusk shouted, his feet pounding heavily along the deck before coming to a stop outside the engine room. Williamson had been examining some maintenance work on the piston that drove the paddle wheel when Lusk, out of breath, leaned in the door.

"What's wrong, Jacob?"

The first mate's eyes flashed at one of the deckhands standing nearby, then back at Williamson. "I just needs you to come up to the texas, Cap'n."

"I'm right in the middle of something, Jacob."

Lusk's face grew even more intense. "We needs you upstairs right away, Cap'n."

Williamson wiped his hands on a rag, retrieved his hat from the back of a cane-bottomed chair, and followed Lusk outside. Once out of earshot of the crew, Lusk looked at him, his face reflecting a fear the captain had rarely seen.

"It's Steven, Cap'n. He's up in his quarters shakin' somethin' awful. One of the crewmen is with him and I've sent for that doctor on board." Lusk hesitated, swallowed hard, then spoke almost in a whisper. "It could be Yellow Jack."

As Williamson broke into a run down the deck and up the stairs, he recalled how Tibedeau had not looked well when he'd talked to him Saturday, but surely they were wrong. He was just overworked. He just needed a couple of days to rest.

When Williamson arrived at Tibedeau's room, the doctor was already there, along with three crewmen, two of whom peered in the door from the deck outside.

"Is he gonna be all right, Captain?" one of the hands asked.

"Sure. Steven's going to be fine," Williamson said, crowding into the small cabin. "That's right, isn't it, Doctor?"

The doctor struggled to look into Tibedeau's eyes amid the violent rigor that shook the very bed where he lay.

"I'm—I'm so *cold*," Tibedeau managed to utter.

The doctor placed his hand on the man's head. "And burning up on the inside, aren't you, son?"

"Yes," Tibedeau mumbled.

"Hell, Steven," Williamson said, offering a rubbery smile, "why didn't you tell me I was working you too hard?" One of the crewmen outside managed a soft chuckle.

"Steven, he sho' works hard, all right," Lusk added.

"I mean, if you wanted a day off you should've said so," Williamson added.

The doctor turned around. "May I speak to you outside, Captain?"

"Yeah, sure." Williamson followed the doctor out on the deck and the two of them stopped several feet down from Tibedeau's door. "He's going to be all right, isn't he?"

The look in the doctor's eyes made Williamson's stomach churn.

"It's yellow fever, Captain. I'm sure of it."

"You must be wrong," Williamson declared. "We haven't had a single case of fever on board the *Paragon*."

"You have now," the doctor said, "and I just came from the *City of Chester*. There's two cases on board there, too."

"But he can't have the fever. I mean, that's why we're down here in quarantine, isn't it?"

"Captain, I'm from Chicago, and I'll be the first to admit I don't have any experience with yellow fever. But from everything I've read, your clerk displays all the symptoms. He's having a rigor in there right now. You saw his complexion. He's as jaundiced as he can be."

"But it couldn't have come on him this fast," Williamson said. "I talked to him just the other day."

"It probably didn't come on fast," the doctor replied. "I suspect he's been ill for two or three days now. It's a testament to his stamina that he was able to keep going as long as he did."

"Maybe it's not Yellow Jack," Williamson said, the desperation showing in his voice. "It could be some other kind of malarial fever. Hell, I've heard of dozens of different fevers up and down the river."

"Yes. It could be. But it's not," the doctor replied.

"You can't be sure yet. You just don't know for sure yet."

"We'll watch his urine output. If it shows blood, then I'm afraid—"

"He's not vomiting," Williamson said. "People with Yellow Jack vomit."

"Sometimes it takes a couple of days."

"What can we do for him?" Williamson asked.

"Like I said, I don't have any experience treating the disease, but I understand quinine is the best initial treatment. I'll start him on quinine immediately. See if someone can fix some flax-seed tea. Try to make him comfortable until we transport him to the pest house."

"No."

"What do you mean, no?"

"I want him to stay here so we can look after him."

"Captain, that's out of the question."

"He's an officer on my boat—one of my best. I'll see to it he's taken care of."

"That's precisely why he needs to go to the hospital."

"We can look after him here. You can treat him yourself."

The doctor placed his hands on the captain's shoulders. "I know you're upset."

Williamson pushed his hands away. "I'm not upset. I just want Steven taken care of."

"Captain, you can't keep a man with yellow fever on this boat."

"I'm the captain of this boat. I can do what I please."

"No. No, you can't. This is a medical condition and your authority does not extend to medical situations. I'll order him off this boat if I have to."

Williamson glanced down the deck in the direction of Tibe-deau's room. "I guess there's no chance of keeping this quiet among the passengers."

"I imagine they already know something's going on. It's best to tell them. Let them know what they're dealing with."

"What *are* we dealing with, Doctor? Does anybody really know?"

"I'll do the best I can for your clerk, Captain Williamson. But I can tell you right now, the prognosis isn't good."

*"The prognosis isn't good." What kind of talk is that?* Williamson thought as the doctor returned to Tibedeau's room. Steven Tibe-deau would be all right. He had to be.

# ≪ 13 ≫

Calina Tyner plopped into a crude chair outside the back door of the yellow fever hospital at Fort Pickering. She let out a long, slow breath, rolled her stiff neck, and looked up at the cloudless blue sky. It was almost two o'clock, and since seven that morning she had been on her feet, moving almost incessantly from one patient to the next, assisting other nurses and administering treatments ordered by the three doctors who had come and gone at various times during the day. When she'd arrived that morning, the room had smelled like rotten hay, polluted by the discharge of dozens of disease-ravaged bodies. The stench had almost overcome her, but somehow she had persevered. Sister Naomi had arrived with two more nurses just after one o'clock, providing this brief moment of respite before she would have to return to the wall-to-wall sickness, the likes of which she had never seen before. There would be anywhere from four to six more hours of this, then the long carriage ride back to the hotel, maybe a chance for a bath if she was willing to trade the sleep, then up at four tomorrow morning, another ride out here, and another day of horror. What had she gotten herself into?

Baldridge had it made. While she was emptying vomit and wiping sweat, today he was talking to Roland, the accountant for the Howard Association, and probably stopping off for a drink somewhere en route. She had definitely gotten the sour end of this deal, and she'd told him so at the hotel the night before during the few minutes they'd had to talk before she'd fallen asleep. She remembered his audacity when he'd asked her what she had found out about the Howard Association.

"Found out about the Howard Association?" Tyner had snapped at him. "How about that they nearly kill themselves taking care of fever patients? How about that most of them work twelve to fourteen hours a day for nearly nothing just to console and treat people who have virtually no hope of recovery? How's that?"

She'd known what he'd meant, but she'd intended to make damn sure he knew what she was going through. Maybe it was only the second day, but it felt as if she had been at that hospital for a week. Watching eleven people die, four of them just that morning, was already taking its toll on her, and she felt an odd combination of respect and pity for the nurses and doctors who had contended with the situation for over a week now.

She knew Baldridge was pushing on with the investigation; he had told her of his encounter with Malachi Baine, and she now recalled clearly how his theories about who had killed Lassiter and the young girl had angered her just before they'd parted that morning.

She had been waiting in front of the hotel for the Howard Association carriage when he'd started asking about the nurses.

"Nurses?" Tyner had challenged him. "How can you think nurses had anything to do with this?"

"It's the only thing I can find that the two had in common."

"How about the fever?"

"Lassiter didn't have the fever."

"Then how could a nurse—"

"His wife did."

"But nobody killed her!" Tyner had reminded him. "She died of Yellow Jack. You said so yourself."

"Yeah, but Baine saw a nurse near his house the day he died."

She had caught sight of the carriage approaching in the early-morning light.

"So? Who else was he likely to see moving around the streets of Memphis that day? Masey, the Howard Association has mobilized a lot of women to meet this fever epidemic. I'd say ninety-nine percent of them are good, decent people. Hell, most of the ones I've met are closer to saints."

"What about that one percent?"

"Why?" Tyner had asked as the carriage approached. "Before they get here to pick me up, just tell me that. Why? Why would a nurse want to harm the patients she had volunteered to help?"

"Mercy?" Baldridge had offered. "Maybe she couldn't stand to watch the suffering anymore."

The carriage had begun to slow, the lantern mounted on its right front wobbling from side to side and casting an eerie amber glow over the two of them.

"I don't believe that for one minute, Masey. Not with what I witnessed yesterday. Anyway, this Lassiter fellow wasn't a patient, and Deke Stayley didn't even die at the hospital. So that ruins your whole theory."

"But he *had been* at the hospital. They found him three blocks away."

The carriage had rolled to a halt in front of the hotel that morning, and the driver had leaned down and opened the door, to reveal Sister Naomi and two other nurses sitting inside.

"Good morning, Sally," Sister Naomi had said.

"Good morning, Sister." As Tyner started to step into the carriage, Baldridge had leaned in close and whispered to her, "Find out who treated Stayley at the hospital, and see if they keep records about who goes to which private home. See if you see the name of a Nurse Chriswell."

"I'll see you tonight, Masey," she'd told him as she'd taken a cramped seat next to one of the nurses.

"Find out for me," he'd urged as the carriage driver called to his horses and pulled away.

Sitting on the back steps of the hospital, Tyner pulled her skirt up slightly to expose her calves and rolled up her sleeves, fanning herself in the absence of any breeze.

*Investigate the Howard Association. Exactly when am I supposed to do that?*

Tyner heard a wagon rattling up the dirt road, heading toward the rear of the building. The driver of the oversized wagon took a wide berth around the back of the building and came to a halt beside a narrow, flat-roofed structure that stood beside the four toilets that served the hospital. The glum-faced driver and a companion climbed down, and upon noticing Tyner, the driver tipped his hat and continued to the back of the wagon. He opened the twin doors and walked with his assistant directly to the small building. A few moments later the two emerged bearing a stiffened corpse wrapped tightly in a sheet, which they placed in the wagon. They were carting out the sixth corpse when Tyner heard someone speak to her from the doorway at her back.

"No matter how many times you see it, it never gets any easier to watch."

She turned to discover Dr. Rice wiping his hands on a wet towel. He pointed at the hearse. "That wagon there—that's ol' John Walsh's boys. Doesn't look much like a hearse, now does it?"

"No."

"That's because it's a converted furniture wagon," Rice said. "Walsh and the other undertakers can't keep up. Walsh has got a hundred men hired to do nothing but build coffins." The driver nodded at Tyner and snapped the reins, and he and his companion slowly rolled away.

"They're probably going to Potter's Field, you know," Rice said, taking a seat on the back steps. Tyner sat down beside him.

"The pauper cemetery?"

"Yeah. It's getting to the point where whole families have died, and if you're the last to go, and you've got no one to see to your affairs, that's where you end up."

The wagon disappeared around the building. "Does it really matter?" Tyner asked.

"What do you mean?"

"It's where we *all* end up, isn't it? It's not like one person's accommodations are better than another's."

She saw a fleeting smile. "You say pretty much what you think, don't you, Miss Tyner?"

"Always have."

"Well, this time you're wrong."

"How's that?"

Rice turned and looked hard into her eyes. "I can tell you firsthand, Miss Tyner, that there are degrees of death."

"I've seen some horrible suffering in the two days I've been here," she admitted, "but I'm sure it's nothing like what you've faced."

"A situation like this fever epidemic brings out unusual behavior in people."

"What do you mean?" she asked.

"Coroner Prescott was overwhelmed with death certifications last week, so he asked me to stop at the home of a wealthy gentleman who had reportedly died of the fever the previous day. He wanted me to certify the cause of death. The man lived alone except for three or four servants who kept his house for him, and you'll never guess what I found when I got there," he said, a smile overcoming him.

"What's that?" Tyner asked.

"The servants, two colored and one white, were sitting around the dining room table dressed in the late gentleman's most expensive clothes. The female servants even wore his late wife's evening dresses."

"Where was the dead man?" she asked.

Rice chuckled. "Sitting right there with them. Propped up in a chair at the head of the table, dressed in his Sunday clothes, while the rest of them ate dinner. If it hadn't been for the glassy stare, you'd have sworn that any minute he would have asked somebody to pass the potatoes."

"That's strange."

"Like I said, an epidemic like this brings out the strange. Brings out the good and bad, too."

"I suppose it does."

"The good is folks like you—folks who help care for the sick and take care of their neighbors. Take Annie Cook, who runs that whorehouse over on Gayoso Street." Tyner stirred slightly, growing uncomfortable with where the conversation was heading. "She sent her whores away and opened that beautifully furnished house of hers to fever patients. I've treated a half dozen in there in the past week, but she's nursing most of them herself. I mean, I wouldn't have thought that a woman like that was capable of such a thing."

"A woman like that?"

"Yeah, I mean being a madam of a whorehouse and all."

"Guess you just never know about some people."

"That's true. I mean, I can see a fine lady like yourself pitching in, but when a whore—"

"And the bad?" Tyner said, trying to change the subject.

"Beg your pardon?"

"You said you'd seen the bad side, too."

"The bad—well, there's plenty of that, too. People stealing from the homes of fever victims, fighting over the inheritance where there's money or property involved—you see it all."

"And this never gets you down? Seeing all this?"

"Of course it does. Two nights ago I saw something I don't think I'll ever forget. A young boy, not more than eight, came up to me while I was treating a patient over on Front Street. The boy was gaunt, peaked, and looked like he hadn't eaten in days. He told me his mother had gotten the fever about four days earlier, and apparently in an incoherent moment had locked herself and her infant baby in the back room of the shack they lived in down in Happy Hollow."

"I've been down there. It's a rough-looking place."

"Anyway, I went inside and the place was dark. The boy found a lantern and I lit it and made my way to the back room. Unable to locate a key, I finally forced the door open and walked in the room." Rice hesitated momentarily, then shook his head. "This is no story to be telling a lady."

"No. I want to know. Go ahead."

Rice looked at her again. "I held up the light and, there in the corner, nearly covered by rats, I saw the top half of the cadaver of the boy's mother."

"Oh God," Tyner said, looking away.

"An infant child, somehow still alive, was lying on her chest, coated in black vomit and still trying to suckle her mother's breast."

Tyner stood up and walked down the steps and into the grassy area behind the hospital. Rice followed her and placed his hand lightly on her shoulder, apologizing for what he'd told her. Tyner wiped away tears.

"It's all right. I asked you."

"You see so much of this, Miss Tyner, and you're so powerless to stop it, that sometimes the best thing you can do is help them die. Put them out of their suffering."

Tyner folded her handkerchief. "You mean, kill people?"

"That's what they want, many of them. I can't tell you how many people have begged me to give them something that will let them die." Tyner looked at him suspiciously. "But I don't," he added. "My job is to heal where I can and limit suffering where I can't."

"But helping them to die does stop suffering," Tyner said, feeling Rice out. "If a person is suffering badly, why not just help them over the line?" The look on Rice's face told her she had gone too far. "Of course, *I* would never do that. But there are probably people who would, don't you think?"

"Yes," Rice agreed. "But I'll tell you this—they won't work in any hospital I'm affiliated with." He started walking back toward the building. "I've got to write up some records now. Will you be leaving soon or are you working into the evening?"

"I'll be here until tonight," she said. "And I suppose I, too, should get back inside. They told me I could take half an hour, but I guess they could probably use me now."

"Better take a full break when they offer it. You never know when you'll get another one." Then Rice added, "Unless you want to help me write up my patient records?"

"But I'm not a real nurse—not trained, I mean. I couldn't write about patients like—"

"No, but you could certainly pull the records for me. That would save me time." Rice smiled. "It would get me back to the patients sooner."

Tyner was starting to believe that Rice had more than a passing professional interest in her, and she suspected he didn't need her clerical help as much as he wanted her company. He was attractive enough, and certainly the most skilled of the physicians she'd encountered, but where the circumstances of all this disease might not bother *him*, Tyner wasn't the least bit interested in furthering his attraction. Something about courtship, vomit, and greenish bile just didn't go together. She was about to decline his invitation when she recalled Baldridge's request. "Dr. Rice, does the office here keep records of all the patients seen at this hospital?"

"We try. That's why I've got to get inside and get to writing. Are you going to help me or not?"

"I don't want to let the other nurses down," she replied, though her eyes argued for inclusion.

"I'll speak to the head nurse. It'll be all right. I think they are staffed sufficiently at least for another half hour or so."

TYNER TOOK A seat near a cabinet containing medical records. As Rice would call out the name of a patient he was currently treating, Tyner would thumb through the alphabetized folders, locate the record, and hand it to Rice. He took two or three minutes to work on the first two records, his concentration intense and his tongue sticking out slightly between his lips as he wrote. When he was in the middle of the third record, Tyner slipped her hand slowly into the file cabinet and, peering out of the corner of her eye, located the "S" marker. Alternately eyeing Rice, then the files, she picked her way to the one marked "Stayley," and with her fingers she spread apart the folder and leaned slightly forward to see inside.

"So have you nursed before?" Rice asked her, prompting her to sit up straight and look toward him.

"No, this is my first time." His eyes had not left the papers before him, so she again leaned into the files as she spoke. "I've already learned so much in just a couple of days."

"It'll go on until the first frost, you know," Rice said.

Tyner's eyes scanned Stayley's record. "Is that right?"

"Yes. The disease seems to dissipate after the first frost. Don't know why. Some doctors claim it cleans the air, but I don't know that I believe that."

"What *do* you believe?" she asked, her eyes searching over the notations. "I mean, about the fever and what causes it?"

"Could be an airborne disease, but if it is, I don't believe it's contagious from person to person. Maybe if you contact the blood, but I doubt that, too. It's got something to do with rain."

"Rain?" Tyner noted on Stayley's file that the attending physician had been Dr. Fledge.

"Sounds crazy, doesn't it? But it seems that fever epidemics tend to be worse after a rainy spring. That's where some doctors get the idea that decaying plants give off a miasma, or a poisonous gas."

Tyner saw the name of two nurses listed as having treated Stayley on September 9 and 10. The document ended with a statement saying that Stayley had disappeared from the hospital. Sister Naomi and Dr. Fledge had signed it. There was no record of a Chriswell, the name Baldridge had asked about.

"What are you looking at?" Rice said sharply, now watching her from his desk.

"Oh, nothing. I was just seeing if I recognized anyone's name on the files." She smiled at him. "I was thinking about what you said about miasma."

Rice watched her for a moment and then looked back down

at his work, adding, "Well, I'm not saying the disease can't be in the air. Lord knows, burning tar and sulfur seems to lessen the incidence of the disease. That's why the city's spending so much money doing it."

"I'm surprised breathing that tar and sulfur doesn't kill people," Tyner said.

"Yes, the odor's strong, but for some reason it seems to work."

Tyner noticed the head nurse standing in the doorway to the office, a scowl on her face, her arms crossed over her chest.

Tyner stood up. "Do you need me now?"

"Oh, yes, my dear," she said in a heavy Scottish brogue that scarcely contained her frustration. "And we'd be a-needin' you for a while now. That is, if the good Dr. Rice dunna need you n'more."

"No, go ahead," Rice said without looking up from the page. "I've only got a couple more to do."

Tyner stepped outside with the head nurse, and sensing her anger, began to apologize. "I'm sorry. Dr. Rice said—"

"I know. Don't you be a-frettin' now, girl," the head nurse said. "It's not your fault." She looked back at the office. "God knows, he's the best there is, but . . ."

"But what?" Tyner asked.

"He's a bit of a weakness for the ladies," she added. "Don't go a-thinkin' you're the first he's asked to help him with his records. Next thing you know, girl, he'll be a-helpin' you with your petticoats."

For the next seven hours, Salina Tyner attended to the suffering of fever victims, now numbering over a hundred. The smell that had nearly overpowered her that morning was now barely noticeable. Except for the brief respite with Dr. Rice that afternoon, she had been on her feet for almost fourteen hours, with relief nurses long overdue. Her shoes were tight around her swollen ankles and occasionally one of her calves would cramp, causing her to halt for several moments before continuing with her duties. At a few minutes before nine o'clock that evening, Sister Naomi, accompanied by the Reverend Dr. Landrum, entered the hospital with four fresh nurses. Tyner had thought they'd never arrive, and as soon as she had completed blanketing a shivering patient, she made her way toward the front door. That carriage couldn't leave soon enough to suit her.

Sister Naomi was introducing the new nurses to the head nurse when Dr. Landrum approached Tyner and escorted her a short distance from the patients.

"Have you and your colleague been successful in locating our problem?" he asked.

"I'll have to talk to Masey back at the hotel tonight, but I'm pretty sure we're closing in on your thief."

"Anything you can share with me? I want to prevent any further losses."

"Not yet. I'd rather wait until we're a little closer to calling in the police."

"I understand," Landrum said. "And for whatever reason you're here, I'm glad you are. I know these patients are, too."

"It's harder than I thought it would be."

"But you're doing very well," Landrum said. "Sister Naomi speaks very highly of you. She says the quality of your mercy is not strained."

"I feel pretty strained," Tyner said, laughing off his remark.

"I'm afraid I have some rather unfortunate news for you, Miss Tyner," Landrum continued, his tone growing serious.

"News? What news?"

"I trust you are acquainted with the people who work on Captain Williamson's boat?"

"Yes, I know several of them," she said. "What's wrong?"

"It seems that sometime this morning a Mr. Tibedeau was stricken with the fever. We're all rather alarmed by that, since he was the first one on—"

"Steven? Steven Tibedeau?"

"Yes, that's correct. Sister Naomi can tell you more. She escorted the nurses to the pest house earlier this afternoon."

Landrum hailed Sister Naomi, and she approached the two of them. Tyner called to her before she could speak.

"Is it true about Steven? Steven Tibedeau?"

"You're talking about the young man from the boat?"

"Yes, on the *Paragon*."

"I'm afraid so. He's rather seriously down with the fever."

"Can I go to him? I mean, is there any way I can see him?"

"You're a friend of his?" Sister Naomi asked.

"We've known each other for almost a year."

"Oh. I'm very sorry to hear that," she said.

"Well, it's not like he's dead. He's not dead yet, is he?"

"No, Miss Tyner, he's not," Sister Naomi said. "But he is gravely ill. They're caring for him as best they can at the pest house."

Any concern for the investigation evaporated when she heard of Steven, and all she could think of was getting out to President's Island. "I want to help," Tyner declared.

"You *are* helping, Miss Tyner," Landrum said, pointing about this room. "Many of these people would be suffering far more without your—"

"I want to help Steven."

"Miss Tyner, we don't usually allow our nurses to select their patients," Sister Naomi said.

"You've got to have nurses out at the pest house, haven't you?"

"Yes," the sister responded.

"Are you taking others out there tomorrow?"

"Yes. Tomorrow at noon."

"I want to go with you," Tyner said.

"But you're needed here."

"Then I'll work here tonight. I'll work another shift. Whatever it takes. But I'm going to President's Island with your nurses tomorrow."

"Miss Tyner, I don't think—"

"Sister," Landrum said, "could we make an exception this time? I think it's very important for Miss Tyner to see Mr. Tibedeau."

"Father, I'm not comfortable with this—"

"I said I'd work another shift tonight," Tyner said forcefully.

"That won't be necessary, Miss Tyner," Landrum observed. "You need to go ahead and get some rest tonight. The carriage to return you and the other day nurses is waiting. Please, go ahead."

"We'll pick you up at the hotel at the regular time tomorrow morning," Sister Naomi said. "Work here in the morning, then, if you desire, I can swing by here on the way to the crossing point and pick you up to go to the pest house."

"I'd appreciate that very much," Tyner said. She was moving toward the door when Reverend Landrum called to her.

"Would you care to have prayer with us, Miss Tyner? We'd be pleased to hold up your friend to the Lord."

Tyner returned to the group, where she kneeled alongside Landrum and Sister Naomi.

"Lord," Landrum began, "move Thy gentle healing hand to Mr. Tibedeau and to all those suffering this malady of fever. Grant them freedom from pain and through Thy divine power, if it be Thy will, heal them of this affliction."

He paused momentarily, and Sister Naomi continued the prayer.

"Many are suffering tonight, Heavenly Father. We pray that You will move through us, Thy servants, to bring them peace, and to make that sacrifice that will be pleasing before You."

Tyner, sensing it was now her turn, felt awkward, and lacking the eloquence of the others, simply uttered, "God, please get Steven well. Amen."

Tyner was already standing by the time Landrum and Sister Naomi got to their feet. She thanked them for the prayer, moved outside, and plopped her aching body into the carriage beside two other nurses. She was asleep before the driver had gone a half mile.

# 14

When Baldridge came to Tyner's room shortly after five o'clock Tuesday morning, he realized he had never seen her so worried. He handed her a cup of coffee scrounged from the hotel kitchen as she finished readying herself for the day's nursing tour. Though exhausted from the hours she had put in the day before at the hospital, she confessed to having slept fitfully, unable to get her mind off Steven Tibedeau. When she told Baldridge of her intention to go to the pest house, Baldridge felt himself resenting the time she was spending nursing for the Howard Association. He needed her help on the case, particularly the missing money. But when he suggested that she should stay in the city and ask more questions at the Howard Association office, she gave him a piercing stare. He'd seen that look before, and he decided he'd rather work both ends of the case than incur the wrath likely to be brought on by pressing the issue.

She liked Steven Tibedeau, perhaps more than any of the other officers on the *Paragon*, with the exception of Luke and Jacob Lusk; and once she set her mind on seeing him, she was not a woman to be easily deterred. So Baldridge figured he would spend the few moments they had left that morning trying to put the pieces together. Despite how she felt about Tibedeau, there was still a case to work. He told Tyner about meeting Mayor Johnson in a back alley behind his house the afternoon before, and how Johnson hadn't been pleased that they still had no one to charge in the thefts. With the additional ten-thousand-dollar grant to the Howard Association due from the city within a couple of days, Johnson was clearly nervous. He wasn't sure how long he could keep the reporter, Washburn, at bay, and he had been particularly incensed that Washburn had cornered him and asked him why he was meeting with a detective. It had taken several moments for Baldridge to reassure Johnson that he had given Washburn no information, and that he would continue to dodge him until the investigation led to a suspect. It hadn't helped any that Tyner had been unable to find a link to the Howard Association nurse Baldridge suspected might be involved, and he pressed her on the matter.

"Are you sure that Chriswell's name wasn't anywhere on Stayley's treatment record?"

"I told you last night. I never saw the woman's name." Tyner dampened a cloth and wiped at a spot the laundress had failed to remove from her blue Howard Association apron. "Only Dr. Fledge and Sister Naomi's names were on the record. I do know that for nurses who work in private homes the Howard Association keeps records at the office."

"Of all home visits?"

"Yes. I remember that Sister Naomi told me so while we were riding out to the hospital the first day. She gave me several blank copies of the form just in case I ended up working in someone's home."

"So if I go over there, do you think I could find a record for Mrs. Lassiter and the young girl?"

"Probably." She pulled a piece of paper from a bedside table and handed it to him. "Here. This is what one looks like."

---

OFFICE OF THE HOWARD ASSOCIATION

Memphis, Tenn., _____ ,187__

Name of Applicant: _____

Wants: _____

Residence: _____

Nurse Assigned: _____

_____Head Nurse

_____Attending Physician

---

Baldridge folded the paper and slipped it inside his pocket.

"I wish I'd known this yesterday. I was over at the Howard Association talking to their bookkeeper, Roland. I could have checked the record."

"Do you think Roland's involved in the missing money?"

"No. His paperwork looked pretty good to me, and though I didn't give him many details about the missing money, he seemed to be conscientious enough. I'm pretty sure he just recorded what he received. The money was culled before it got to him. Landrum's right about Roland. He seems like a pretty straight-laced fellow. My money's on that fellow Roe you followed, and that policeman named Deaves."

"What about the other merchants in Ward Two?" Tyner asked. "Have you talked to any of them?"

"Yeah, the ones I could find open for business. A lot of places are shut up as tight as a drum."

"Did anybody cooperate?" Tyner asked.

"Not really. I could find only one or two people—a cobbler on Main and a dressmaker over on Jackson Street—who even admitted to making a contribution to the Howard Association.

The dressmaker said the amount she gave matched what was in the paper the following day. But the cobbler," Baldridge said, his eyebrow raised, "I'm pretty sure he wasn't telling me everything he knows. He was way too nervous for a man with nothing to hide."

"Did Officer Deaves collect from him?"

"Yep."

"Then he's scared, Masey, just like Snowden. Deaves is threatening them. I'll bet on it. I suspect they're afraid Deaves is going to come back to them if anyone finds out he's skimming money."

Baldridge walked over to the window and tossed out the grounds from the bottom of his cup.

"I think you're right about Deaves. Now I just wish you'd found out something at the hospital."

"I did," Tyner replied. "I found out that your theory about a Howard Association nurse having something to do with these deaths is ridiculous."

"I just thought that—"

"Masey, the women who volunteer for this nightmare *don't* want people to die. Nobody would go through something like this if they didn't want to save lives."

"You're going through it," he said.

"Yes, I am. And I took the job because of the investigation. At least at first."

"Oh, so now you're going to be a nurse, eh?"

"No, Masey, I'm not going to be a nurse. I *am* a nurse. I'm helping these people. And do you know what? I like it."

"You didn't much look like you liked it last night."

"The work is hard. And sometimes I want to quit, I'll admit that. But when I got back here last night, I had this sense that for once in my life something I was doing mattered."

"All right. Whatever you say. I just need to find a connection between these deaths. That's why I asked you to find out about Stayley. The only thing that Stayley, Lassiter, and the girl had in common was Yellow Jack."

"You said Lassiter didn't have the fever," Tyner said, putting the final touches on her hair.

"No, but his wife did. That's my point. Stayley died after wandering from the hospital—where Howard Association nurses were working—"

"Masey, I told you—"

"No, no, just bear with me for a minute," he said. "A Howard Association nurse was seen in the vicinity of Lassiter's home shortly after, or at least around, the time he was killed."

"There are Howard Association nurses all over this town."

"And a Howard Association nurse treated his wife."

"Masey—"

"And that precious young girl died right under the nose of a Howard Association nurse," he said.

"But you know for a fact that it wasn't the same nurse for Stayley and the girl."

"True. But I'm going to find out who Lassiter's wife's nurse was."

"Why? That doesn't mean that's the same person Malachi Baine saw. For that matter, I'm not sure I'd believe Malachi Baine anyway."

"Why are you so unwilling to admit the possibility that someone in the Howard Association might be involved?"

"Because I'm working with these people every day, Masey. And I can tell you right now, I'd trust my life to any one of them."

"You may have to," he said.

"I'm ready," Tyner said, grasping a small crocheted bag, and the two of them went downstairs to the street.

Baldridge slipped into the hotel kitchen and brought Tyner a cup of coffee that she sipped while they waited for the carriage. She told him about some of her experiences at the hospital the previous day, and it wasn't long until the details got to be too much for Baldridge.

"Listen, I haven't even had breakfast yet," Baldridge told her. "So if you don't mind, could we talk about something else?"

"All right. If you can't take it . . ."

"I can take it," Baldridge protested. "I just don't want to. Not this time of morning."

"I don't think you could take it."

"Nursing? Ha!" Baldridge laughed.

"Oh, you think it's easy, do you?"

Baldridge didn't answer right away, then under his breath muttered, "I could do it."

"Sure you could," Tyner replied. "Five minutes in there and you'd be on your knees in front of the toilet puking your guts out."

"And you're saying you haven't?"

"I've wanted to, but I haven't yet," she said proudly.

"Well, *somebody's* got to work the case," Baldridge declared.

"So are you going to follow up on the money? Are you going after Deaves and Roe?"

"First thing this morning," he said, "as soon as I get you off to the pest house." He grinned. "That's a pretty good name."

Tyner's eyes flashed. "What?"

"Pest house. And you going there and all . . ."

"Are you calling me—"

"Carriage is here," he said, stepping forward and opening the door. "Good morning, Sister."

"Good morning," Sister Naomi replied from inside. "Are you ready, Sally?"

"Yes." She handed Baldridge her empty cup and placed

her foot on the step. Baldridge grasped her by the arm.

"I ... uh ... want you to be careful," he said awkwardly, gazing down at the ground. "Out on President's Island, I mean."

"I'll be fine, Masey," she said, climbing into the carriage.

"Well, see to it you are," he said, slamming the carriage door. As the driver hurried away, Baldridge watched them disappear down the street and wondered what would happen if she got Bronze John. How would he work these cases without her? What would he do? The thought gave him a chill. Or was it the brisk morning air? Cooler than usual this morning. That's what it was.

BALDRIDGE MIGHT NEVER have noticed had the streets of Memphis had the usual traffic, but with so few people out and moving about, the rider who had been following him on the chestnut mare was bound to stand out. The man had kept too far away to be recognized since leaving the Overton Hotel, so Baldridge made the turn on Market Street, brought Nashville Harry into a trot, then broke into a gallop as he raced around the city block. As he returned full circle and again made the corner on Main, he startled the rider by pulling up hard beside him and grasping his reins.

"What the hell are you doing?" Baldridge demanded.

"Mr. Baldridge! How pleasant to see you this morning," a surprised Miles Washburn said.

"Must be pleasant. You've been following me since I left the hotel."

"Sir, I don't—"

"Don't feed me any horseshit. Why are you following me?"

Washburn fought through his embarrassment. "Because I'm a newspaper reporter."

"So you follow everybody?"

"I'm looking for the truth, Mr. Baldridge."

"The truth? Well, I'll give you some truth," Baldridge said. "The truth is that you're getting in the way."

"In the way of what, sir?"

"Something more important than your raggedy-ass newspaper."

"I doubt that, sir. There is little on this earth more important that the people's right to know."

"Don't give me that 'right to know' business. You're out to sell newspapers." He led his horse up tight beside Washburn's. "But you can't do it with this story."

"What, Mr. Baldridge? Tell me what you're investigating on behalf of the mayor. I know now that Malachi Baine was arrested for the murder of a Mr. T. R. Lassiter. Why was he released?"

"Baine has been released?"

"Yes. This morning. You didn't know that?" Baldridge offered no answer. "Whatever it is you're investigating on behalf of the Big River Detective Agency, I just might be able to help."

"Washburn, you can help by keeping your nose out of this."

"Why, Mr. Baldridge? Why are you so determined that I not know the truth here?"

"Because people's lives are at stake, that's why."

"All the more reason for the people to know. This has something to do with the Howard Association, doesn't it? That's why your female detective is working with them, isn't it?"

"Sally Tyner is working as a nurse for the Howard Association. She's taking care of fever patients just like all the other nurses."

"Right. That's exactly what Reverend Landrum told me when I asked him that question last evening. But frankly, Baldridge, I've talked with the good reverend on several occasions in the past, and I don't think I've ever seen him that nervous." Washburn took a deep breath. "You? I understand why you would lie to me. You're a detective. But the reverend surprised me. This must be pretty big for a minister like him to start lying."

"Miss Tyner is a nurse."

"Who just happens to be a detective, who happens to be staying at the same hotel with you, who's also a detective working on some kind of murder investigation on behalf of the mayor."

"Listen, Washburn, leave this alone. At least for right now."

Washburn removed some notes from his pocket. "I did a little checking up yesterday." He reviewed one of the pages. "A fellow on the police force who I help out occasionally told me what Chief Athy wouldn't. Seems that day I saw you and the chief at that boardinghouse, there had been a murder. That young girl they brought out of the boardinghouse had been killed. And Malachi Baine was arrested in connection with yet another murder—a man named Lassiter. Why are the police hiding this investigation?"

"You'd have to ask the police about that."

"I have. Officially, they're admitting nothing. That's where you come in. I say you've been hired to help the police solve these murders. I say they've got something to do with the Howard Association, otherwise that Tyner woman wouldn't get within a mile of the yellow fever hospital. How am I doing so far?"

"What do you want from me, Washburn?"

"The truth will do. Otherwise, I'm going to print on Wednesday with what I've got. Maybe a front-page story will get other people asking what's going on. Maybe then we'll get some answers."

"You won't wait a week?"

"A week?"

"Yes. I need you to give me a week before you print your

story. If you do, I'll tell you everything you need to know."

"A week's too long, Mr. Baldridge. If I'm right, and people are being murdered, and somehow the Howard Association is involved, the citizens of Memphis deserve to know it."

Baldridge studied Washburn's face for several seconds. His pale blue eyes never blinked, his expression never changed, and Baldridge knew he was dealing with a man who meant exactly what he said. Baldridge knew he couldn't finish his investigation with Washburn following him around; with no chance of the inquisition letting up, or any hope for a delay on his story, Baldridge figured he had only one option.

"Okay, Washburn. I'll give you the whole story. But you've got to ride with me, go where I go, do what I do, and stay out of my way."

Washburn's face brightened. "I understand. Where are we going first?"

"Pete Flanagan's."

"The saloon?"

"That's right."

"I don't see why that's—"

"Do you want this story or not?"

"All right," Washburn said as Baldridge led Harry away. "I'm right behind you."

For the next hour, Baldridge emptied the better part of a bottle of whiskey, keeping Washburn's glass full as he told him about the investigation. When the reporter tried to refuse another drink, Baldridge reminded him of their agreement.

"Go where I go, do what I do, and stay out of my way," Baldridge said. "I'm drinking. I expect you to drink, too."

Baldridge disappeared momentarily and emerged a few moments later from the back room of the saloon with Pete Flanagan right behind him.

"Get on your feet," Baldridge told him. "Let's go."

Washburn rose on shaky legs, steadying himself on the table. "Where are we going?"

"For a ride."

"A ride? I don't feel like a ride. I don't want to—"

"Go where I go, do what I do . . ."

"Yeah, yeah," Washburn said with a thick tongue. "But I—I ain't drinking any more whiskey with you." He gave him a wide-eyed, reeling look. "I don't see why you're not drunk. You had more than I did."

"Let's go, Washburn."

The reporter struggled to mount, and finally got into the saddle. He and Washburn rode down to Chickasaw Street and halted at an isolated row of sheds some three or four hundred feet from the river. Baldridge dismounted.

"Come with me," he told the reporter.

An unsteady Washburn landed awkwardly on the ground, his hand going immediately to his forehead. "My head's hurting. I think I may have had a little too much whiskey."

Baldridge limped toward the sheds. "Are you coming or not?"

"What are we going to see?"

"Something for your story."

"A body?" Washburn asked, his eyes dancing with excitement as he fished into his pocket for some paper and a writing instrument. "You don't have a body in there, do you?"

"Not yet," Baldridge mumbled.

"What?" Washburn said.

Baldridge produced a key from his trousers pocket and unlocked the middle shed of three in a row. The inquisitive Washburn stepped up immediately and stuck his head inside.

"There's nothing in here but empty bottles," Washburn said. "Who owns this place?"

"A friend of mine."

"What's it got to do with—"

"Washburn, I hate to do this," Baldridge said, "but I just can't let you publish that story." He grabbed him by the collar and shoved him into the shed, his feet kicking over whiskey bottles as he tumbled into the corner.

"Baldridge, Baldridge, we had a deal!" Washburn said, struggling to stand on whiskey legs. "I went where you went. I did what you did . . ."

"That's right," Baldridge said, lifting his good leg and kicking Washburn back into the corner. "And now you're going to stay out of my way." He quickly slammed the door and locked it.

"Baldridge! Baldridge! Let me out of here." He was banging on the walls as Baldridge mounted. "You can't do this." As Washburn pounded on the door, Baldridge heard him slip inside and fall on the loose bottles.

"I'll be back for you," Baldridge said.

"Baldridge!"

"Go ahead and yell," he told Washburn, spurring Harry away. "Ain't nobody within a mile of this place."

"Baldridge!"

BALDRIDGE SEARCHED THROUGHOUT Ward Two, and it was midafternoon before he spotted a policeman who, based on Tyner's description, had to be Officer Deaves. For almost two hours he kept his distance, determined not to be as obvious as Washburn had been, shadowing Deaves from alleys and backstreets as he moved about the ward. Along streets that resembled a ghost town, Baldridge saw him go to several homes and visit a half dozen businesses—one of which was the fidgety cobbler's Baldridge had told Tyner about. Baldridge figured him to be gathering more subscription money for the Howard Association, and if he was, this might be Baldridge's best chance to see where the money ended up. Only three or four carriages passed while Baldridge followed Deaves, and perhaps a dozen pedestrians came and went during that time. One of the undertaker wagons of Holst and Brothers made a collection in front of a store on Adams Street. The family who lived above the store had lost someone, and Baldridge watched as Deaves assisted them in bringing the body to the wagon. From almost a block away, he could hear the gut-wrenching wail of a young woman who clutched at the sheet-wrapped body of the loved one she could not bear to see taken away. As the wagon rattled away over the Nicholson pavement, he watched Deaves standing beside the family, offering condolences and being the very epitome of a concerned public official.

It was almost four o'clock when Baldridge finally saw what he had been looking for. A gentleman in a carriage slowed as he passed Deaves on the street, then turned into an alley and reined up beside a feed store, well out of sight of the street. Baldridge eased Harry around the corner of a building and toward the feed store. Deaves glanced hurriedly up and down the street, then disappeared into the alley. Riding past the alley, Baldridge scanned between the buildings and saw Deaves talking to someone in the buggy, though the black canvas roof shielded the driver from view. Deaves noted him passing and Baldridge quickly averted his eyes to look straight ahead, then turned down the corner and waited, out of sight. In a few moments, he heard the buggy rumble out of the alley and onto the street; from his post he watched the driver move east. Based on what Sally had seen, he had a pretty good idea of who the driver might be and where he was headed, so he moved north and cut over on a parallel street so Deaves would not see him following. There would be plenty of time to take care of Deaves.

The Roe Novelty Company was exactly where Tyner had said it was, and when he circled the block and scanned the back of the warehouse from across the vacant lot she had described, Baldridge was not surprised to see a buggy and four horses tied to the mimosa tree out back. He dismounted, removed his .45 from its holster, opened the loading gate, and checked the cylinder. Satisfied with the load, he replaced the weapon in the holster and made his way around the edge of the vacant lot to the back door. He found the key, opened the door, and slipped inside. He crept up the steps and stopped outside the door, where he could hear another dice game in progress. He considered drawing a weapon and bursting into the room, but being unsure of how many men he faced on the other side, that didn't make much sense. He would just walk right in as if he were expected.

Opening the door, Baldridge stepped inside, bringing an instant halt to the conversation. The dice rattled against the wall and came to rest, leaving the room silent.

"Can I get in this game?" Baldridge asked, walking toward the five men who were huddled along the far wall. One of them, a tall gentleman in a business suit, rose from his kneeling position.

"Who are you?"

"Just a fellow who likes a good game," Baldridge replied, still closing in on them.

"How did you get in here?"

"The door—same as you, I reckon." Baldridge glanced at one of the rough-looking characters to his right. "Didn't you tell him I was coming?"

The tall man glared at the fellow Baldridge had addressed.

"Do you know him?"

"Hell, I ain't never seen this man in my life," the scrubby fellow said, moving away from the rest of the group.

"This is a private game," the gentleman said.

"A private game. With public money. That's illegal, ain't it?"

"I don't know what you're talking about," the man said, glancing at his companion, who was standing near the window. Baldridge caught a motion out of the corner of his eye. Reaching across his body, he grasped the bird's-head handle of his Colt, mounted in a reverse grip on his left side, and in one quick, fluid motion, drew the weapon, cocked it, and leveled it on the man by the window.

"Go ahead!" Baldridge challenged. "Go ahead and pull that pistol on me! This forty-five will put a hole in you big enough to pitch them dice through."

The tall gentleman immediately began to protest. "What do you want? What are you doing here?"

"Roe, I know who your are, and I know what you're doing. You're stealing money from the Howard Association." Baldridge glanced around. "And now folks are going to know what you're doing with it."

"What are you talking about? I don't—"

"Don't bother trying to lie to me," Baldridge said. "My associate followed you here last week. And now I've got you myself."

"But I don't—"

One of the other men addressed Roe.

"Roe, is this fellow tellin' the truth?"

"Keep quiet, Martin."

"No. I want to know. Is that money from the Howard Association? 'Cause if it is, I don't want no part of this."

"Shut your mouth, Martin."

"No, I ain't gonna shut my mouth. Howard Association

money's supposed to be for sick folks." The man looked at Baldridge. "Mister, I was just here shootin' some dice. I didn't know nothin' about no stolen money."

Roe looked at Baldridge. "No. You're not doing this to me. I'm Gerald Roe. You can't accuse me of something like this."

"I'm not accusing you of anything," Baldridge said. "I know you did it. I know about you and your buddy Deaves. I saw you meet him this afternoon."

"You can't prove it. Deaves will never admit to something like that."

"Maybe. Maybe not. But you've got to wonder what a jury of your peers—folks who have lost loved ones to the fever—would do with a man who steals money like this."

"I'll swear that you came in here with a gun to rob us. I'll swear it in a court of law. I'll swear it." He pointed at the others. "So will they."

"I ain't swearin' nothin'," the man by the window said.

One of the others chimed in. "We just wanted to shoot some dice, Roe. I'm not getting involved in this." He started to walk away.

"Not so fast, there, mister. I'm going to need you to come with me."

"I ain't goin' nowhere with you. You ain't the law. You ain't—"

Baldridge brought his weapon to bear upon the man. "You ain't gonna keep talking, are you?"

The man got quiet.


BY NIGHTFALL, BALDRIDGE had escorted Roe and his friends to the Central Station House. One of the officers sent for Athy, who arrived by eight o'clock, and Baldridge explained what he and Tyner had discovered about Roe and Deaves. Athy appeared stunned.

"Deaves has been an officer for five years."

"Maybe so. But now he's just a thief."

"How come the mayor didn't tell me about this investigation?"

"That's between you and him."

"But he should've told me. He should've let me handle this. Sounds like he doesn't trust me."

"I doubt that's it, Athy. The mayor's got his reasons. I'm more concerned about what you're going to do about Deaves."

"We'll bring him in and question him. But unless he admits to something, all we've got is your statement and what that Tyner woman who works with you says. And neither of you actually saw any money change hands."

"For God's sake, Athy, the man was shooting dice with Howard Association money!"

"Right now, it's your word against his," Athy said. "And he'll claim that's his own money."

"What about the fellow I brought in with him?"

"He may confirm the dice game, but I doubt he knows where Roe gets his money."

Baldridge hated it when Athy was right.

"What about the store owner, Snowden?" Baldridge asked. "And the others Deaves threatened, like that cobbler?"

"We'll talk to them. Maybe someone will be willing to testify once Deaves is off the street and out of the ward," Athy admitted. "Don't get me wrong, Baldridge. I want to see these men pay for what they've done just as much as you do—particularly Deaves, what with him being a member of my force. But I've got to prove it in a court of law, and frankly, short of Deaves confessing and implicating Roe, I'm not sure we're going to be able to hold him.

Roe's a prominent man. Most people like him, and they aren't going to want to believe he would do this."

"You know he's guilty."

"Knowing it and proving it are two different things," Athy said. "I operate within the law, Baldridge. Maybe you don't—"

"Is that why you released Malachi Baine?"

"There's no evidence against Baine," Athy said. "We questioned him. So did you, I understand. Hell, I even had that newspaper reporter, Miles Washburn, come by here to talk to him. Didn't much like that, but I couldn't really stop him. The last thing we need is Washburn getting his teeth into this murder investigation. He's like a dog with a bone. Once he gets hold of something, you can't get it away from him."

Baldridge smiled as he picked up his hat. "Unless you chain him up."

"Good luck. I haven't seen anybody do it yet." Athy called to him as Baldridge started for the door. "Where are you headed?"

"I'm not rightly sure," Baldridge said. "Maybe I'll go find Baine again. If he didn't do the killing—and I'm not convinced of that yet—he may still have seen something he's not telling us." Baldridge paused as he opened the station-house door. "But I do know one thing. Finding the money leak at the Howard Association was just half the job the mayor hired me to do. There's still a murderer on the loose out there, and whether you folks here at the police station like it or not, I'm still getting paid to find him."

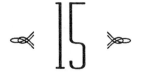

## WEDNESDAY, SEPTEMBER 24

og rolled off the water and seemed to climb up the river bluff south of Memphis as First Mate Jacob Lusk and Captain Luke Williamson rowed a tiny skiff toward the shore. The sun would be up in less than an hour, burning away the fog and increasing the chances that they would be spotted by the guards stationed every quarter mile along the shore. To slip past the quarantine, they planned to maneuver a tiny boat into a draw south of Fort Pickering. Williamson would climb up the face of the bluff and Lusk would cover the boat with branches and await his return. Williamson's face was tight, his expression intense as they rowed perpendicular to the current.

"Been a while since we done this, ain't it, Cap'n?" Lusk whispered.

"Not long enough, as far as I'm concerned," Williamson said.

"Where do you figure to find a doctor who'll come out here?"

"I don't know. I can't very well show up at the yellow fever hospital at Fort Pickering. They'll know I broke quarantine and I may never get back."

"You ain't the first person who's broke quarantine, Cap'n. I heard tell they're ferrying folks across the river at night from Hopefield, on the Arkansas side."

"I've got to find somebody to help Steven," Williamson said. "Somebody who knows what he's doing."

"That doctor on board seemed like a pretty smart fellow— the one who said Steven had Bronze John. If he hadn't up and took sick himself, then—"

"But he did," Williamson snapped. He realized his tone of voice, and calmed himself down. "And I'm not letting Steven die because no decent doctor will come out to the pest house. I'll find somebody who knows what he's doing if I have to bring him at gunpoint."

"That doctor who was lookin' after Steven last night—that Doctor—"

"Fledge."

"Yeah. Are you sure he don't know his business, Cap'n?"

"The man's a fool. Hell, I can see that myself, and I'm no doctor. He was trying to sweat the fever out of Steven, and Steven was just getting worse." Williamson drew the oar handles back hard toward his chest. "I'm not going to let him die, Jacob. I'm not going to allow it."

"Cap'n, that may not be for you to say."

"The hell it isn't."

The two men drew their craft into switch willows at the foot of a long, narrow draw that led up and wove in behind the bluffs where guards watched the river. Williamson said good-bye to

Lusk and began clawing his way up the draw on his hands and knees, then, just as the glow of daylight began to spread off to his right, he slipped out to the main road and started walking to the city. It would be a four-mile walk unless he found a horse, which wasn't likely given the value of a healthy mount during the epidemic. He thought of the horse that Salina Tyner had rented to that man at the depot last week. He was captain of one of the finest steamboats on the Mississippi, owned a half dozen excellent horses, and had a reputation for honesty. So why was he rowing a skiff to shore and sneaking into town on foot like a common criminal? In his heart he knew it wasn't Baldridge and Tyner's fault—except for maybe taking this case in the first place. The fever caused this for sure, but it seemed to make him feel a little better to blame someone for what he had to do. If they hadn't taken this case, maybe he would have sailed the day before the quarantine had taken effect. Maybe Steven would not have come down with the fever. But he knew it was just as possible they'd all be sitting in a backwater slough somewhere upriver with half the passengers and crew dying from the fever and the other half starving.

Williamson entered the Overton Hotel at seven o'clock that morning and inquired as to Baldridge's room. When a knock on the door produced no reply, he went down to the kitchen, where he found Baldridge nursing a plate of biscuits and gravy. Baldridge almost choked on a bite when Williamson walked up.

"Luke?" He chewed quickly and swallowed, wiping his mouth with a towel. "What the hell are you doing here? I thought the quarantine—"

"Shhh," Williamson said, glancing at two men occupying a table nearby. "It is." He pulled up a chair and took a seat.

"You want some breakfast?" Baldridge asked.

"Where can I find a doctor?" Williamson asked. "A good one—one who knows what he's doing."

"Luke, there's doctors all over town, but most of them are busy with fever cases. Are you talking about a doctor for Steven Tibedeau?"

"He's dying."

"I'm sorry. I heard he was sick. Salina found out from the Howard Association people who went out to the pest house. Don't they have doctors out there?"

"Nobody I trust," Williamson replied. "We had a doctor on board the *Paragon*—a pretty good one, I'd say—but he's come down with the fever himself. And the doctor who came out from the Howard Association yesterday isn't worth a dime."

"What was his name?"

"Fledge."

"I know him."

"He's going to mess around with his insane treatments and let Steven die. I've got to find someone else. I've got to—"

"You've got to keep anybody from recognizing you," Baldridge said. "They'll put you in jail for breaking the quarantine."

"There's not enough cells to hold all the people breaking this ridiculous quarantine," Williamson said. "They can't stop people from coming and going. People are going to do what they have to, and there's not enough law to stop them."

"Maybe not," Baldridge said, "but a man of your stature . . . they'd be liable to make an example of you."

"Let 'em try," Williamson said. "I'm going to find me a doctor and I'm taking him back—no matter what I have to do."

"I know a doctor," Baldridge said. "He seems like he's miles ahead of these others."

"What's his name?"

"Rice. Sally and I met him investigating the missing money at the Howard Association." Baldridge smiled. "We found out who was stealing. Turns out that a policeman named Deaves was in cahoots with a fellow—"

"The *doctor*, Masey. Tell me about the doctor."

"I was just bringing you up to date on the case," Baldridge said.

"That's fine, Masey. I'm glad you solved it."

"Oh, we're not done yet. We've still got—"

"I'm about to lose one of my best crewmen if something isn't done. I don't care about the case. I want to find this Dr. Rice."

"Well, I know he works some with the Howard Association nurses out at the yellow fever hospital. Sally's worked with him before. Says he's about the smartest they've got out there."

"So we could find him there?"

"Probably. He goes to people's homes, too, though, so I don't know—"

"Come on," Williamson said, grasping Baldridge by the sleeve.

"What are we doing?"

"You're coming with me. I want you to find this Dr. Rice and talk to him. Convince him to come back to President's Island with me."

Baldridge stood up reluctantly. "Luke, I don't think—"

"Do you want to see Steven die?"

"Hell, no."

"Then you've got to help me find Rice."

"All right, I'm coming," Baldridge said, reaching back to grab a biscuit he had not yet drowned in gravy.

WILLIAMSON HID IN the trees about a hundred feet from the back door of the yellow fever hospital. For almost twenty minutes he'd watched Baldridge waiting outside to see Dr. Rice, then Rice had finally emerged. The two men spoke briefly, but Williamson was too far away to hear what was being said. Then the doctor followed Baldridge a few steps out into the grassy area behind the hospital. In a moment, Baldridge called to him.

"Luke," he said, motioning him out of the trees. "Come over here."

As Williamson approached, he watched Rice's face for signs of contempt at his having broken the quarantine, but he saw none of the condemnation he had expected.

"So you're Captain Williamson?" Rice said, extending his hand. "You're rather famous on the river."

"Doctor, I know I shouldn't have broken the quarantine, but I've got—"

Rice chuckled. "That quarantine is the stupidest idea to come along in years. Several of us meet with the mayor the day after tomorrow to try and convince him to lift it. Yellow Jack is not contagious from person to person. I stake my life on it every day."

"One of my crewmen has the fever," Williamson explained. "He's getting pretty bad off."

"Mr. Baldridge tells me he's being treated at the pest house."

"That's right."

"Dr. Fledge, right?"

"He's the man who's been coming out since the quarantine began. But Steven—that's my crewman—Steven's not getting any better."

"A lot of folks don't, Captain. The fever is—"

"But I don't think he's being treated right," Williamson said. "This Dr. Fledge is losing a lot of patients."

"We all lose patients to the fever, Captain."

"Not Steven. I'm not going to stand by and watch him die. I want the best care possible."

"Captain, it's common knowledge that Dr. Fledge and I don't see eye to eye on handling yellow fever. But the truth is, Fledge is an experienced doctor," Rice said. "And while his ideas on treating the fever are not necessarily what I would do, and I've publicly stated as much, professional courtesy prevents me from—"

"Professional courtesy?" Williamson shouted. "How can you talk about professional courtesy in a situation like this?" Williamson moved closer to him. "For God's sake, man, if you have a better treatment for yellow fever than Fledge, you have to administer it."

Baldridge stepped in. "Luke, back off."

"I *am* treating people, Captain," Rice said. "Right here at this hospital, and at individual homes all over the city, too."

"But what about the patients at the pest house?"

"That's why there are other doctors," Rice said.

"Not for Steven. Not for one of my crewmen."

"Captain Williamson, has it occurred to you that you are not on the river anymore?" Rice asked. He pointed at the building. "This is a hospital. You can't show up here and order people around. And you sure can't order the fever to go away, as much as all of us wish you could. Now, I'm sure that Dr. Fledge is doing the best he can with the situation."

"That's not good enough," Williamson said. "Salina Tyner says that you're the best."

"That's very kind of Miss Tyner, but she's rather new to treating yellow fever herself, and I'm not sure her opinion—"

"She's a good judge of people," Williamson countered. "If she says you're the best, that's good enough for me."

"Captain, even if I could come to the pest house, what would you have me do?" Rice pointed again at the hospital. "Would you have me leave the two dozen patients I have in there to come and care for *one* person? I can't justify that."

"All I know is that Steven will probably die if something isn't done. And I'm telling you right now, if he dies—and there is something you could have done to save him—I'll be coming after you."

"Are you threatening me, Captain?"

"Luke, don't," Baldridge said. "Dr. Rice, I don't think he means—"

"You're damn straight I mean it," Williamson said.

Rice stepped back two steps. "So if I won't abandon all those people in there to die without a doctor at least trying to save them, in order to come and treat your crewman, you're going to kill me?" Williamson offered no reply, as the rage inside him at the thought of losing Tibedeau overwhelmed him. "Then why don't you just go ahead and do it right now?" Rice raised his hands in the air. "Just shoot me right now. I heard tell you do that to people trying to get on your boat, anyway."

Williamson reached inside his jacket and grasped the handle of a navy Colt revolver. "That man left me no choice."

"Well, neither am I, because I'm not leaving these patients. Go ahead. Shoot me. You'd keep me from having to walk back inside that hospital and watch a nine-year-old boy vomit his insides out and die in a violent seizure. Come to think of it, getting shot doesn't sound nearly as bad."

Williamson walked to a nearby hickory tree, where he began chipping away at the bark with the toe of his boot. He was making a fool of himself and he knew it, but if that was what it took to save Steven, he would accept it. The problem was, it wasn't going to save Steven. Rice wasn't coming, no matter what he said or did. When Williamson could find no words, Baldridge spoke up.

"How about suggesting a treatment? Doctor, could you outline some of the things you do for fever patients? Maybe Luke could go back and get Dr. Fledge to try them. He wouldn't have to say they came from you. He wouldn't have to say anything. For that matter, he could see to the treatment himself."

For the first time in the last twenty-four hours, Williamson had a sense of hope. He turned to face Rice. "Would you at least do that? Would you prescribe something—anything—I could do to help Steven?"

Rice agreed. Promising to return, he disappeared inside the hospital for a few minutes and eventually emerged with some written instructions, which he proceeded to explain to Williamson. Producing a dark brown medicine bottle, he handed it to Williamson, explaining the dosage and intervals of administering it.

"I believe Miss Tyner's been assigned to the pest house today," Rice said. "She's familiar with my treatment procedure, having worked with me for a couple of days. She should remember what to do."

Williamson offered his hand to Rice. "Doctor, I'm sorry for the things I said. I had no right."

"It's all right, Captain. Go and see to your crewman. I'll do the best thing I can do for him from here," Rice said. "I'll pray."

Baldridge and Williamson rode double on Nashville Harry until they came within a quarter mile of the spot where Williamson had left Lusk and the boat.

"Thanks, Masey. I appreciate what you did. I'm sorry I'm not able to help you much on the case, but—"

"You've got more important things to worry about," Baldridge told him. "I'll take care of the case. You take care of Steven."

"I will."

"And say hello to Sally for me. Tell her I'm going back to see the preacher."

"What?"

"Never mind. I'll explain it to you some other time."

Williamson slipped down the bank and rendezvoused with Lusk.

"Where's the doctor?" Lusk asked.

Williamson held up the medicine bottle.

"Don't look like no doctor to me," Lusk said, uncovering the boat.

"It's all we're going to get," Williamson said.

They began rowing for the channel, and having reached no more than fifty feet offshore, someone shouted to them to stop and return to the bank. But they never looked back. The men watching from the bluff were tasked with stopping people from coming ashore; they had little concern for, and less inclination to stop, anyone foolish enough to go *to* President's Island.

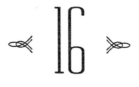

aldridge rode back into the city in search of Malachi Baine. As much as he hated to admit it, Baine was still his only real lead in the murders, and as limited as that may have been, he couldn't figure out where else to turn. As far as he knew, Chief Athy had developed no new information since the murder of the young girl, nor had he or his men uncovered anything that would suggest a suspect in Lassiter's death. With no solid proof that Nurse Chriswell had done anything wrong, and with Tyner unable to establish any connection between that particular nurse and Deke Stayley's death, Baldridge felt little closer to locating the killer. But the impression of that cross pressed into the flesh of each victim kept nagging at him, and when it came to crosses, Baine seemed to be the most prominent prophet peddling one; thus another talk with him might shake loose something he could use.

Before looking for Baine, Baldridge went by the Overton Hotel, where he picked up some water and cold biscuits, then stopped down by the river to check on Washburn at his temporary lodging. He had completely forgotten about the man when

Williamson had arrived that morning, and for the entire ride over to the shed by the river he had felt guilty at having left him in that shack overnight without food or water. The last thing he needed to do was mess around and kill the little bastard—then he'd have to go to the trouble of getting rid of the body and, frankly, he didn't have time for that right now. When Baldridge unlocked the door of the shack, Washburn raised his hands over his face and turned away, blinded momentarily by the sudden influx of daylight.

"You all right in there, Washburn?" Baldridge asked.

"I'll have you jailed for this, you know," Washburn grumbled, struggling to get to his feet and tripping yet again over the loose bottles.

"You really ought to straighten this place up before you hurt yourself, Washburn." Baldridge glanced over his shoulder to make sure no one could see him from Chickasaw Street; but the deserted street offered no prying eyes.

Washburn made it to his feet. "You had no right to do this to me." He rotated his shoulder to relieve the stiffness. "Leaving a man locked up in here overnight and half the next day . . ." He held out his hands. "Look at my hands. They're raw from banging on these walls."

"I told you that no one would hear you, Washburn." The reporter stepped around the corner of the shack and Baldridge followed.

Washburn glared at him over his shoulder. "Do you mind?" He began unbuttoning his pants. "I've been about to die to take a piss."

"Sorry about that, Washburn," Baldridge said, moving back around the corner and placing the water and food on the floor of the shack. And he was genuinely sorry—at least until Washburn kept on talking.

"You're going to be sorry, all right," Washburn called to him.

"I meant to get back and check on you, but—"

"I'm going to tell the law what you've done," Washburn shouted from around the corner of the shed. "I'm going to write my story about all this and tell everyone what you and the mayor and the chief of police have been up to." Washburn buttoned his pants and returned to face Baldridge. "I'm going to see to it you pay for this. I'm going—"

Baldridge grabbed him by the sleeve. "You're *going* back in the shed!" Washburn struggled with Baldridge, but being much smaller, he was easily overpowered. "Don't make me hurt you," Baldridge shouted as he wrestled the man to the floor.

"Don't lock me back in here, Baldridge. Don't do it. I can't stand it. I swear!"

Baldridge slammed the door shut. "There's food and water for you on the floor."

Washburn banged against the door, groaning as his sore hands hit the wood. "I won't write the story. I promise I won't."

"You're lying," Baldridge said, securing the lock.

"No. I swear. I'll wait until you tell me it's all right to print the story."

"You're a lying son of a bitch, Washburn."

"To hell with you, Baldridge," Washburn said, kicking the door. "I hope you rot in hell!"

"It could happen," Baldridge said, mounting up.


BALDRIDGE SEARCHED FOR over two hours, riding around Ward Two and checking Baine's usual circuit without ever catching sight of the man. The sun was dropping as Baldridge eventually rode for Baine's shack behind Fontaine's store, and the gradually increasing wind from the west carried the acrid smoke from the evening's tar and sulfur fires throughout the city. Baine had probably stopped preaching for the evening, Baldridge figured, and when he found the proprietor of Fontaine's locking up his store for the night, he stopped.

"Is ol' Malachi in his shack?" Baldridge asked.

"Haven't seen him all day," the proprietor said, rattling the door to ensure that it was locked. He glanced up and down the deserted streets. "Don't know why I'm bothering to lock up," he mumbled more to himself than to Baldridge. "You a friend of Malachi's?"

"I guess you could say that," Baldridge said, dismounting and leading Nashville Harry to a hitching post beside the building.

"You a preacher, too?"

"Me?" Baldridge tied off the reins. "No, not hardly."

"Too bad. I was going to ask you to pray that I get some business around here."

"Afraid I can't help you there."

The proprietor, looking forlorn, slipped a door key in his pocket. "I'm not sure anybody can. Say hello to Malachi for me."

"I'll do that," Baldridge said, walking by the side of the store and some fifty feet to the rear of the building, where a tin-roofed, one-room shanty sat beneath a broad-spreading elm tree. Baldridge noticed that the upper branches had been hit by lightning some time ago.

*If a preacher ain't safe . . .*

Baldridge rapped on the door but received no answer.

"Malachi? Are you in there?" He peered into a dusty window beside the door but saw only a dim light and no movement within. When he tried the door, he found it unlocked, so he slowly entered the room. The smell he noticed at Lassiter's home—dried blood mixed with that of oil from a lamp—nearly overpowered him as he stepped inside. As he gazed across the room, dust particles danced through a beam of dying sunlight that pierced the window, and Baldridge's eyes followed the ray of light across the floor to the far wall. The orange light of the fading sun illuminated the bloody face and chest of Malachi Baine, seated on the floor, his back wedged into a corner. Baldridge rushed to him and checked his neck for a pulse, but quickly realized he was long since dead. The rigidity of the corpse told him he'd been there hours, maybe even all day. Baldridge moved to the window and parted the ragged curtains to allow more light, and when he returned to the body, he saw it—the unmistakable impression of a crucifix on his right temple, just below the hairline. Gazing about the room, Baldridge noticed no evidence of a struggle. There was little blood on the floor and he could find none on the chair or the bedspread nearby. And since most of the blood had soaked Baine's shirt all the way down to his pants, Baldridge figured he had died quickly, more or less where he fell. Removing his hat, Baldridge walked over to the door, opened it wider, and took a deep breath. He wasn't sure what was worse—the tar and sulfur outside or the smell of death inside.

First Stayley, then Lassiter, then the young girl, and now Baine. What was the connection? What did they have in common? Who would want them dead? And why? He glanced back across the room at the body.

"I guess you're no longer on my list of suspects," Baldridge muttered.

When he had pulled himself together, he stepped carefully back inside and examined the room. A flame in the oil lamp across the room still flickered, leading Baldridge to believe Baine had been killed the night before, or early this morning, before daylight. That certainly explained why he couldn't find him preaching anywhere that afternoon. But who would want Baine dead? And why didn't he fight to protect himself?

On the bed not far from the corner where Baine's corpse rested, Baldridge noticed a worn Bible. He picked it up carefully so as not to disturb the pages and placed it on a table. The same person who killed Lassiter had killed Baine. Both men apparently knew their killer, or at the very least believed they had nothing to fear from him. Both men had been slaughtered like animals, their throats slit wide open. One man was killed in his home while praying, his Bible open to the beatitudes. The other had also been killed in his home—maybe praying, maybe not. Baldridge couldn't tell that. Each man had a crucifix mark on his body. Baldridge sat down at the foot of the bed and went over the details in his mind. What connected Stayley and the little girl had no connection to Baine. Baine and Lassiter were enemies, but had nothing to do with Stayley or the child. He sat there ruminating until the sun had set and, except for the dim light of the lantern, the room had grown dark. He kept asking himself the question, Whom did they know in common? It provided the only link between the murders, and a tenuous one at that, especially since Baine was a man of few friends. He kept coming back to the Howard Association, and the nurses, but even then he couldn't isolate one nurse or doctor who was acquainted with all the victims. Then he recalled something Baine had told him in jail. Baine had claimed to know Sister Naomi. Baldridge rose from the bed and walked over to the lantern. He looked down at Baine's corpse and was abruptly cognizant of how quiet the room was. That booming, accusatory voice was forever silenced. He blew out the lantern, closed Baine's door behind him, and rode to notify the police.

After he had given instructions on how to get to Baine's shanty, and described what he had found there, Baldridge rode for number 12 Court Street. Inside, he found Dr. Landrum working alone at his desk. The door was open, so he tapped on the facing.

"Dr. Landrum?"

Landrum glanced up from his papers and looked at him over his eyeglasses. "Mr. Baldridge." He pointed to a wing-backed chair beside a row of books. "Please, come in." Removing his eyeglasses, he pushed his chair back from the desk and crossed one leg over the other. "What brings you by here so late, sir?"

"I want to talk to you about one of your workers."

"Of course," Landrum replied. "I received your message about the arrest of Mr. Roe. That's excellent work, Mr. Baldridge. Excellent work. I trust the other culprit—this Officer Deaves—is in custody?"

"Not yet," Baldridge said, "but I expect he will be before long."

"Excellent. I cannot tell you what a load off my mind this is. Although I must admit to feeling rather awkward when that newspaperman showed up here asking questions."

"Washburn?"

"Yes, that was his name. I'm not a very practiced liar, Mr. Baldridge. I'm afraid he wasn't exactly convinced—"

"Don't worry about Washburn."

"He won't be writing a newspaper story?" Landrum asked.

"Not for a while."

"Oh, that is a relief. With so much to do to administer the Howard Association, I do not want to have to worry about a fund-raising scandal."

"No, Reverend, you don't. You've got bigger problems."

Landrum appeared startled. "I beg your pardon? I thought you had solved the issue of the contributions."

"This isn't about the contributions."

"It's not? Then, sir, what is it about?"

"Murder."

"Murder? What are you talking about?"

"Reverend Landrum, four people have been murdered in Memphis in the last two weeks."

"That's terrible. But what does that have to do with me?"

"Nothing personally. At least I hope so," Baldridge said. "But I believe it's got something to do with the Howard Association."

Landrum uncrossed his legs, placed his hands on his knees, then ran them all the way down his legs to his shoes and slowly back up again. "What could possibly lead you to such a conclusion?"

Over the next few minutes, Baldridge explained the deaths he had been investigating at the request of the mayor, and then told of finding Baine.

"Dear Lord," Landrum said in a near whisper. "I didn't agree with ol' Malachi's theology, but I have to admit I respected his dedication."

"As I told you, the Howard Association is the only connection between the other murders," Baldridge said.

"Perhaps. But the Howard Association had no affiliation with Malachi Baine."

"Maybe the organization didn't, but I think one of your people did."

"Who? In what way?"

"Baine didn't have many friends," Baldridge said. "Most people were put off by that hellfire preachin' he was constantly spittin' out around town."

"Yes, I'm sure they were."

"But he did have one friend. Or at least he thought he did."

"Who?"

"Sister Naomi."

Landrum looked at him incredulously. "*Our* Sister Naomi?" Baldridge nodded. "You're talking about the woman who administers our nursing program."

"That's right."

"Mr. Baldridge, what you say may be true, but Sister Naomi is well-known and respected all over Memphis. She's practically up for sainthood among people who've had family members suffering from the fever."

"I'm sure that's true."

"And she may have known Malachi Baine, but I don't like what you seem to be suggesting."

"What I'm suggesting is that Sister Naomi knew Baine, Stayley, and the Lassiter family."

"I hardly think that makes her a candidate for a murderer, Mr. Baldridge," Landrum said. His face grew stern. "The woman is simply attending to her duties—and mightily so, I would add. The Howard Association couldn't be successful without her. That she would have a tie to these people is not so extraordinary."

"My associate, Miss Tyner, checked the records. She was one of the last people to see Deke Stayley alive."

"You said yourself that Mr. Stayley was killed several blocks from the hospital."

"That's right. But how did he get there? He was down with the fever. How could he have walked that far without help?"

"I don't know, Mr. Baldridge, but that hardly means that Sister Naomi had anything to do with it."

"I believe she helped him out of the hospital. And I'll bet she had been at Lassiter's home, too. The neighbor saw two nurses the day Lassiter was killed. I'm betting Sister Naomi was one of them. Only, she went back to the house for a second visit that afternoon. I think Baine knew it, too. He just didn't want to tell me."

"Why wouldn't he tell you that?"

"Maybe because she was his friend. Other than that, I don't know."

"But where's the connection with the young girl who died? Are you saying Sister Naomi was her nurse? Because I can check those records right here." Landrum got up and walked over to a file drawer. "We keep a copy of all the nursing assignments made to private homes." He opened the drawer and thumbed through the files, eventually removing two. "Here," he said, taking the file to Baldridge and pointing at the entry. "See? Right here. It says that Miss Chriswell was the nurse for that little girl."

"I already knew that," Baldridge said.

"Then why would you accuse—"

"Look at the bottom of the form." Landrum scanned the page as Baldridge continued. "Who assigned the nurse to that child?"

"Sister Naomi," Landrum read from the page.

"And Mrs. Lassiter?" Baldridge asked.

Landrum examined the file. "It says a Mrs. Cromme was her nurse . . . ," he said, pausing momentarily, then he added, "and Sister Naomi as well."

"Didn't you tell me that the sister visited her nurses and checked up on their work?" Baldridge asked.

"Yes, but that is just to be expected."

"Miss Chriswell specifically told me she had talked to Sister Naomi about the child she was caring for."

"I still fail to see that just discussing a patient makes the sister guilty of anything."

"She knew the girl was at the boardinghouse," Baldridge said.

"Still, Mr. Baldridge, what possible reason would someone

210 | JAMES D. BREWER

have for killing a child, or the husband of someone who had died of the fever?"

"I don't know," Baldridge said, coming to his feet, "but I want to talk to Sister Naomi."

"She's not here. She's out with her nurses," Landrum said.

"But she does stay here, doesn't she?"

"Well, yes, at least since the epidemic started. Normally she lives at St. Brigid's, but she's been staying here for the past two weeks. She says it saves her time each day in coming and going."

"I'd like to see her living area."

"I don't know, Mr. Baldridge," Landrum said, closing the folder. "I'm not sure that's appropriate."

"Maybe not. But somebody's murdering people around here about every three days, and I know damned well *that's* not appropriate. I hope I'm wrong. I hope it's just a coincidence that the good sister seems to be connected to these dead folks. But I'm not going to know that until I check."

Landrum appeared to wrestle with the request, but eventually agreed to show Baldridge to Sister Naomi's living area. Using a passkey from his desk drawer, he opened the door to a room at the end of the hall and lit a lamp mounted on the wall. Modest, as Baldridge had expected, only the bare minimum of furnishings—a chair, a writing desk, a chest of drawers, and a small bed—filled the twelve-by-eight-foot room. Maybe it was because she was a nun, and he was nosing around her belongings, but Baldridge felt uneasy from the moment he stepped through the door. Landrum didn't seem any more comfortable.

"Let's get this done as quickly as possible, Mr. Baldridge," Landrum said.

"Where was Sister Naomi last night?" Baldridge asked him.

"Attending to her duties," Landrum replied as he watched Baldridge. "What, exactly, are you looking for, anyway?"

"I don't know." Baldridge bent down to check under the bed. "What time did she return here?"

"It was just before I left to go home. I finished the records about ten-thirty and I was putting on my jacket when she came in. We spoke briefly about the next day's nursing requirements, and I bid her a good evening and walked to the parsonage. It's only about four blocks from here."

Baldridge opened an old chest of drawers and felt through each drawer.

"Mr. Baldridge, must you do that?" Landrum said, glancing over his shoulder. "Those are the sister's undergarments."

Baldridge glanced back at him as he felt through the second drawer. "If you're afraid I'm doing this because I like it, you needn't worry. Now, if she was a dance-hall girl . . ."

"I beg your pardon?" Landrum said.

"Nothing." Baldridge suddenly stopped, his hand meeting what felt like a book. With both hands he parted the garments and removed a Bible from the drawer. "What do we have here?"

"Mr. Baldridge, I hardly think that finding a Bible in a nun's room is—"

"Just a minute," Baldridge said, tracing with his hands a gold chain that disappeared between the pages and into the closed book. "Odd place for a nun to store her Bible, don't you think?"

"I wouldn't know," Landrum said.

With his fingernails, Baldridge parted the book where the remainder of the chain lay creased into the binding, and grasping the chain, he lifted it from the page and held it up in front of Landrum. A small golden crucifix dangled at the end, the lamp-light glinting off it as it rotated slowly.

"Well, I'll be damned," Baldridge said, then he corrected himself. "Excuse me, Reverend."

"Mr. Baldridge, a nun possessing a Bible and a crucifix hardly seems unusual. Sister Naomi has several crucifixes—she always wears one around her neck. She's never without it."

"Would you say this crucifix is similar to the one she wears?"

"Yes, I think it is," Landrum agreed.

"This looks to be about the same size as the marks I saw on those bodies," Baldridge said.

"Are you sure?"

"No, I'm not sure of anything. I'm just—wait a minute," Baldridge said, examining the pages he found marked by the crucifix. He felt a chill as he considered the possibilities, then began reading aloud.

> "And seeing the multitudes, he went up into a mountain;
>    and when he was set, his disciples came unto him:
> And he opened his mouth and taught them, saying,
> 'Blessed are the poor in spirit; for theirs is the kingdom
>    of heaven.' "

"The beatitudes," Landrum said. "That's one of Sister Naomi's favorite passages."

"Must've been. She underlined several of them."

"We've discussed the passage often."

"Discussed it how?" Baldridge asked.

"Oh, just what the Lord meant by 'blessed.' And who he meant in each of those statements."

"Who did he mean?" Baldridge asked, barely containing his excitement.

"Well, I think he was talking about different kinds of people."

Baldridge grew frustrated. "*What* kinds of people. Talk to me, Reverend."

"The Greek word for 'blessed' is *karikos*. It means 'to be happy.' "

"I don't understand," Baldridge said.

"Mr. Baldridge, the Lord was saying that happiness is not in the unfortunate conditions of this world," Landrum explained, "but in the glorious rewards to come."

"You mean in Heaven?"

"I think that's what the passage means."

"Reverend, do you think it's possible that Sister Naomi could love God so much, and despise suffering so greatly, that she would take a person's life just so that she might send him to Heaven?"

"That is a horrible thought."

Baldridge pointed at the passage of scripture. "And the people? Who are the 'poor in spirit'?"

"Most theologians think that means people living outside the Lord."

"Like Deke Stayley?"

"I didn't know Mr. Stayley."

"And those who mourn?"

"Means pretty much what you think," Landrum said. "People who are in mourning."

"Like a man whose wife had died of the fever? Like Lassiter?"

Landrum nodded, his face revealing a growing realization. "Yes, like Mr. Lassister."

" 'Blessed are the meek,' " Baldridge read from the text. "A child is meek." He continued reading. " 'Blessed are they which hunger and thirst after—' "

" 'Righteousness,' " Landrum said, with sorrow in his eyes as they met Baldridge's. "Yes, Mr. Baldridge. Like Malachi Baine." Landrum sat down in the cane-bottomed chair beside Sister Naomi's writing table and buried his face in his hands.

"I've known Sister Naomi for ten years. No one is more dedicated to treating fever victims. Back in the epidemic of '67,

I watched that woman nearly kill herself trying to keep the nurses organized and getting care to people who needed it." He peered over his fingers at Baldridge. "I simply cannot believe she would *take* a life."

"Try *four* lives, Reverend. At least that's how many we know of," Baldridge replied.

"Perhaps the pressure of this work was too much," Landrum speculated. "Maybe we asked—maybe *I* asked too much of one person."

"You didn't cause this, Reverend, but you can help me put a stop to it. When do you expect her back here tonight?" Landrum's hands dropped to his knees and his face appeared puzzled and frightened. "What's wrong, Reverend?"

"She's not returning tonight," he said.

Baldridge stepped closer. "What do you mean she's not returning? I thought you said she spent the night here."

"Usually she does, but there have been occasions when she's remained at the hospital—sometimes for up to two days. It depends on the number of cases, how available nurses will be, and—"

"Where is she tonight?"

"When I talked to her here last night, she indicated that she would be staying at the pest house tonight."

"I've got to get to President's Island before somebody else turns up dead," Baldridge said.

" 'The merciful,' " Landrum more muttered than spoke.

"Beg your pardon?"

"Next on the list—'the merciful,' " he added.

Baldridge scanned the page in the fifth chapter of Matthew, and read it aloud. " 'Blessed are the merciful; for they shall obtain mercy.' " Baldridge looked at Landrum. " 'The merciful'—what does this scripture mean? Who would be 'merciful'?"

"Those who minister unto others, who support others in

suffering," Landrum said, then added in a near whisper, "like nurses."

"Nurses. Sally!" Baldridge handed the Bible and crucifix to Landrum. "Contact Chief of Police Athy and don't let these out of your sight. Tell Athy what we've found out and that I'm going to the pest house."

"Mr. Baldridge," Landrum yelled as Baldridge left the room and hurried down the hall. "Mr. Baldridge, Sister Naomi is a good servant of the Lord."

Baldridge called back to him. "*Was*, Reverend. Right now she's just a murderer."

# 17

## THE PEST HOUSE
## WEDNESDAY, SEPTEMBER 24

Steven's shakin' somethin' awful, Miss Tyner," the ship's steward assigned to watch Tibedeau said as he tried to spread a blanket to cover him.

"He's having another rigor," Tyner said, returning from attending to a patient farther down the row of beds. Tyner placed the back of her hand against Tibedeau's forehead and found it warm and damp.

"Dr. Fledge!" she called down the length of the ward. "Dr. Fledge, can you come here?" She gazed down at Tibedeau, his face contorted and his teeth rattling from the violent shaking. "It's going to be all right, Steven. The doctor's coming." In the several moments it took for Fledge to make his way to Tibedeau, Tyner recalled the cycle she had seen since her arrival Tuesday. In the less than twenty-four hours she'd been at the pest house,

Tyner had seen the man experience no fewer than four such episodes, and she wondered how many more he could stand. It would begin with Tibedeau complaining of pain in his head and the small of his back, then the rigor would set in—like the one he now experienced—to be followed by intense sweating and high fever. The crisis would pass, and for an hour or more Tibedeau would seem to rebound. But weak from nausea, he was scarcely able to walk, and the times he had tried to move about, he had felt faint and been returned to his bed. Late last night Dr. Fledge had given him quinine, and followed it with a second dose that morning, neither of which had prevented another rigor and sweating before noon. That, too, had passed, leaving him weaker than the previous episode, and he could not bear talk of food or nourishment. With a cool cloth, Tyner dabbed the sweat from Tibedeau's forehead, noting how his skin had now turned a bronzed yellow and that his eyes were suffused. The vomiting would likely begin again, too, and she glanced down the ward to see how much longer Dr. Fledge would be. That had been the hardest part—the vomiting. Tibedeau's entire body had retched and heaved as he spewed forth the tarry-looking substance that she recalled Dr. Rice calling bile. As with her experiences at the yellow fever hospital, the noxious odor had made her light-headed, and several times she'd gagged and thought for sure she, too, would vomit. But she had maintained herself, and of that she was proud. Again she looked down the ward.

"Dr. Fledge!"

Moments later Fledge appeared, glaring at Tyner.

"Young woman, surely you realize I have other patients here," Fledge said. "And you do as well, if you call yourself a Howard nurse."

"Steven needs you," Tyner said.

"They all need me, Miss Tyner." Fledge motioned down the

ward. "Look at them. There are far more here than I can care for. I need three, maybe four, more doctors, and nurses as well. When is that other shift of nurses due to arrive from shore?"

"They will be running late tonight," Tyner said, running her fingers through her hair. "But Sister Naomi promised they'd be here no later than ten o'clock."

"Going back, are you?" Fledge said, examining Tibedeau.

"What?"

"Back to shore. Back with the other nurses. You're going back, aren't you?"

"No, Dr. Fledge, I'm not."

"You'll need to rest. Tomorrow's—"

"I'm staying with Steven," Tyner said. "I'm not going to leave him."

"We don't have any private patients out here, Miss Tyner," Fledge said. "If you stay here, you'll be expected to attend to *any* patient who needs you."

"Not if I'm off duty," she replied.

"Look around you. There is no off duty out here. This isn't the Fort Pickering hospital, Miss Tyner. This is the pest house." Fledge placed his fingers on Tibedeau's arm to sense his pulse. "You know why they call it the pest house, don't you?" He did not wait for her answer. "They say it's a short term for 'pestilence,' but I think it's because people with a disease are pests. They're pests to the community. They make life difficult. They get in the way of business and social life."

"But the quarantine is—"

"The quarantine is the right thing to do, all right," Fledge said. "I urged it myself. But look around you. How many other doctors do you see out here?"

"None."

"That's right. Most of them are treating patients at the hospital in Memphis or in private homes. You don't find them out here in the sticks, do you?" Tyner knew he was right about one thing—Fledge was the only doctor she had seen since she'd arrived, and from what one of the other nurses told her, he was the only one who regularly came to the island. He had slept perhaps two hours since she'd been there, and she figured his temper being short led him to his outburst. Fledge continued. "Some of them don't want to work alongside me because they think I'm too old to know what I'm doing. They say I'm not current in my medical thinking." He lowered Tibedeau's arm. "The truth is, Miss Tyner, the mortality rate of my patients is no higher than anyone else's. What do you think about that?"

She had a pretty good idea he was referring to his encounter with Luke Williamson. The captain, upon witnessing one of Tibedeau's rigors, had demanded Fledge ease his suffering. They'd exchanged words, with Williamson insisting that more should be done and Fledge declaring that he had administered every acceptable treatment he could offer.

"It will just have to run its course," Fledge had told the captain—an answer that had sent Williamson storming out of the hospital and vowing to "find his own goddamned doctor."

"His pulse is irregular," Fledge said, parting Tibedeau's quivering lips with an instrument. "See the tongue?" he said, drawing Tyner over for a closer look. "It's broad, indented at the margin, and looks almost like a flabby oyster." He removed the instrument. "Did you see that the milky white coating is starting to turn yellowish brown?" Tyner nodded. "That's not a good sign," Fledge whispered to her. "We're nearing a crisis here, Miss Tyner. The next few hours will tell the tale. I want you to keep an eye on his pulse. If it starts to bound, call for me." Fledge took a cloth from his bag and wiped his hands. "What about his kidneys? Has he passed anything?"

"Doctor," the steward said, somewhat hesitantly, "I got him to the toilet a little over an hour ago—when Miss Tyner was down the way—and he was pissin' awful dark. I couldn't really tell, but I 'spect they was some blood in it."

"His back is hurting him, too," Tyner said. "He says that—"

"Kidneys," Fledge said. "It's his kidneys."

"What can we do for him?"

Fledge picked up his medical bag. "Just try to keep him quiet. Once this chill passes—*if* it passes—if he's still in pain, I'll give him a one-thirty-second grain of morphia."

Fledge moved down the long room to attend to another patient and Tyner adjusted the blanket around Tibedeau's feet and took a seat beside the bed. She had been sitting there perhaps an hour when Luke Williamson came dashing in the far door. He stopped, out of breath, beside the bed, with Jacob Lusk close behind him.

"How is he?" Williamson asked.

"He's just had another rigor. Dr. Fledge was with him a few minutes ago," Tyner replied. "It's not good, Luke. The next few hours will tell the tale."

Williamson dropped to one knee beside Tibedeau's bed and began unwrapping a bottle he had rolled up in a cloth. "I met a Dr. Rice in Memphis. Masey said you knew him."

"I worked with him for a couple of days."

Williamson handed her the bottle and from the inside pocket of his jacket produced a piece of paper. "Rice said to give him quinine. It's in the bottle here."

"Luke, Dr. Fledge already gave him quinine. Two doses since last night."

"Did it help?"

"Some, maybe. I'm not sure there's much more we can do right now."

"There's more we can do," Williamson snapped. "There *has* to be more we can do."

Tyner placed her hand on the captain's arm. "Luke, I think he's just going to have to fight through it."

Williamson pointed at the paper. "What about tea? Dr. Rice wrote here that beef tea can help."

"Look at him, Luke," Sally said. "He's scarcely conscious. He can't take tea."

"Well, then we'll try it when he comes to."

"We can try it, Luke."

"Dr. Rice says that rest and nourishment are the key. We've got to get him to eat something."

"I doubt he could keep it down. Luke," Tyner said, her fingers pressing against his arm, "I'm afraid the disease is in his kidneys. He's had pain in his back, and his urine was—"

Williamson shoved the paper at her. "Mustard packs," he said. "It says so right here. We'll apply mustard packs for the pain."

"That may help the pain, Luke, but—"

Williamson stood up. "I'm going to the *Paragon*. I'll have Anabel prepare a beef broth for when he comes around."

"Luke, I'm not sure I'd leave if I were you."

"He's *not* going to die. Do you understand? Steven's *not* going to die." Williamson looked at Lusk. "Stay here with her, Jacob. Send for me if you need anything."

"Yes, Cap'n," Lusk replied.

Tyner watched him hurry out of the building, then turned to Lusk. "Jacob, doesn't he understand? Can't he see what's happening?"

"He don't want to see, Miss Tyner. The cap'n is the bravest man I've ever known. But there's one thing he's scared of—sickness."

"Luke?"

"Yes, m'am. I've seen the cap'n face down armed men, run a riverboat that draws six foot through five foot of water, and risk his life to save one of his men. But he can't stand being around no sickness."

"Why, Jacob?"

"That's what took his parents. The malaria killed 'em when he was just a young man. Wasn't nothing he could do to stop it, and he ain't never got over it."

"Nobody could have stopped that," Tyner said.

"Maybe not. But the cap'n is a man used to being in charge. He fixes things. Makes things right," Lusk explained. "With Steven here dying right before his eyes, it might as well be him dying. He loves Steven. Always has." He placed his hand on Tibedeau's head. "So have I."

Almost an hour passed, and Tibedeau's body temperature began dropping. Tyner sent the steward to get Williamson, and Dr. Fledge arrived to attend to Tibedeau, noting that his pulse was bounding, ranging from fifty to more than a hundred. In moments of lucidity, Tibedeau began speaking to them. It was just a jumble of words at first, only occasionally taking shape as coherent sentences. Tyner could read the alarm on Fledge's face as he listened to Tibedeau's heart. Suddenly Tibedeau opened his eyes wide and spoke in a loud, clear voice.

"Captain, I'll be up right away."

"Steven?" Tyner said.

"Steven, it's Jacob," Lusk added.

"I've got to check that load of firewood for the boiler, and I've—" He lapsed into mumbling.

"Steven," Lusk said, a tear creeping down his black cheek, "Steven, ain't no firewood here. You in the hospital."

Tyner dabbed his forehead with a cloth as Fledge again checked his pulse.

"It's falling. It's down to forty-five."

Tyner heard the door at the end of the building, and rising to her feet, she ran to meet Williamson.

"Luke, come quick!"

Without another word, the two of them ran to Steven's bedside, where Jacob Lusk held his hand tightly. Dr. Fledge had stepped back from the bed, where Williamson addressed him.

"Doctor?"

Fledge shook his head. "His heart is weak. The fever's damaged it badly."

"Give him some medicine," Williamson said.

"There's nothing I can give."

Williamson grabbed Fledge by the collar with both hands. "I said give him something."

Tyner pushed between them. "Luke, stop it. Stop it!"

"I'm not letting him die," Williamson said, fumbling for the bottle of quinine beside the bed.

Fledge grabbed his arm. "It's no use. It won't help." Tyner saw in Williamson the eyes of a helpless boy as he looked up at Fledge, who shook his head and said, "I'm sorry, Captain."

Williamson took Tibedeau's right hand, and with Lusk holding his left, he spoke gently to him.

"Steven, I'm here. Steven, you've got to make it. I—I don't know what I'll do if you don't make it." Williamson's tears began to fall on the blanket that covered Tibedeau's legs.

"I'm almost across, Captain," Tibedeau said. "Can you hear me, Captain?"

"I hear you, Steven."

"Tell Jacob I'll send a boat back for both of you," Tibedeau said, his voice growing weaker.

"I'm here, too, Steven."

When Tyner heard the rattle in Tibedeau's throat, she

stepped close behind Williamson and put her hands on his shoulders. "We love you, Steven."

"It's beautiful over here," Tibedeau said, then in more of a moan than in words, he said, "The trees are . . ."

"What, Steven? What about the trees?"

"Captain, I'm sorry. I—I—"

A long, slow breath drifted from Tibedeau's parted lips, and his tensed brow, bronze from the disease, relaxed until his face was as smooth as a sleeping baby's. Tyner saw Williamson release Tibedeau's hand and rise slowly to his feet, his face a portrait of disbelief.

"Jacob," Williamson began sobbing, "Jacob, he's gone. Steven's gone."

Lusk placed his muscular arm around Williamson, who buried his face in his first mate's chest and cried like a child. Dr. Fledge offered his condolences, wrote down the time of death as 9:48, and covered Tibedeau's face with the blanket. Salina Tyner said a prayer.

STEVEN'S DEATH HAD shaken Salina Tyner more than anything she'd experienced in a long time; and as the night breeze blew against her face, cooling her cheeks still wet with tears, her thoughts went to Luke. He and Jacob Lusk had returned to the *Paragon*, and when he'd left the pest house, she had never seen him so distraught. This powerful, decisive man whom everyone turned to for answers seemed frailer, more vulnerable than she had ever realized. She thought about what Jacob had said—how the fever had taken Williamson's parents—and her soul ached as much for him as for Steven. Steven was gone. There was nothing she or anyone else could do for him now. But Luke was another matter. She knew he was hurting, and part of her wanted to go to him and cradle him in her arms and tell him that everything would be all right. But she doubted he would allow it even if she went, preferring, if possible, to maintain that impenetrable exterior that had always been able before to ward off pain and heartache.

As she looked out over the river, listening to the current lapping the water against the bank, someone called to her out of the darkness.

"Who's there?" she asked.

"It's Sister Naomi." Tyner could make out a silhouette against the distant lights from the pest house.

"Sister?"

"Yes, Sally, it's me. I thought I might find you out here." She had arrived some time before with the relief nurses, and though she had offered her condolences to Tyner immediately upon arrival, the demands of the patients had kept them from talking. The sister extended her right hand to take Tyner's and slipped her left hand around her shoulder. "May the Lord comfort you in your hour of sadness, my dear."

"I'm afraid it's going to be more than an hour, Sister." Tyner began walking toward the pest house, with Sister Naomi's arm still around her shoulders.

"Yes, I suppose so. I'm sure your riverboat captain friend is mourning as well," Sister Naomi said.

"Luke's not taking this very well at all, Sister. I've known him for some time, and I know he was close to Steven. Outside Jacob Lusk, he was closer to Steven than any of the rest of his crew."

"Yes, it is difficult to lose those we love. But the Lord has a purpose in all He does," Sister Naomi assured her.

"I'd love to know what it is."

"Few of us can know the Lord's will, Sally. About the best we can hope to do is be instruments of His divine plan."

"Well, I'm glad you take comfort in that, Sister," Tyner said, "but if it's all the same to God, I'd rather have Steven back."

"Do you wish to return to Memphis?" Sister Naomi asked. "I have the boat standing by, although I am of the opinion that that would not necessarily be the best way to handle your grief."

"What do you mean?"

"Sometimes, when we lose someone like this, it is best to lose oneself in ministry. Returning to shore would leave you with much time to ponder your loss, whereas remaining here and continuing the ministry of mercy to those who still suffer would help to keep you busy and keep your mind off what has happened."

"I suppose you're right, but I'm worn out. I don't think I can offer much until I lie down for a while."

"Of course," Sister Naomi said. "There is a building not far from the pest house. I could arrange a place for you to sleep—"

"Thanks for the offer, Sister, but I believe I'll just return to the *Paragon*. I maintain a room on board."

"You have a room on Captain Williamson's ship?"

"Like I said, I've known Luke for quite some time."

"I see," Sister Naomi said. "Then by all means return to the ship and get some rest." She removed her arm from around Tyner. "I can send someone to wake you in a few hours. I'm sure we'll need the help."

"Not too soon, Sister."

"I'll make certain you get plenty of rest," Sister Naomi said.

"Thank you."

As they neared the steps of the pest house, Tyner could hear the all too familiar sound of someone vomiting, and the foul smell of urine and bile emanating from the building and drifting toward the water.

"This must be what Hell is like," Tyner said in a near whisper.

"Do you think so?"

"Listen to them," Tyner said. "I don't see how it could be much worse."

"Perhaps. But God reserves Hell for the wicked, Sally. I hope your friend Steven was a child of God."

"I suppose so. It's not something I ever asked him."

"If he was a child of righteousness, then God's sacrifice through Jesus has been made that he might be redeemed."

"Redeemed. Yeah, I hope so."

"It always takes sacrifice to satisfy God. I will pray for your friend Steven's soul tonight."

"I appreciate that, Sister," Tyner said, turning to walk away.

"Your cabin?" Sister Naomi inquired, holding her arm gently. "Where we can find you later?"

"Alabama Room. On the *Paragon*."

"Very well," Sister Naomi said, her hand gently touching Tyner's cheek. "God loves you, Sally. Blessed are the merciful, for they shall receive mercy."

"Thank you, Sister."


TYNER REMOVED HER dress and skirts, washed her face and hands to remove the awful smell of the pest house, and checked her riding watch before sitting down on the edge of her bed. It was one-thirty in the morning as she closed the case and placed the watch on top of the Saratoga trunk she kept in her room. She sat recalling a conversation she'd had a few minutes earlier. On her way to her room, she had gone up to the crew's quarters, and despite the lateness of the hour, she'd walked slowly by Williamson's cabin. Light leaked around the curtain in his window, so she'd pressed her ear against the door and her heart had ached at the low, nearly muffled sound of a man sobbing. She had tapped lightly on the door.

"Luke?"

She'd heard him rustling about.

"Who's there?"

"It's me. Sally. Are you all right?"

Williamson had hesitated before answering, summoning, she suspected, his composure. "Yes, I'll be fine." He'd made no movement toward the door. "Why are you still up?"

"I spent a while talking with Sister Naomi. She's head of the Howard Association nurses."

"Oh."

She had wanted to just open the door and go inside and hold him in her arms and comfort him, but, though she'd reached for the knob, she could not bring herself to enter.

"So are you going to get some sleep now?" she asked.

"Yeah. Eventually. How about you?"

"Yeah. Me, too. I'm going on down to my cabin now." A few moments of awkward silence had passed. "Better rest while you can. The sun will be up in a couple of hours."

"I will," Williamson had said in a low voice.

"And if I know you, you'll have a million things to do by eight o'clock," Tyner had said, adding a forced laugh.

"It won't be the same," Williamson had said, "without Steven."

"I know, Luke. I'm sorry. I'm so very sorry."

"Thank you."

She'd waited about fifteen seconds, but Williamson had offered no other comment.

"Well, good night. Or I guess I should say good morning."

"I'll see you later today," Williamson had said.

"Right. Uh, Luke?"

"Yes?"

"I may be up awhile. I may not be able to get to sleep." She'd paused a moment. "I'm just saying, if you need somebody to talk to . . ."

"I appreciate it. I'll be all right."

"Well, good night."

Satisfied that Williamson would not take her up on her offer to talk, Tyner blew out the light beside her bed and pulled the sheet up to her chin. The weight of the day, and the gamut of emotions she'd experienced, took their toll, and in moments she was asleep. How long she had slept she wasn't sure, but something was wrong. Was she dreaming or awake? Did she have the fever? Was it Steven she saw lying in state beside her, his hands folded over his chest? He seemed to sit upright upon her notice of him, and turning his head in an ominous glare he spoke to her.

"Tell the captain I'm sorry," he said. "I didn't want to go. I didn't want to go. I didn't want to go." He just kept repeating the words, louder and louder, his face a menacing portrait of pain and sorrow. "Don't come!" Tibedeau shouted. "Stay away from me! Don't touch my skin!" Tyner could feel something surrounding her, and though she realized she was dreaming, the feeling did not go away. Suddenly, she couldn't breathe. Something was covering her face, and in her half-dream state she sensed it was the sheet covering Steven's body. He seemed to turn to her under the sheet, his eyes begging her to stay away.

Tyner could taste cloth in her mouth and her lungs ached for air. Her arms flailed and she grasped someone's shoulder. It wasn't a dream. Someone was in the room. Someone was hovering over her. As she tasted the cloth against her mouth, she knew—someone was smothering her. Each of her hands grasped a wrist as she struggled to lift a pillow from her face, and overcoming the exhaustion of the previous day, Tyner somehow found the strength to pull her assailant's arms away from her face. Gasping for breath, she shoved her attacker backward, to tumble over the trunk and land hard against the wall. She strained in the darkness to see the shadow of an individual rising from the floor. Tyner bolted for the door to her stateroom, reached the handle, and had the door partially open when someone grabbed her arm and slammed her against the wall. Her head struck the wall hard enough to rattle her teeth, and in the light from a lantern burning on the deck outside, she saw the glint of light against steel.

"Help me!" she shouted. "Somebody help me!"

Ducking to her left, she tried to push past her attacker, only to feel a biting pain in her right shoulder. Spurred on by the stinging pain, Tyner pulled free and leaped for the partially open door. Landing on her stomach, she rolled over on her back, and the lantern on the deck trim above her revealed a woman rushing toward her with a knife. Realizing she could not get to her feet, Tyner lifted her hands and caught the wrist of her attacker as she bore down on her with the blade. Her opponent's strength seemed enormous, and as Tyner began to weaken under the pressure, the knife was drawing ever closer to her throat.

"Help me!" she called again, and from the corner of her eye she saw a light come on in the cabin next door. *Hurry*, she thought. *Hurry*.

Tyner could resist no more, her arm shaking from the exertion, and the knife moved within an inch of her throat. Angry, frustrated, and terrified, Tyner searched the eyes of her attacker to discover the face of Sister Naomi.

"Why?"

"The wrath of the Lord," Sister Naomi said as she strained against Tyner's weakening grip, "must be satisfied."

Tyner saw a coldness in her eyes that had driven out the warmth of earlier that evening, and her voice, quivering from the strain, was methodical and unfeeling.

"The sins of the wicked must be . . . covered by the blood—the blood . . . of the innocent," Sister Naomi said.

Tyner knew she could not last, and only now was the door to the cabin next door opening.

"What's going on out here?" a gentleman, wearing only his pants and suspenders, demanded as he looked down the deck through sleepy eyes.

Tyner took what she expected to be her last look at Sister Naomi and spat in her face.

"Go to hell," Tyner shouted.

The report of a weapon from down the deck to her right was followed immediately by a sudden release of pressure against her arms. The knife stopped moving toward her, and now Tyner was pressing it back. Sister Naomi stared down at her, her face showing no expression of pain, and she momentarily toppled to the deck beside her. Tyner pushed away and slid from beneath her, struggling to her feet and running in the direction of the shooter. The man who had peered out of his cabin had quickly ducked back inside, the bullet having missed him by only inches. Tyner saw Masey Baldridge standing on the deck some ten feet away, his revolver hanging from his right hand, pointed at the ground, the smell of powder in the air.

"Sally? Are you all right?"

She ran toward him and threw her arms around him.

"Masey."

"You're hurt," he said, noticing the nasty slash on her shoulder.

"I'll be all right."

"You need a doctor."

By now, several passengers had opened their doors and were cautiously peeking outside to determine the source of the excitement. Tyner glanced over her shoulder and, to her horror, she saw Sister Naomi, her arm over the deck rail, pulling herself to her feet.

"Masey, she's getting up," Tyner said, her grip tightening on his arm.

"Don't move," Baldridge called to her, but Sister Naomi continued to pull herself upright. "You people stay in your cabins," Baldridge called to the onlookers, who were now emerging from cabins all down the deck. "Stay in your cabins!" Several doors slammed.

Sister Naomi, using the rail for support, began dragging herself along the deck toward them. Tyner saw no anger in her face; rather, she seemed to have a look of complete peace, and was moving as deliberately as though she were preparing for a mass.

"Don't make me shoot you again," Baldridge said. "There's been enough killing."

"A sacrifice," she said, struggling to breathe, "must be . . . rendered unto the Lord."

"Like you sacrificed Deke Stayley, and Lassiter, and that little girl."

"The blood . . . of innocents . . . of the righteous," Sister Naomi said, still clawing her way toward them, "taketh away . . . the sins of the . . . multitude."

"If you take another step, I'll kill you."

Tyner saw Sister Naomi halt momentarily, then a strange smile appeared, and her eyes seemed to be looking far away.

"Father, into Thy hands I—I commend my spirit." In a final burst of strength, Sister Naomi lurched at Tyner, knife drawn high above her. But instead of reaching Tyner, she met a blast from Baldridge's revolver that drove her backward and left her sprawled facedown on the deck. A gaping exit wound in her back gushed blood that cut a crimson trail to the edge of the deck, dripping over the side and into the water below.

# ⊰ 18 ⊱

aldridge lurched at the touch on his shoulder, which drew him from a deep sleep. He coughed and cleared his throat, and through half-open eyes looked up at the cabin steward standing beside him.

"Mr. Baldridge, Cap'n said I should wake you," the steward said.

Curled up in the rocking chair where he'd fallen asleep shortly before daylight, he drew back the blanket someone had placed over him and began slowly bending his stiff left leg.

"Cap'n said you'd be needin' your breakfast," the steward said, placing a whiskey bottle and a glass on the table.

"You tell the Captain that I don't think that's funny," Baldridge said through a pasty mouth. He opened the bottle and poured himself a glass anyway.

"Cap'n said you'd be wanting to know—"

"Cap'n said, Cap'n said," Baldridge mocked. "Is that all you can say? How come the captain doesn't come here and say it himself?"

"He's attendin' to Mr. Tibedeau's service," the steward said solemnly.

Baldridge felt terrible. He had forgotten about Tibedeau's death. Glancing down the deck toward Tyner's cabin, he noticed a crewman scrubbing the deck, removing the bloodstains from where Sister Naomi had fallen.

"What time is it?" Baldridge asked.

"Near about ten o'clock, sir."

Baldridge rubbed his neck, stiff from sleeping in the chair. He had fully intended to find himself a cabin after the incident; but after the shooting, he had taken the opportunity to talk with Tyner and brief Luke Williamson on the events of the past two days. He figured he must have fallen asleep.

Baldridge got to his feet. "Is Miss Tyner awake?"

"Yes, sir. She's been up for almost an hour," the steward said. "Can I get you something to eat, sir?"

Baldridge finished off the whiskey in the glass. "No, thanks."

"Sir, Cap'n said—" Baldridge glared at the man, and after hesitating momentarily, he continued. "Cap'n told me to tell you that the quarantine's over."

"What? When?"

"Word came this morning about eight o'clock," the steward said. "Seems they took another vote in Memphis and this time they said ain't gonna be no more quarantine."

"I guess Williamson's happy about that," Baldridge said.

"No, sir. He ain't happy 'bout much of nothin' today," the steward replied.

"Well, I am," Baldridge said, walking toward Tyner's door.

"Sir?" the steward followed after him. "Sir, you forgot your bottle."

"Thanks," Baldridge said, taking it from him.

Baldridge knocked on Tyner's cabin door.

"Just a minute," she called from inside.

In a moment she opened the door, dressed in a black dress

with lace high up the neck, and a broad black hat. After little or no sleep the night before, she looked quite nice.

"Good morning," Baldridge offered. "How's your shoulder?"

"One of the stewards changed the dressing this morning," she replied. "I think it'll be all right."

"Dr. Fledge put some stitches in you last night, didn't he?"

"Don't you remember?"

"I think so. I was so tired last night I fell asleep in a chair on deck."

"I know. You fell asleep right in the middle of a sentence while talking to Luke. I brought you a blanket after Dr. Fledge stitched me up."

"That was you? Thanks. But why didn't you wake me up so I could go to bed?"

"Looked to me like you were *in* bed," Tyner said. "I didn't have the heart to wake you."

"You look mighty nice this morning," Baldridge offered.

"Well, *you* don't. You look like hell," she said, returning to the room, where she retrieved some black mourning beads. "You need a shave. You need a bath, and you definitely need a change of clothes."

"That don't seem like much of a way to talk to the man who saved your life last night."

"I told you last night I appreciated what you did," she said, placing the beads around her neck and turning her back to him.

"I just figured I'd get more of a—"

"Fasten this," she said, indicating the beads.

"Please," he said, placing his bottle and glass on a nearby table.

"Please," she echoed.

"Who pissed in your drink?"

"Masey, I've had maybe three hours of decent sleep, I nursed fever patients for two days solid, somebody tried to smother me last night, I saw a woman gunned down in front of my eyes," she said, "and I'm about to bury a friend." She turned around and faced him, her dark eyes flashing. "Now, who wouldn't be a little peeved?"

"Yeah, I'm sorry about Steven."

"We're *all* sorry about Steven," she replied.

"I liked him. He was a feisty character, all right. I remember one time we docked at Helena and—"

"Please, Masey. I don't think I can stand to hear that right now." She placed her hand lightly on his chest. "I know you mean well, and maybe in a day or two I'll listen to your story. Probably tell you one of my own." She took a deep breath. "But not this morning."

"Did you hear they lifted the quarantine?"

"Yes, I heard that."

"I figured I'd get a boat on back to Memphis and see if I can round up Deaves, that is, if the law hasn't already found him. That would just about wrap this thing up and we could—"

"You're not serious," Tyner said, her face evidencing her disbelief.

"Yeah. I figured I'd head on over—"

"And not go to Steven's service?" Her penetrating eyes forced Baldridge to look away.

"Sally, I ain't sat for a funeral since my wife, Rachel, died back during the war. Don't figure to go to another one until my own."

"That's the most selfish thing I've ever heard," Tyner said. "Steven was a friend of yours. You said so yourself."

"Sally, Steven don't care if I'm there or not. It won't do him no good either way."

"Maybe not. But what about me? Maybe it would do me some good to have you there."

"Sally, I—"

"And Luke. Don't you care what he thinks? Don't you figure it would help Luke if you were there?"

Baldridge looked down at the floor. "I don't know, Sally, I'm just not much for going to—"

"For God's sake, Masey, can't you think of somebody but yourself for a few minutes? How much would it really hurt you to get cleaned up and show up to support Luke? He's done plenty for you."

"I pull my weight around here," Baldridge said. "Worked this case by myself, didn't I?"

Tyner's hands went to her hips. "By yourself?"

"Well, no, not exactly. I mean, sure, you helped and all. But I—"

"*We* worked this case," she said. "And just because Luke wasn't in Memphis didn't mean he wasn't part of it."

"I know. I know. But the case ain't over until we see to it that Deaves is brought to task for his stealing. And I just thought I'd go on and attend to that—"

"It can wait, Masey. It can wait until after Steven's service," Tyner said slowly, trying to contain her anger. "If Deaves found out that you turned Roe over to Athy, he's long gone anyway. And if he doesn't know, then a couple of more hours won't make any difference."

She stood in front of him, staring at him, clearly expecting a response.

"When is this funeral, anyway?" Baldridge asked.

"Eleven-thirty. Luke decided that since the quarantine is lifted, he'll take the *Paragon* out into mid-channel. Steven always said he wanted to be buried in the river. Luke intends to honor that."

"Good thing they lifted the quarantine," Baldridge said.

Tyner smiled slightly. "In this situation, do you think for one minute that would have stopped Luke?"

Baldridge smiled. "I suppose not."

"So? What's it gonna be?" Tyner asked.

"All right, Sally. I'll go clean up."

"And change your clothes."

"Yes, and change clothes."

"And shave."

"Will you stop this? I'm not a child. I know how to get dressed."

"Then what are you waiting for? The boat will pull away at eleven." She checked her riding watch. "That's thirty minutes from now. That means you've got less than an hour to get yourself ready." She began to usher him out of the cabin. "Go on. Go on. You'd better not be late coming up on deck. They're holding the service on the back deck." Baldridge stalled in the door. "What are you doing?" Tyner asked.

Baldridge reached inside and retrieved his bottle and glass. "I'm at least having a drink first," he said.

"Now, that's a big surprise," she said, pushing him out of the cabin and closing the door behind him.

THE RAILINGS ON the second and third decks were lined with passengers who pressed forward to view Steven Tibedeau's interment in the Mississippi River. The ship's orchestra was positioned on the port side of the rear deck, near the paddle wheel, which churned the brown water as it rotated slowly to maintain the *Paragon*'s position amid the current in mid-channel. Some two dozen men and women of the crew, clad in immaculate white uniforms, white gloves, and white hats, stood in line along the starboard side of the ship. Eight officers in dress-blue uniforms formed a line in front of them, and Luke Williamson stood at front and center of the officers. Baldridge had squeezed into a spot beside Tyner on the hurricane deck, where he observed the spectacle below. The ship's orchestra had been playing "Rock of Ages" when Baldridge made his way beside Tyner. She immediately took his hand and looked at him, tears in her eyes, forcing a smile. She squeezed his hand.

"Thanks for coming," she whispered.

Baldridge said nothing, and returned his attention to the deck below. The orchestra concluded the song and the crowd of onlookers grew silent as Captain Williamson took two sharp steps forward from the row of officers, executed a crisp right-face toward the body of the ship, took three more steps forward, and addressed the crew beside him and the people crowding the railings above.

Baldridge's heart ached as Williamson began to speak, for he'd known the captain long enough to realize he was fighting back tears with every word.

"This day, we the officers and crew of the *Paragon* gather to mourn the loss of one of our own. As captain of this ship, I have known and worked with Steven Tibedeau for more than six years. I served with him during the war and saw his valor and dedication to duty. Every day, for all these years, I watched this man go about his duties—always doing every task with everything he had to give. As chief clerk on the *Paragon*, Steven knew every ounce of freight, every passenger, and every dollar spent or taken in on this boat. No captain could have asked for a more loyal, decent, hardworking officer than Steven Tibedeau." Williamson hesitated, his emotions scarcely obeying him as he struggled to continue. "And no man could ask for a more dependable, reliable friend. So today, I invite you, the passengers, to join with my officers and crew to bid a sailor's farewell to one of the finest rivermen I've ever known." Williamson, now clearly fighting back tears, turned and gave a nod to the orchestra. During an introductory bar of music, four of the white-clad crew members stepped from the formation and stood in the center of the rear deck, near Williamson, where they began to sing.

> "Shall we gather at the river,
> where bright angel feet have trod;
> With its crystal tide forever,
> Flowing by the throne of God."

In rich harmony, the quartet sang as Baldridge watched six of the officers, led by Jacob Lusk, march momentarily out of sight toward the lower cabin area. Another crewman lowered to half-mast a U.S. flag that extended from the deck above, dancing in the light breeze. As the six officers emerged again into sight, they carried, at shoulder level, Steven Tibedeau's corpse. The body, wrapped tightly in a white sheet, lay on a flat shelf some three feet wide, covered loosely by an American flag that was bound to the shelf along the edge but open at the far end. The quartet continued to sing.

> "Yes, we'll gather at the river,
> The beautiful, the beautiful river,
> Gather with the saints at the river
> That flows by the throne of God."

From the back row of crewmen, where the singers had emerged, seven men marched from the group, executed an about-face, and each shouldered a rifle pointed out over the starboard side of the ship. The officers bearing Tibedeau turned left and moved between two lines of the remaining white-uniformed crewmen. They halted at the edge of the deck, Tibedeau's body still resting on the shelf they held on their shoulders. The quartet sang on as the captain positioned himself beside the riflemen.

> "Soon we reach the shining river
> Soon our pilgrimage will cease
> Soon our happy hearts will quiver
> With the melody of peace."

The singers completed the tune and the orchestra stood silent as Luke Williamson commanded the riflemen.

"Ready, aim, fire," he ordered. Twice more he repeated the command, and the men lowered their rifles and executed an about-face as the smoke from their firing drifted away on the wind.

Williamson addressed the gathering in a loud, clear voice. "Lord, we commend to the river the body of Steven Tibedeau, our friend and fellow crew member, so that his spirit might rest in the water of everlasting life."

"Amen," echoed some of the officers bearing his body as they raised the end of the shelf nearest the center of the boat. Williamson signaled someone on the upper decks and the *Paragon's* distinct five-tone steam whistle blew loudly enough to startle Baldridge and Tyner. They watched as the officers lifted the shelf slightly higher, until Tibedeau's body, shrouded, tied, and weighted, slid from the shelf and splashed into the river, disappearing beneath the muddy current. The whistle stopped momentarily, then issued forth again—this time in a long, low moan that lasted for about ten seconds. Williamson returned to the center of the lower deck, thanked his crew and the passengers for their reverent attention, and ordered his crew to make for the Memphis wharf.

Baldridge and Tyner located Williamson in the pilothouse, and after talking with him for about half an hour, during which time Baldridge explained Sister Naomi's killing streak through the city, they told him of their intention to find Deaves and finish the case. But Williamson's mind was no longer on the case the mayor had hired them to investigate, and Baldridge knew why. Once the *Paragon* docked at the wharf boat, it was clear to Baldridge that Williamson was anxious to leave for St. Louis. He made no promises to hold the boat until they finished the case; rather, he told them he intended to stock what provisions could be had, and leave by three that afternoon. He indicated he would, barring bad weather or new quarantines, return to Memphis in four days; and wishing them success with Deaves, he put them ashore with Nashville Harry and a horse for Tyner.

Baldridge and Tyner went first to Athy's office at the central police station. Baldridge introduced Tyner, and Athy invited them inside, where he was unusually cordial. He offered them seats and took his own behind his desk.

"Reverend Landrum came by here this morning and told me about Sister Naomi. He brought in the Bible and crucifix you found." Athy paused. "We got Baine down at Coroner Prescott's." Athy scratched his head. "I'll have to admit that he has got the same markings as the others. You may be right, Baldridge. Sister Naomi could've been the killer."

"Could've been?" Tyner said. "The woman—"

"Yes, I got word just before lunch about the shooting last night on President's Island."

"It wasn't on the island. It was on the *Paragon*," Baldridge said.

"I understand you came upon the sister attempting to kill Miss Tyner here," Athy said.

"That's right. I had to shoot her. She had a knife."

"That's too bad," Athy said. "Because I guess we'll never really know for sure if she was the killer, will we?"

"I know," Baldridge said.

"And I'll have the scars to prove it," Tyner added.

"Yes, I know. But proving it in a court of law would have been tough." Athy looked first at Tyner, then at Baldridge. "Why did she do it? What I don't get is why a God-fearing, dedicated woman of the church would kill four people."

"I don't know," Baldridge said. "I think somehow she figured she was doing what God wanted—"

Tyner interrupted. "I think, in her own way, she was trying to save the city."

"Save the city? By cutting people's throats?" Athy said.

"Somehow, somewhere down the line, I think maybe Sister Naomi had seen far too much suffering," Tyner explained. "She believed that God was angry, and that was why He sent the fever—to punish people."

"That sounds like Malachi Baine," Baldridge said. "I think they both thought some of the same things. I think they both believed the fever was a scourge from God."

"But Baine wasn't killing people," Athy said.

"No. From what Masey's told me, ol' Malachi was preaching repentance. That's what he believed would free the city of the fever."

"And the sister?" Athy asked her.

"Sister Naomi took a more direct approach. She talked to me a lot, and in those conversations one thing came through clearly. She believed that only some kind of sacrifice would stop God's anger."

"So she killed people as a sacrifice?"

"I'm afraid so," Tyner replied.

"But not just anybody. She was following the beatitudes," Baldridge added. "Sally was to be her next victim."

"Sounds pretty crazy to me," Athy said.

"Do you need some kind of statement from me about the shooting?" Baldridge asked.

"Won't be necessary. It's not my jurisdiction. The shooting didn't actually happen on the island; and it's not the sheriff's jurisdiction either, since it happened on that steamboat. If the captain of the boat is satisfied it was self-defense, that's just fine with me."

"Captain Williamson knows all about the shooting. He knows that I had no choice."

"Very well, then. Let's hope you were right and there are no more murders," Athy said, smiling slightly. "I'll have to admit, I had my doubts about you, Baldridge. That first day at the undertaker's, I didn't want you involved in any of this."

"I know."

"But, all in all, you've handled yourself pretty well."

Baldridge, growing uncomfortable with the praise, asked about Deaves, bringing about a sudden shift in Athy's pleasant demeanor.

"Officer Deaves has been relieved of duty," Athy said.

"Relieved? He'd better be in jail!" Tyner said.

"Miss Tyner, he's not been formally arrested yet."

"Did Roe admit Deaves was involved?" Baldridge asked.

"No. Mr. Roe has not been very cooperative with our investigation. Without an admission of guilt, or a statement from whoever was working with Roe, we may not be able to prove anything."

"Have you questioned Deaves?"

"Yes, we brought him in for questioning on Wednesday. But he's not talking either."

"What about the store owners like Snowden? Won't they admit that Deaves was stealing money from their donations?"

"None of them have admitted anything," Athy said.

"That's because they're afraid," Tyner said. "They're afraid you won't lock Deaves up, and then he'll be out to get them."

"I doubt Officer Deaves will be getting anyone," Athy said.

"Oh, yeah? And why is that?" Tyner challenged.

"He was taken with Bronze John yesterday morning."

"Is he at the hospital?"

"No. He refused to go. My men tried to take him, but he insisted on staying at his home."

"And you just let him stay there?" Tyner said in disbelief.

"Believe me, Miss Tyner, he's not going anywhere."

"Who's caring for him?"

"A nurse from the Howard Association, I think."

"Anybody talk to him since?" Baldridge asked.

"Every officer I've got is busy just keeping this city from coming apart. We haven't time to—"

Tyner was incensed. "You haven't time? The man is being cared for by the very people he stole from, he'll probably die anyway and you'll lose your only chance to convict Roe, and you say you haven't got time?"

"We'll get someone over to see Deaves just as soon as we can. Don't worry, Miss Tyner, in his condition, he'll still be there."

"You'll mess around until it's too late," Tyner said. Baldridge could feel her growing anger. "I know. I've been nursing fever patients for the past week."

"Miss Tyner, I assure you—"

"I think maybe you don't want to go and talk with Deaves again because he's a policeman," Tyner said. She looked at Baldridge. "What do you say, Masey? Maybe Chief Athy here doesn't want to face the fact that one of his own men is a thief."

"Look, Miss Tyner, I'll admit that I didn't like it one bit how the mayor went behind my back on this investigation and hired your detective agency."

246 | JAMES D. BREWER

"Well, at least you admit it."

"But even if Deaves is involved with Roe, he'll probably die. And if he was involved, the stealing will stop."

"But what about Roe?" Baldridge asked.

"Like I said, I'd like to convict him. But I need more evidence."

Tyner stood up. "All right, Chief. You want more evidence, Masey and I will get it for you." She took him by the arm. "Let's go, Masey."

"Where?"

"To see Deaves. If the police don't have the time to visit him, we will." And without another word, Tyner pulled Baldridge out of the office. After obtaining Deaves's address from one of the officers at the main desk, Baldridge and Tyner rode over to a small cottage on Adams Street. At their knock on the door, a Howard Association nurse whom Tyner recognized answered. Over her greeting, Baldridge could hear a plaintive wail from a back room.

Tyner talked for a few moments with the nurse, who confirmed Athy's assessment of Deaves's condition. A doctor had been there about two hours earlier, and after examining Deaves expressed to the nurse that he doubted Deaves would make it through the night. The nurse, concluding she was on a death watch, accepted Tyner's offer to relieve her for an hour to get some supper, gathered up her belongings, and departed.

"Smells like the hospital," Tyner commented as they walked toward the back room of the cottage. They found Deaves curled up in a near fetal position, his face dripping with sweat and the bedclothes around him wet with perspiration. He looked up at them, his eyes yellow where the whites should have been, and immediately recognized Tyner.

"What are *you* doing here?" he asked, frightened, drawing away.

"I'm relieving your nurse," Tyner said.

"You're—you're not a nurse," Deaves said. "You're not wearing a uniform."

"I'm all the nurse you're going to have for the next hour," she said. For several minutes, Baldridge and Tyner talked with Deaves, whose level of awareness varied throughout their conversation. But even though Deaves's mind drifted, he heard enough of Tyner's careful, calculated description of how Yellow Jack patients suffered before they died to make him highly agitated.

"I mean, it's one of the saddest things I've ever had to watch," Tyner told him. "When a grown man vomits his innards out, he cries like a baby. Messes up his clothes, too. It's a hell of a way to die, Deaves. And about all the nurse can do for you is make you comfortable—or perhaps, if she knows how you tried to steal money from the Howard Association—maybe she'll let you just lie in your own vomit until you dehydrate and die."

"You're not going to tell my nurse, are you?" Deaves asked.

"It'll be hard not to," Tyner said.

Baldridge took his cue from her. "It would be easier if you had told us the whole truth."

Reluctantly, Deaves began to relate the story of his relationship with Roe, interrupted occasionally by fits of crying and bouts with the pain in his back. Locating some paper and a pencil, Baldridge wrote as he spoke, taking down every detail Deaves offered. Deaves admitted to taking a 25 percent cut from the money he'd culled from contributions, and he claimed to have no idea what Roe did with his share. As Baldridge had suspected, their little operation might never have been found out had not the Howard Association begun publishing the amounts each contributor gave. Deaves then found himself having to keep people quiet, and his threats to burn down their businesses, or refuse them police protection, had worked effectively enough to keep them from talking.

Exhausted by the ordeal of his confession, Deaves eventually rolled over on his side, his face toward the wall. Baldridge grasped his shoulder and rolled him back over to face them. Deaves growled from the pain and urinated on himself. The smell was strong, forcing Baldridge to step back.

"One more thing, Deaves," Baldridge said.

"What—what do you want?" Deaves asked weakly.

Baldridge held a paper in front of Deaves and pointed to the bottom of the page. "Sign it."

"What? What is—"

"It's your confession. The truth is, Deaves, you're going to die." Deaves began sobbing. "At least you can meet your maker knowing you did one good thing."

Deaves raised a quivering hand and took the pencil, then slowly, and with effort, he wrote his name at the bottom of the page, dropping the pencil on the soiled sheet beside him.

Baldridge folded the paper and slipped it into his pocket, then stepped away from the bed, in strong need of a breath of fresh air and a drink of whiskey.

Deaves mustered his strength to speak. "I—I done right by you," he said. "I know I ain't gonna live. I know it." He pointed to where he had soiled his clothes and the sheet beneath him. "But I—I don't want to die like this. You gotta help me."

"Like you helped all those people who needed the money you were supposed to be collecting?" Baldridge said.

"You gotta help me," Deaves moaned.

"What do you want us to do?" Tyner asked. "The doctor's already been here, and you've got a nurse."

Deaves slowly lifted his weak, trembling hand toward Baldridge. "I told you what you wanted to know." His voice weakened as he continued. "Now . . . you've got to do right by me," he said, nodding toward Baldridge. Baldridge looked at his jacket, then at Deaves, whose eyes implored him.

"What do you want?"

Baldridge did not realize what Deaves was staring at until he pulled his jacket to the side to reveal his revolver. Deaves nodded slowly.

Tyner looked at Baldridge. "He doesn't mean . . ."

"That's exactly what he means," Baldridge replied. "And he wants my gun to do it with."

"Do right by me," Deaves groaned.

Baldridge moved closer and removed the revolver from its holster.

Tyner took his arm. "You're not going to do it?"

As Deaves struggled to reach the weapon, Baldridge cocked it and aimed it at his head. Deaves sank back in the pillow, tears rolling down his cheeks and mingling with the sweat of the fever.

"Please," he said. "Please shoot me." His body began to shake. "Please."

Baldridge sighted down the barrel at Deaves's forehead.

"Masey! Stop this!" Tyner shouted, glancing into the other room and expecting the nurse to return at any moment.

Deaves was sobbing, out of control, as Baldridge stood beside him pressing his finger against the trigger. But Baldridge placed his thumb over the hammer and, pulling the trigger, he allowed the hammer to return slowly to the body of the weapon without discharging a shot.

The fear in Deaves's eyes grew stronger. "No! Please! Don't make me—"

"You know," Baldridge said, returning his weapon to its holster, "a righteous man once told me that the wicked shall have no escape from their deeds." He put his arm around Tyner's shoulders and led her into the other room.

"Please!" Deaves's weak voice called out to them as Baldridge opened the door of the cottage.

"Please!" Deaves called again.

"Masey, you were talking about Malachi Baine when you mentioned that righteous man to Deaves, weren't you?"

Baldridge slammed the door to the cottage. "Yeah," he replied, removing his flask from his pocket.

"Do you really believe he was righteous? I mean, the way ol' Malachi told people that they got the fever because of their sins? That's just plain cruel."

"I said he was righteous." He unscrewed the lid. "I didn't say I thought he was right."

"So you think a man can be wrong and still be righteous?"

Baldridge took a long, slow sip of whiskey. "I sure as hell hope so."

SWINGING BY THE central police station, Tyner waited outside while Baldridge presented a surprised Chief Athy with Deaves's signed confession, informed him of the officer's deteriorating condition, and told Athy that he and Tyner could be found at the Overton Hotel if he needed any further information. Athy shook Baldridge's hand, and for the first time since meeting him, Baldridge believed the man truly appreciated what he had done. Arriving at the Overton Hotel just before dark, Baldridge turned over the horses to a boy who worked in the livery across the street, then walked into the lobby and registered the two of them for rooms through Tuesday—the day Williamson and the *Paragon* were due to return. In the lobby, Tyner was speaking with a messenger boy and had just dismissed him when Baldridge approached with the keys. He held them out to her.

"You know, just say the word and I could give one of these back," Baldridge said with a grin.

Tyner rose to her feet, took the key from his hand, and with a playful smile said, "And where would *you* sleep?"

"Mr. Baldridge!" someone called from the hotel's large double doors. Baldridge saw Mayor Johnson entering the building. "A moment, sir?"

Johnson, dressed in a freshly pressed suit, his beard manicured to perfection, extended his hand. "I just want to thank you for everything you've done for me and the city of Memphis. I just spoke with Chief Athy, and from what I hear, you've both done a marvelous job," he said. Johnson reached inside his coat pocket and produced an envelope. "Based on our agreement, this should cover what the city owes the Big River Detective Agency, with a little bonus included."

Tyner intercepted the envelope as Baldridge reached for it. "Thank you, Mayor Johnson. The agency was glad to be able to help."

"You did more than help," Johnson said. "You did your work in confidence. That prevented a panic and saved a lot of lives."

"That's good to know," Baldridge said. But something about the mayor's words bothered Baldridge, though he couldn't put his finger on what it was. He was forgetting something.

"Miss Tyner, I understand you worked with the Howard Association during your investigation," Johnson said.

"That's right."

"Well, you should be particularly pleased to know that because your agency stopped the theft of Howard Association funds, I was able to authorize the city's gift of ten thousand dollars to fund more nurses and buy more medicine."

"That's wonderful, Mayor," Tyner said with a smile.

"Of course, I'm sure you won't be nursing any more now that the investigation is over, but I thought you'd like to know anyway."

"That's not true," Tyner replied. "In fact, I'll be returning to the yellow fever hospital tomorrow morning."

"Tomorrow?" Baldridge said. "Sally, you haven't slept more than three or four hours in three days."

"I'll sleep tonight. I sent a message a moment ago to have the nurses' buggy stop by for me here in the morning. The work must go on, Mayor. One of the other nurses has agreed to take over Sister Naomi's job as director of nurses."

"But you need to catch up on your rest," Baldridge said. "The case is over."

"Maybe," Tyner said, "but the fever's not. And until it is, the city needs nurses."

"That's admirable of you," Johnson replied.

"No, Mayor. It's not admirable. It's just necessary. Even with the quarantine lifted, the city is held prisoner to this disease. I'm going to be here four more days, maybe longer. I might as well do something to help."

Baldridge's gut tightened at Tyner's words, his face growing pale as he stared toward the double doors at the front of the hotel.

"Are you all right, Mr. Baldridge?" Johnson asked.

"Uh, yeah. I'm fine." Baldridge turned to Tyner. "Sally, I've got to go somewhere."

"Right now?"

"Yes, right now," Baldridge said, still eyeing the front door.

"What are you looking at?" Tyner asked, turning, herself, to look toward the door. "Who's that raggedy-looking man staring at you from the door?"

When Baldridge didn't answer, Johnson chimed in. "Looks

like Miles Washburn, but I can't say I've ever seen him in that shape." Washburn stood in the doorway of the hotel, his shirt torn, his face filthy, his hair tossed wildly about his face.

"Baldridge!" Washburn yelled across the nearly empty lobby.

"I've got to run," Baldridge told Tyner and Johnson, limping away as quickly as his bad leg would carry him.

"Baldridge, you're gonna pay for what you did!" Washburn said, rushing across the lobby.

"Mayor, don't believe a word that man tells you," Baldridge said, opening a door to the hotel kitchen. He closed the door behind him and started for the back entrance to the hotel, then halted and returned to the door. He opened it slightly to see the disheveled Washburn in animated conversation with Johnson. Baldridge poked his head around the door. "And if you do believe him, just don't let him print it."

Incensed by the comment, Washburn started after Baldridge again, but found the door locked from the other side. Baldridge slipped out the back of the hotel and got to Nashville Harry only seconds before the livery boy was to unsaddle him.

When he took him by the reins, the boy called to him, "Hey, mister, I thought you told me to put him up for the night."

"I did," Baldridge said, tossing the boy a coin.

"Then why you leavin'?" the boy asked.

"Baldridge! Stop!" Washburn demanded from the doorway of the livery.

Baldridge spurred Harry and broke him into a trot that sent Washburn diving into the hay to avoid being run over as the horse's hooves clambered onto the wooden pavement.

"When you comin' back?" the livery boy shouted at Baldridge.

"Just in time for the next boat," Baldridge replied, disappearing down Main Street, riding Nashville Harry at a gallop.

# EPILOGUE

The first frost came ten days later on the morning of October 7, killing off the *Aedes aegypti* mosquito, and effectively putting an end to the scourge of yellow fever in Memphis that year. More than 2,000 men, women, and children died between late August and the second week of October 1873; and despite the heroic efforts of the medical community and the self-sacrifice of volunteers with the Howard Association, still no one knew what caused the fever or how to prevent it. The debate over quarantine, mode of transmission, and origin of the disease split the medical community for years to come.

Bronze John would return five years later to Memphis, and between early August and the first frost, some 6,000 people would go to their graves—making that visitation of yellow fever the severest epidemic in the history of American cities.